The Next Competitor

Also by Keira Andrews

Gay Amish Romance Series
A Forbidden Rumspringa
A Clean Break
A Way Home
A Very English Christmas

Contemporary
Arctic Fire
Reading the Signs
Beyond the Sea
If Only in My Dreams
Valor on the Move
Cold War
Holding the Edge
Where the Lovelight Gleams
The Chimera Affair
The Argentine Seduction
Eight Nights
Daybreak
Love Match
City of Lights
Synchronicity

Historical
Semper Fi
The Station

Paranormal
Kick at the Darkness
Fight the Tide
A Taste of Midnight (free read!)

Fairy Tales (with Leta Blake)
Flight
Levity
Rise

THE NEXT COMPETITOR

BY KEIRA ANDREWS

The Next Competitor
Written and published by Keira Andrws
Cover by Dar Albert
Figure Skating Icon made by Freepik from www.flaticon.com is licensed under CC BY 3.0

Copyright © 2016 by Keira Andrews
Print Edition

ISBN: 978-1-988260-12-9

This is a work of fiction. Names, characters, businesses, places, events and incidents are either the products of the author's imagination or used in a fictitious manner. No persons, living or dead, were harmed by the writing of this book. Any resemblance to any actual persons, living or dead, or actual events is purely coincidental.

Dedication

To all the skaters putting in long hours in cold arenas who've inspired me with their athleticism, artistry, and work ethic.

Thanks to Becky, Mary, Anara, and Rachel for their support and friendship, as always.

Author's Note

I wrote the original version of *The Next Competitor* in 2009 and published it as a YA novel in 2010. I always thought there was more potential in it, and I've rewritten and updated the book extensively for this new adult romance edition.

It takes place in the not-too-distant future, and although several real-life skaters are mentioned briefly, the characters and story are completely fictional. For example, when I conceived the character of Kenny Tanaka, it was long before Yuzuru Hanyu started training in Toronto. Any similarities to actual skaters are coincidental.

It was interesting to look back at my old story and see what had changed in men's skating (quads are no longer optional!) and what hadn't (you still can't win in the short program, but you can lose). I hope you enjoy this story of love, discovery, and blood, sweat, and tears on ice.

CHAPTER ONE

I F PAVAROTTI CAN hit that high note, I'm going to land my goddamn quad.

The powerful surge of violins echoes in the frosty arena as I thrust out my arms dramatically, "Nessun Dorma" from the opera *Turandot* building to its first crescendo, my left leg stroking the ice powerfully as back crossovers take me around the corner of the rink and diagonally across.

Sucking in a deep breath, I visualize my quad Salchow, a.k.a. the jump that will vault me to the top of the Olympic podium in four months. I pull in and up off the back inside edge, arms crossing my chest tightly—one, two, three—

Slam!

My tangled feet hit the ice, my ass following as I crash down before completing the fourth revolution. Sliding to a dejected stop, I curl my hands into fists. The music dies, and I brave a glance at Mrs. C behind the boards on the other side of the rink.

In AP English senior year, we read a Yeats poem with the line: "A gaze blank and pitiless as the sun."

Mrs. C in a nutshell.

Beneath the elegant mink winter hat over her silver hair— pulled back into an impossibly tight bun as always—her stare doesn't falter. Her tailored leather coat hugs her petite frame. Diamonds glint from her earlobes, rings catching the harsh fluorescent light as she claps her hands once with an echoing *crack* in the frigid air. "Again, Alexander."

Everyone else calls me Alex, but I guess it's too friendly for Mrs. C. I don't bother wiping off the seat of my pants as I haul myself up since they soaked through half an hour ago. I haven't landed my quad Sal once today, and Mrs. C won't let me continue my long program until I do.

Her last name is Cheremisinova, but no one can pronounce it properly outside Russia. Her first name, Elena, is easy to say, but she might seriously kill me if I ever dared call her that. They'd find pieces of me buried in the huge snow bank the Zamboni makes behind the arena.

As I skate back to my starting position, "M&M" whiz by hand in hand. Mylene Bouchard and Matt Savelli are the two-time Canadian pairs champions and definitely candidates to end up on a Wheaties box. I'm not sure if Canada even does Wheaties boxes, but M&M are perfect for it: wholesome, hardworking, and very nice.

In short, very Canadian. He's twenty-four and she's nineteen, and Mylene has some personality, at least. I suspect Matt might be made entirely of chiseled cardboard. He never seems to get mad, and if he sighs heavily or puts his hands on his hips, that's his equivalent of throwing a hissy. I have to wonder if he even cares about winning.

As I take my position at center ice for the zillionth time, Matt and Mylene—pronounced "Mee-len" because she's French Canadian—practice a pairs spin in the corner. They whirl in place, Matt holding her close as Mylene yanks her foot up behind her with both hands, right to the back of her head in a Biellmann.

A lot of skating moves are named after the people who first performed them: Axel, Salchow, Lutz, Ina Bauer. Others just have boring names like loop and flip. The pairs do death spirals, but they aren't quite as dramatic as they sound.

Mylene is doing the heavy lifting in the spin, but then Matt does the literal lifting as they skate down the rink and he smoothly hoists her overhead, his T-shirt stretching across his muscles...

I apparently shouldn't have skipped my morning jerk-off session, and I give my head a shake to refocus as the familiar strains of opera fill the air. After the intro of my program, I reel off a quad toe-triple toe combo, then emote through my choreography and circle the rink to build speed for the quad Sal. Up, up—

Down.

I bite back a string of curses, Mrs. C's merciless gaze heavy as the music is silenced. My ass is numb and wet, and I just can't get the damn jump around today. At this point, I'll take a two-foot landing if it means staying on my feet.

I skate the long way around the rink, giving myself extra time to shake off the fall, a bruise on my hip smarting. Annie Frechette, one of the top Canadian women skaters, glides out of my path with a sympathetic smile. We all have time each day to play our music and do run-throughs, and the other skaters stay out of our way.

Kenny—really Kenjiro, but only his mother calls him that— Tanaka is at the other end of the rink, listening intently to Mrs. C's assistant coach, Rick. Kenny's been a Japanese national silver medalist twice and he trains in Toronto because skaters are rock stars over there and he can't leave the house in Tokyo without being mobbed by hordes of teenaged girls.

His mother sits in the second of the few rows of bleachers lining one side of the rink, watching silently, as she does every single day without fail.

I don't bother looking at Mrs. C as I take my spot again. Five more times the scenario repeats itself before I finally get the damn jump around and landed on one foot. There's scattered applause from the other skaters, coaches, and dedicated parents in the stands, and I know everyone is just happy not to have to listen to the same minute and a half of music over and over again.

The music plays on, and I nail my triple Axel, a jump that has always come easily to me, thank every deity in existence. In the old days—2010, to be exact—you could still win without the quad, but not the Axel.

These days, we need a quad in the short program and at least two in the long—preferably three. Some guys are doing four or five or even trying for six, but the rest of their skating isn't as polished. God help me if that changes.

Now we need the perfect combination of quads, footwork, spins, and artistry. Every moment of every program has to be jam-packed to rack up the points, and any day now someone will start doing a quad Axel or some crazy shit. The Axel is actually a revolution and a half since it takes off forward, and three and a half is the max anyone is doing.

For now.

Sailing into a flying camel, I catch air before landing on my right foot and spinning, my left leg extended straight behind me at waist level, upper body leaning forward, one arm reaching to the ceiling as the world rushes by in a blur. The music suddenly cuts out, and I jerk up, skidding to a stop.

"Free leg needs to be straighter. You're lazy."

I gnaw on my tongue. Spins are one of my best elements, and Mrs. C rarely criticizes them. This day *sucks* and it's barely even light out yet. I accept the inevitable as she regards me with cold eyes before issuing the dreaded order.

"Again."

ON MY WAY to the gym mid-morning, I stop by a wall of windows to peer at the swath of trees surrounding the country club housing the rink. Here in the north part of the city, I can almost imagine we're miles out into the country. Off to the right, clusters of people in visors and slacks—mostly rich seniors—play on the Valley Club's golf course, still a vibrant green in the warm late September.

Maybe I should go for a run on the trails instead of the treadmill, but it's too easy to twist an ankle. No, I have to be smart and stay focused. No unnecessary risks. Definitely not in an Olympic season. I snap a picture of the landscape and Instagram it with a caption about how lucky I am to train in such a beautiful place. Hashtag blessed.

Carrying a pile of textbooks, Mylene approaches, her flip-flops slapping. She wears jeans and a T-shirt proclaiming: *I'm not short—I'm just concentrated awesome.* At five-one, she's pretty damn short, but that's one of the things that make her perfect for pairs. She smiles brightly, which is her default expression and one of the other qualities I imagine make her a great partner. Too bad Matt's so bland.

"*Salut!*" She stops and eyes my running shoes and workout shorts. "Going to the gym?"

No, I'm going skiing. Even though sarcasm tends to be the first thing to always pop into my head, I'm working on keeping it there, so I bite back the automatic snark. "Yep. What are you learning today?" Mylene's taking a few classes at the University of Toronto, which frankly boggles my mind in an Olympic season.

"European history." She doesn't really say the letter *h*, so it sounds more like *istory.*

"So a bunch of white men building castles and oppressing people?"

She laughs. "Yep."

If I wasn't gay, I'd totally be into Mylene. Even though she's tiny, she still has hips and boobs, and her wide smile is killer. The French accent is adorable, and her curly brown hair and green eyes gleam. Her skin is light brown since her mother's white and her dad African-American. Well, African-Canadian, I guess, but so far I haven't heard anyone in Canada use that term.

"I don't know how you can worry about school when the Olympics are coming."

She shrugs. "It's nice not to think about skating all the time."

"Not think about skating all the time? I'm not following." I exaggerate the furrow of my brow, and she laughs on cue.

Then she gives me a shrewd look. "You know you really should take a break once in a while."

"I'll take a break when I win gold in Salzburg. You don't understand what it's like to *actually* be a contender. You'll be, what? Top ten at most?" I run through the pairs in my head like a TiVo on fast-forward. "Yeah, I think the best you can hope for is seventh, and that's assuming you land all your jumps and throws. So we're not really on the same level, you know?"

Holding the textbooks to her chest, Mylene blinks, her warm smile vanished. "We're aiming for the podium just like you. You're not the only one here with Olympic dreams."

Shit. "Oh, of course! I didn't mean..." She stares and offers no help as I flounder. "You guys are great, don't get me wrong!"

She laughs, short and sarcastic. "How would anyone ever get you wrong, Alex?" With that, she marches off.

Part of me wants to chase after her and apologize, but I have a workout schedule to keep. Besides, I'm not wrong, damn it. The only way she and Matt will make the podium is if a bunch of teams ahead of them implode. But that doesn't mean they won't make it in four more years—pairs are sometimes in their thirties by the time they build as a team and put it all together to win.

So not thinking about skating all the time is fine for her right now. But me? I'm going to be Olympic champion. I'm going to win. I *have* to win.

The gym—a bright, mirrored room containing several cardio machines, free weights, foam rollers, mats, TRX bands, and a weight machine circuit—is predictably deserted. Weekends are busy with club members, but on weekdays outside of summer we skaters have it mostly to ourselves. Our trainers come in a couple times a week, and I strictly follow my workout instructions.

Before hopping on a treadmill, I go to the mirrors and tug down the collar of my T-shirt. Running my fingers over the spot just below my right collarbone, I imagine the tattoo I'm going to have inked after I win gold in Salzburg. It'll just be the Olympic rings in black—simple and totally cliché. But I've dreamt of this tattoo since I was a kid doing single Axels and I saw a Russian skater on TV with the rings inked on his bicep.

"You're going to do it. You can do it. You can beat them all." Staring at my reflection, I nod decisively, then turn to the treadmill and crank up the volume on my iPod.

I have a lot of hip-hop and dance playlists, but sometimes I listen to the songs I've skated to in the past. As I run up an imaginary hill, arms and legs pumping, I close my eyes and relive my long program from last season, one of my favorites of my career.

The music is so familiar now it's practically been imprinted in my DNA. John Williams's score from an old Spielberg movie called *Empire of the Sun* soars, driving my pace as I pound the treadmill.

Sweat beads on my forehead as the hill steepens, but I'm a million miles away in my head as the music swells and I perform a textbook triple Axel-single loop-triple Salchow sequence—in the second half of my program too, so ten percent bonus on the score.

In my memory, the crowd cheers so loudly the music is almost drowned out as I move into my footwork sequence. My feet fly across the ice as I weave my way down the rink, changing edges constantly, twisting one way and then the next, staying deep in my knees. My blades carve the ice effortlessly, body and mind in perfect unison, the endless training paying off.

This is the program I skated in Cincinnati seven months earlier when I won my first US national title, and I remember the surge of elation and roar of the crowd as I whirl into my final spin as if it were yesterday.

With a shout of triumph, adrenaline pumping, I thrust up my arms. In the moment of silence before the next song on my playlist, there's applause that's most definitely not in my head. I open my eyes to find Matt and Kenny standing by the weight bench, laughing and clapping.

My face flushes hot, sticky embarrassment sparking to anger as I yank out my earbuds, their laughter grating my nerves. I jab at the treadmill screen to stop my workout, then open my mouth to bark out a couple of insults so they'll feel as awkward and embarrassed as I do.

Kenny approaches. "Are you big winner?"

Looking at his smile, I force my lungs to expand, pressing my lips together. Being mean to him is like kicking a puppy. Even though Kenny's a medal contender and my competition, he's so sweet I can't resent him. Believe me, I've tried.

I manage a laugh. Okay, I must have looked ridiculous, cheering for myself on a treadmill. "Yeah, the big winner. That's me."

Kenny ducks in a little nod/bow and shakes my hand to mock congratulate me while Matt racks weights on a barbell, smiling. It still irks that Captain Cardboard is laughing at my expense—he doesn't even *know* me—but I hop off the treadmill and ignore him and his stupidly perfect smile.

Matt and I have barely said more than a few words to each other in the couple months I've been training at the rink, but something about him rubs me the wrong way. He's so calm and smiley, not to mention annoyingly good looking.

He's several inches taller than me and more built. Yet he's still long and lean, and not huge like some of the male pairs skaters. His dark brown hair is full and glossy, his thick eyebrows prominent over hazel eyes.

While we haven't talked much, one day in the locker room I caught him frowning at me in obvious disapproval while another skater and I gossiped about the worst new costumes of the season. Sorry not sorry, but Tatiana Safina's yellow, feathered monstrosity makes her look like Big Bird.

Matt's clearly a total killjoy and goody two-shoes, as my Grandma would say. I'm not really clear on what that means, but I'm going with it. So as hot as he is, I'll take a hard pass on Matt—not that I'm looking to hook up, or that he'd want me anyway. I suspect he's gay, since there's something about the way he *doesn't* look at beautiful women around the rink, but I'm sure he's banging dudes just as buff as he is.

Regardless, I jerk off to sleep most nights and again in the morning, and that's enough until I win gold.

Kenny says to me, "Busy later?" He pauses, seemingly searching for a word. "Saturday?"

I only moved to Toronto this summer and know no one outside the rink, which is perfect. But Kenny's so sweet he's hard to say no to. I groan internally, bracing myself. "Just training. Um, what's up?"

"My birthday. We go eat and dance. Salsa."

An excuse automatically cues itself up on my tongue, but looking at his hopeful face, I can't pull the trigger. "Sounds fun. I can't stay out late, but I'll come for a bit."

With a grin, Kenny does his little nod/bow again. The truth is, he kind of worships me. I'm popular in Japan, and even though Kenny's a huge star himself now, when we toured over there in early summer, he still stuck to me like glue.

With the language barrier it's hard to really have deep and meaningful conversations, which makes Kenny the perfect friend. We can just smile and have fun once in a while, and that's that.

Kenny lowers himself to the weight bench and picks up the

barbell as Matt stands just behind his head, spotting. Kenny grunts as he lowers the weight, and I marvel that anyone that small and skinny can reel off quads. For him it seems so easy, and I choke down a dark spike of resentment.

Settling on the rowing machine, I put my earbuds back in and play a workout mix. I quickly find a rhythm that matches the thumping beat, pulling with my arms as I push with my legs, feeling it in my glutes.

When I found out Mrs. C was moving her coaching operation from New Jersey to Toronto, and that Kenny was leaving his coach in Japan for her, I wasn't sure what to think. But training with him pushes me to be better, and it's nice to have at least one person around who adores me, since Mrs. C sure doesn't.

I yank on the rowing cable, regulating my breathing in time with my strokes. Admittedly, I'm not always the easiest person to get along with. I've had four coaches since I was fourteen, and I'm twenty now. My last coach was way too motherly and coddling, and the one before that didn't push me enough either. For all my bitching about Mrs. C, I need her. Warm and fuzzy won't get me to the top.

In the past year, I won my national title and got the bronze medal at Worlds in March. I'm now one of the men to beat at the Olympics, and I have Mrs. C and her pitiless gaze to thank.

She was the Russian pairs champion a million years ago with her husband, Boris, and they won gold at Worlds a bunch of times and twice at the Olympics. Boris died a couple of years ago, so I never met him. Mrs. C has never mentioned his name once, but it's not like we sit around and braid each other's hair and talk about our feelings.

Now if I can only master the quad Sal, I'll be on my way to the gold medal. Tanner Nielsen can do the toe, the Sal, *and* posted videos of training the quad Lutz this summer. The smug bastard.

I jerk a towel over my sweaty face, yanking harder on the rowing cable as images of Tanner and his golden hair, sky blue eyes, and perfect, dazzling smile invade my head. He's the classic all-American jock, and he wouldn't know true artistry if it bit him in the nuts.

Across the room, Kenny bounds up from the weight bench and smiles at me, flexing his slight biceps as Matt takes his place. I give Kenny a leering wink, and he giggles. He's not gay, but we joke sometimes that he's my skating boyfriend. It's not like he has any competition off the ice anyway.

A lot of people outside skating think we're all gay, but the majority of the guys are actually straight, even with their sequins and ruffles. Some of us are gay or bi, but every job in the world has LGBT people in it. Skating isn't really that different.

It even has crappy homophobia too, which I know all too well. I'm not super popular with the people in charge of the United States Figure Skating Federation. To be fair, part of the reason is because I have a tendency to say things to the media that are…controversial. I like to think of myself as honest, but as Mom puts it, I was born without a filter between my brain and mouth.

Sometimes honesty isn't the best policy, especially now with social media, where one offhand comment gets tweeted and dissected to death.

But regardless of my flaws, homophobia plays a role too. American networks love a champion with a beautiful wife or girlfriend they can show in the stands. If a male skater is married with kids, the commentators usually mention it approximately a zillion times. Things are changing, but not soon enough for me. For the Federation, the sun beams out of Tanner Nielsen's hetero, muscular ass, and they weren't too happy when I won the title.

Rowing harder, I revel in the memories of beating Tanner by seven glorious points at Nationals. Sure, he missed two of his jumps and basically handed me the victory on a silver platter, but I still won that gold fair and square.

Tanner is the poster boy for American skating, and advertisers love his perfect hair, square jaw, and beautiful girlfriend—who still reigns as America's sweetheart after winning gold at the last Olympics.

Lisa Ackles promptly retired at nineteen after her surprise Olympic victory and now spends her time touring with ice shows or doing her bit looking gorgeous and fresh-faced in the audience cheering on Tanner. Her hair is so blond it practically glows, and she's the spokesperson for American Girl makeup and a whitening toothpaste.

On the other hand, I have plain brown eyes and dirty blond hair I highlight so it isn't a totally mousy shade. Even though I'm in damn good shape, I don't ripple with muscles like Tanner.

I glance across the gym to where Matt is pressing the barbell, sweat glistening on his skin like it's been sprayed there. He and Tanner are definitely cut from the same buff, six-pack-abs cloth.

I've always been on the thinner side, although at least I don't look as if a stiff wind will blow me away like Kenny. I used to have a snaggle tooth I had fixed with veneers that weren't cheap. Still, my smile isn't quite as straight and flawless as Tanner's or Matt's. At five-seven, I'm not technically short, but I avoid standing next to Tanner without my skates on.

As for a camera-ready girlfriend in the stands, I definitely don't have one of those. While I don't wear a rainbow flag pinned to my costume, I've never really hidden my sexuality. I knew by the time I was ten that I wanted to kiss boys, not girls.

Granted, I've still barely kissed anyone, which is a little embarrassing at my age. But it's only because training has consumed my life, not because I'm confused.

When I gathered my courage in junior high and told my parents I was going on a date—my first and pretty much last so far—with an ice dancer named Kevin, they just gave me twenty bucks and told me to be home by ten.

There are a few out skaters, like Rudy Galindo, Matty Marcus, Eric Radford, and Adam Rippon. Brian Boitano, but he took decades. They're all retired, and even though I know it would probably be okay to come out officially, I need every tenth of a point to beat Tanner, and you never know which judges might have prejudices. I'm not giving him any advantage.

So it's not a *secret* I'm gay, but I'm not prepared to put myself out there publicly. The girls in Asia love me because I'm the cover boy for *Non-Threatening American Male Monthly*. I make a good amount of cash over there doing shows, and now that I'm US champion, I made a King Sub sandwich ad in Jersey. It's not much, but I need it to pay the bills, and I have an agent to try and get me more deals.

I make prize money when I do well at competitions, but skating is *hella* expensive. There's ice time, lessons with Mrs. C, costumes and choreographers, trainers and physio, ballet classes, my boots and blades, sharpening, traveling costs for competitions and bringing Mrs. C with me. Never mind rent, food, gas, etc., etc., etc.

The Federation helps with some expenses, but to pay off my parents' double mortgage—which they took out for my skating— and buy myself another car when my beater Honda Civic throws in the towel, I need endorsements.

Ugh, just thinking about it makes me want to reach for the Tums.

After my daily half-hour stretching routine, I nod to Kenny and Captain Cardboard and make a pit stop in the locker room to change back into my skating clothes.

A ratty old T-shirt and black stretch pants are all I usually wear in practice, although at a competition, my practice gear is new and color-coordinated since the judges are watching. With some judges, every impression counts. It's not really fair, but welcome to figure skating.

In the club's lounge, one wall of the sizable room is glass over-looking the rink a story below. On the other side there's a small café with a few round tables and chairs. I buy a can of Coke, knowing Mrs. C is on the rink. Her face would pinch like she'd just chomped a lemon if she spotted me, but I need the caffeine boost.

Flopping on a soft brown leather couch by the large window, I pull my lunch from my gym bag. As I eat my peanut butter sandwich on enriched white—I can't stand whole wheat even if it's better for me—I watch Mrs. C coaching a young Latvian pair, Oksana and Maxim.

Maxim's twenty and little Oksana's only sixteen and not even five feet tall yet. Blond Maxim's a jokester, always with big smiles, but she's serious and shy, often saying little and watching instead while she winds her dark ringlets around her finger.

They came from Latvia to train with Mrs. C, and they rent rooms in her large house in the northern suburbs of the city. They drive in every morning with her and go home with her every night, and I fully expect them to go batshit within six months. I can't imagine *living* with Mrs. C. Her house is probably like a museum where you can't touch anything or relax, and she gives you that death stare when you take the last banana.

Chantal Penault, M&M and Annie Frechette's coach, joins Mrs. C and makes a few comments about Oksana and Maxim, motioning to them as they practice a lift. Chantal never got very far as a skater herself, but she's had a ton of success as a coach. Middle-aged, blond, and plump, she has a warm smile and a sing-songy voice.

Chantal and Mrs. C share opinions about each other's skaters and offer suggestions, but aside from supportive smiles and a few comments now and then, Chantal doesn't have anything to do with my training.

Mylene isn't back yet, but I watch as Matt returns to the rink, gliding around it with powerful strokes, black Lycra clinging to his long legs. He reels off a gorgeous triple Lutz-triple toe-double toe, which I grudgingly admit is impressive for a pairs skater since their side-by-side jumps tend to be easier.

Mylene appears, bending to remove her skate guards before gliding onto the ice. As Matt nears, he extends his hand, and she takes it without even looking. A strange jealousy pulses in me, low and prickly.

It's stupid, since I'd be a terrible partner. First off, I'm not tall enough, but more importantly, I get so mad at myself when I make mistakes that I'd probably be a complete dick to the poor girl stuck with me.

Still, as I watch M&M circle the rink hand in hand, I can't help but wish I had a big, strong man to be by my side and catch me when I fall. Obviously not Matt, since he'd probably put me to sleep being so pleasant and bland all day long, but…

Snorting, I take a big bite of my sandwich, the peanut butter sticking to the roof of my mouth. Sure, maybe I want a boyfriend sometimes, but I have zero time for that. Zilch, nada, nope. I have my hands full with my own bullshit, let alone someone else's.

Soon I'll be competing on the Grand Prix circuit in my two assigned events, trying to get enough points to make the final in December. The top six skaters or teams overall in each discipline square off at the final, and the momentum from a win there will be vital heading into the Olympics. I have to win. Have to prove I'm the best.

And Jesus, then I have to defend my title at Nationals in January. I can't be beaten by Tanner. I *cannot.*

Washing down the sandwich with my forbidden Coke, I try to calm my racing heart. The nails on my left hand dig into my palm, leaving accusatory half-moons.

On the ice, Matt and Mylene are still holding hands, stroking around the rink with easy smiles for each other.

I crumple the Coke can, and when I get on the ice, I put on my broad, beaming competition smile and pretend the judges are already watching.

CHAPTER TWO

"N O!"

I skid to a stop, snow flying from my blades. Mrs. C stands by the boards, her mouth a thin line. I just popped my Lutz—the worst thing to do when jumping.

If you try and fall, you can still get points for the rotation even if you blow the landing. But if you pop—bailing out of the jump in the air and only doing a single or double—the points nosedive. Mrs. C has a strict no-popping policy.

"It just didn't feel right in the air." I don't know why I bother defending myself. I only pop jumps when I'm not concentrating or I'm afraid I won't land it and I don't fully commit. There's no excuse.

Accordingly, Mrs. C doesn't dignify my explanation with a response, simply ordering, "Again."

Today we've taken a break from my quad Sal and are working on elements in my short program. I restart the segment with my flying camel spin, reaching my limbs and pointing my toe. After completing the revolutions, I launch myself into the connecting steps leading to my Lutz.

Extending my left leg, I plunge my toe pick into the ice, vaulting into the air for the jump. My right shoulder drops and I can't hold the landing, gravity toppling me over, my hip throbbing from all the quad falls earlier in the week.

Mrs. C nods. "Better. But stay in circle."

As long as I don't pop, she doesn't mind me falling. I mean, she *minds,* but as long as I commit to the jumps, it's okay. Nodding, I return to the end of the rink where M&M are practicing their side-by-side triple Salchows.

They have to get the timing perfect to take off and land in complete unison. They've been skating together for six years, so they have the timing down pat. However, Mylene's having trouble, not getting high enough to do the three revolutions cleanly. Today she's either two-footing her landings or coming up short and falling.

As she pushes herself off the ice with a grimace, I refocus and zone them out. Spin, footwork, then triple Lutz—up, around, keeping my body straight up and down—what they call "in the circle" as I rotate. Then I'm down and gliding back on my right foot with as much speed as I had going into the jump, left leg and arms extended.

Grinning widely, I turn to Mrs. C, who actually cracks a smile. "Perfect." When she compliments you, at least you know she means it.

I take a break to drink water and scarf down a banana, leaning against the boards in the corner while Mrs. C corrects Kenny's flying sit spin, his mother following every movement like a hawk from the stands. In another corner, Annie watches while Chantal skates on the rink with her and demonstrates footwork.

Meanwhile, Mylene slams onto the ice again on her triple Sal. On her ass, she bursts into tears, and I can sure as hell relate. It's so goddamn frustrating when you can't get something right, no matter how hard you try.

Matt gently lifts Mylene to her feet and folds her into his strong arms, her head barely reaching his shoulder. Holding her close, he lets her cry, murmuring something I can't make out, enveloping her protectively.

I wonder what perfect Matt smells like, and how warm his body would feel even in the chill of the rink…

Matt's gaze meets mine, a furrow forming between his brows.

I wheel around as Mrs. C approaches, tossing my banana peel into a garbage can beyond the boards. Of course I miss, and even though she's only standing a few feet from it, Mrs. C waits for me to skate to the exit halfway up the rink, put my blade guards on, and clomp back over to throw away the peel.

When I return to the ice, Mrs. C comes with me, and we go through the positions on my combination spin. At times she stops me and places my limbs just so, and I do my best to extend exactly the way she wants.

After a long afternoon, I heave a sigh when it's time to leave, so ready for a quick dinner at my bare-bones apartment, more stretching, and an early night. Dropping onto a bench in the locker room, I unlace my skates, wincing as I coax one cramped foot out.

"Rough day?"

I look up to find Matt a few feet away, coming in from the bathroom and pulling his sweaty purple tee over his head. His chest is broad and dusted with dark hair, especially around his pink nipples…

Jerking my head down, I yank off my other skate. "Rough? Not for me." I hate admitting weakness to other skaters, even if I don't compete against them. Matt sees more than enough of my weaknesses in practice every day.

"Mylene is trying her best, you know."

Blinking, I stare up at him. "Huh?"

Matt eyes me in that even, watchful way he has that makes me squirm. "You probably think she's weak for crying, but some of us need to vent our emotions."

"When did I say anything about Mylene?"

His thick eyebrow arches. "I saw you looking earlier. I can

imagine what you were thinking."

I was thinking about what a good hugger you seem to be. Too bad about the sanctimonious streak.

"I wasn't thinking anything."

Matt shrugs. "Okay. If you say so."

I just said it, didn't I?

He balls up his shirt and shoves it in his duffel bag before tugging on a sweatshirt. "I just don't want anyone putting more pressure on her. She puts enough on herself because she's afraid she's letting me down. I know you don't care what people think, but she does."

With that, he heaves his bag onto his shoulder and walks out of the locker room. Shoving my aching feet into sneakers, I lace them too tightly. Mylene's cool and even though I might say dumb things sometimes, I'd never side-eye her for falling on jumps.

But Matt's right about one thing—I don't care what people think, especially not *him.*

AFTER MY FIRST round of practice the next morning, I collapse on a bench and chug a bottle of water. I landed seven perfect quad toe-triple toe combinations, and I should be happy. But last week I landed nine in one practice, and I haven't matched it since.

And the less said about the quad Sal, the better.

My plan was to have it eighty percent consistent by Skate America, my first Grand Prix event. At this point I'll take fifty, and not meeting my goals makes me twitchy and anxious. I'll be in front of a home crowd, which is a huge advantage, but also adds a ton of pressure.

On the way to the gym, my phone chirps out a cheesy Celine Dion love song, which my little sister, Rachel, added as my ringtone when I told her I was moving to Canada. I probably should change it to something less lame, but it makes me smile every time.

After a glance at the display, I tap the screen. "Hi, Mom."

"Hi, sweetheart! How was practice?" She's spent almost as much time in skating rinks as me over the years, and has my schedule memorized.

"I only landed one clean quad Sal."

"That's better than none, isn't it?"

I scoff. "Barely."

"Don't be so hard on yourself. Remember, that new quad isn't everything. It's only one jump."

Yeah, right. One jump that Tanner Nielsen and Vladimir Sidorov can perform consistently. If I want to beat them, I need more than just the quad toe. We're allowed to do triples or quads twice in a long program—once on its own and once in combination. If I want a third quad, it has to be another jump other than the toe, and the Sal is my best chance.

"I'm going to get it. Don't you think I can?" I cringe at my sharp, defensive squawk.

"Of course I do," she answers calmly. "You know what I'm saying. Don't put all your focus on this one jump and forget about the rest of your skating. Don't obsess so much about what the other guys are doing. Be your best you."

I exhale a long breath. "I know, Mom. Don't worry, okay?" The odds of me not obsessing over the other competitors are about zero, and obviously she's well aware I'll be obsessing no matter how many assurances I give. Mothers always know, or at least mine does.

"Okay. I should get back to work. Be good, and please say hello to Mrs. C. Love you."

"Same. Tell Dad and Rach I said hi."

When we hang up, I lean in the hallway by the big windows

over the golf course and let the homesickness wash over me, a barbed ache I struggle to breathe through. We moved around a couple times because of my dad's job in software and then my training, but my folks have settled in New Jersey. It was perfect when Mrs. C was running her school out of Trenton, but now here we are.

Giving myself an actual shake, bouncing and shimmying my limbs, I refocus and continue to the gym. It's empty except for Matt of all people, because of course. Ignoring him and his bicep curls, I scroll through my iPod to find the right song. I definitely do not look twice at the way Matt's dark chest hair pokes above the scooped collar of his tank top.

It's possible I have a few fantasies in my spank bank involving chest hair and jerking off on it, getting my cum all smeared and caught...

Jabbing the iPod, I crank the volume and hop on the treadmill farthest away from Matt.

Half an hour later, I'm counting out my tenth rep on the prone leg curl machine when I break down and glance at Matt's reflection in one of the mirrors as he works his quadriceps on the machine behind me. He's breathing hard, and I have no idea why I can't just ignore him since I don't even *like* him.

Matt's one of those guys I bet most people think is straight, despite the figure skating thing. Since so many pairs end up dating, a lot of people probably assume Matt and Mylene are a couple. However, my gaydar has never let me down, and I'm sure he's playing for my team. Not that it matters, since *ugh*.

I finish my last set of leg curls and gulp down some water before heading over to the weight bench. In the reflection, Matt says something and motions to me, but I can't hear it over classic Eminem. I press pause. "What?"

"I'll spot you."

I stretch out on the bench and reach up for the loaded bar.

"Nah, don't worry about it." I don't need any favors from him.

Suddenly Matt looms over my head. "Well, it's not really safe. You should always have someone spot you when you're lifting that much weight."

I roll my eyes. I doubt Matt has ever broken a rule in his life. "Okay, okay."

Lowering the bar to my chest, I push it back up again as Matt hovers over me. Staring at his upside-down face, I wonder what it would be like to kiss his plump, reddish lips.

He's clean-shaven for competitions, but at the moment, stubble covers his cheeks and chin, and the crazy urge to rub my face against his grips me. The few kisses I've had were before the boys I knew really had facial hair.

Ugh, kissing Captain Cardboard would be like kissing a girl. No sparks. Matt would probably keep his mouth closed and not use tongue, and would be all boring and rule-abiding. It would be like kissing that cartoon Mountie—Dudley whoeverthefuck, who'd been in a few of the Canadian YouTube vids Rachel had sent so I could "prepare for the unrelenting niceness."

I don't even know why I'm thinking about this, and I concentrate instead on lifting the barbell up and down, my chest muscles flexing. I put more weight on the bar than I normally do, and my arms tremble.

Matt says, "Come on, you can do it. Three more." He puts his hands out so he can help me with the bar if need be.

A grunt escapes as I heave it up and down. My arms shake now, and on the last rep, Matt helps me lift and places the bar back in its holder for me.

"Good job!" He gives me a smile, and upside down it certainly looks genuine. He sounds like he's for real, and my chest flushes warm with pleasure. Which is ridiculous since why should I want his approval?

I sit up and stretch my arms back. It hurts, but no way in hell

I'll admit it. "Want me to spot you?" I ask. I kind of have to now.

"Sure. Thanks."

He adds extra weight to each end of the bar before we switch places. He lifts it with no problem at first, but after twenty reps, starts to tire. I count out five more for him, and he makes them all without my help.

"Um, good job, dude." I'm not sure why, but I feel the need to make conversation. "Were you practicing a singles routine yesterday?"

Matt sits and wipes his forehead with a towel. Sweat drips down the hollow of this throat, his legs spread as he straddles the weight bench. As I wait for him to answer, I chug from my water bottle, my throat suddenly dry.

"It's just for fun, really. We both competed in singles at Nationals, but Mylene dropped it this season. I still might give it a go. Keeps my jumps sharp."

"Good idea. Can I do another set?"

We swap positions, and Matt removes the extra weight from the bar. This irritates me, which I know is completely irrational, but I want to prove that I can lift as much. That I'm just as good as he is. I'm about to tell him to put the weight back on even though I never go off-plan when Mylene and Annie burst in, chattering in French at the speed of light. They wave before hopping on elliptical trainers, still talking.

I choke down my competitive stubbornness and do my set with the lower weight, managing to finish all the reps without any help. When I sit up, I murmur, "Can you understand them?"

Matt smiles. "A little. Usually they're too fast for me to keep up. I was better when we were training in Quebec, but most of the time I don't know what they're saying."

"Seriously doubt they have many deep thoughts you're missing out on." I smirk.

Matt's smile vanishes. "Why would you say that? You don't

know the first thing about them."

Shit. Why *would* I say that? Maybe because at my last training center, the cattiness was off the charts, and it became automatic. Or maybe because I'm an asshole. Either way, defensiveness spikes through me. "Look, I was just kidding."

"Mylene and Annie work hard. So what if they gossip and giggle and let off steam sometimes?"

He's right, of course. "Sorry, I didn't mean—"

"Mylene and I have Skate America soon. We're both stressed."

"I know. So am I."

"She has school, and I have shifts four nights a week in the restaurant here. We're working really hard."

"So am I!"

Before I can say anything else, Oksana appears, her typically serious face positively solemn. "Alex." She points in the general direction of the rink. "You go."

Crap. I've been summoned. This can't be good. I turn back to Matt, but he's racking the weights, ignoring me. Okay, so I know I shouldn't joke about his partner, especially since I like her and Annie both. Sometimes I just feel the urge to be bitchy. I'm not proud of it.

In the rink, Mrs. C sits in the vacant stands, a few rows above the ice. She looks the same as always: silver hair pulled back, face made up with dark red lipstick shining on her lips, an expensive and stylish leather coat buttoned to her throat, where a brooch sparkles. I sit a couple feet away and wait. I've tried to figure out what I'm in trouble for, but I can't think of anything.

After leaving me hanging for what feels like an eternity, she finally speaks, her narrowed gaze still on the ice, where junior skaters practice with Rick and Chantal. "Tell me about phone call."

Oh *shit*. The bottom drops from my stomach. Okay, so I might have made one teeny, tiny mistake.

I try playing dumb. "What call?"

She shoots me a glare that could turn you to stone.

"Mrs. C, I just told the truth. The Federation doesn't support me the way they do Tanner. Everyone knows he's their favorite. He's been assigned Skate America for the last five years in a row. This is the first time they've ever given it to me, and you know they only did because I won Nationals and it would have sent a message to the skating world if they sent me to China and Russia like usual. And of course Golden Boy got the other spot."

"So you told this to reporter?"

I swallow hard, my throat suddenly dry. I simply nod.

She says something in Russian that I can't understand. In English, she tells me, "You are very foolish boy."

The problem is she's right. That filter between my brain and mouth is clearly a work in progress. I'm a total idiot, and my stomach churns, shame coursing through me, hot and prickly. I hang my head. "Did that guy from the website mention it in his story?"

"Of course. It is going to be headline. He called to get quote from me."

Uh-oh. I can just imagine how much the Feds are going to love me now after I stir up bad press for them. "What did you tell him?"

"Maybe that it wasn't such a good idea for story. Maybe he should leave that out."

A ray of hope cuts through my misery. "Really? What did he say?"

"We talked for little while, and he came around to my way of thinking."

I seriously think this woman might be in the Russian mob. She's five foot three and probably a hundred pounds, but she is a force of nature. Eventually, everyone comes around to Mrs. C's way of thinking.

"Thank you. I don't know what to say."

She turns her gaze on me, making me feel about two feet high. "Say you won't be stupid boy again. At Skate America, you will say only nice things to reporters. Only nice things to everyone."

I nod vigorously and wait to see if I will escape unscathed. When she dismisses me with a flick of her hand, I gratefully scuttle away, vowing to make sure my mouth won't get me into trouble again.

"COULD THIS PLACE be lamer?"

Of course, the music hits a lull as soon as I say it, and everyone hears me. Even if Kenny doesn't quite understand the words, he definitely catches my tone. Hurt flickers across his face.

"I think it's awesome!" Mylene grins and slings her arm around Kenny, kissing him on the cheek.

Matt chimes in, "Yeah, it's great."

Oksana, Maxim, Annie, and a few other skaters from the rink follow Mylene and Kenny to our table, which is right near the dance floor of this Spanish restaurant/salsa club. We're by far the youngest people here, and I guess it's just me, but I feel incredibly out of place. Because the restaurant is actually really cool and hip, and I *so* don't belong.

"Why do you have to be like that?" Matt has lingered behind.

"Like what?" I ask, even though I know exactly what he means. I tug on the collar of my green Henley. Maybe I should tuck it into my jeans. Am I dressed too casually? Are people staring? I should have worn leather shoes instead of sneakers.

"Can't you just relax and have fun?" Matt's wearing a maroon light-weight sweater that hugs his lean muscles, and dark jeans that accentuate the curve of his ass. His black boots are perfect and shiny. "You're always so cynical."

"Relax? It's—"

"An Olympic season," Matt finishes for me. "I know. We all know. This is one night. It's Kenny's birthday. Try and unclench for, like, five minutes."

I can't think of a witty comeback, so I shrug and brush past him. As if Captain Cardboard knows how to have fun. At the table, I sit and wait until the waitress has taken our drink orders to give Kenny his birthday present, which is part joke and part serious. The joke part is the porno DVD, and Kenny blushes furiously when he unwraps it and sees the bare breasts on the cover.

Everyone whoops with laughter, and I tell him, "Don't let your mother see that!" In all seriousness, Kenny could probably use some porn. I'm amazed his mom let him come out with all of us tonight without adult supervision even though he's turning eighteen. "Oh, and there's something else inside."

Kenny pops open the DVD case and pulls out two front row, first-base tickets to the last regular season Blue Jays game. It's against the Yankees, so it should be a good one. His face lights up. "Baseball!" He does his nod/bow. "You will come?"

Even though I cringe at the thought of taking time away from training—or resting for training—I tell him I'd love to and hope he's forgotten my earlier dickish comment. He opens the rest of his gifts, and as we eat heaping plates of paella, a live band starts playing in the corner. Those of us nineteen or older are sharing pitchers of sangria, but Kenny and Oksana totally steal some gulps as well.

After our plates are cleared away, Kenny and the girls hit the dance floor, shimmying their hips. Maxim watches Oksana longingly, but doesn't join them until she rolls her eyes and comes back to tug him over by the hand.

Part of me wants to give it a try, but the thought of people watching me keeps me rooted in my wooden chair. Maybe it's weird for a figure skater to not want attention, but it's different on the ice. I know what I'm doing there, and I prefer to have all my moves choreographed by a professional.

"Not so bad after all?" Matt raises an eyebrow and looks pointedly at my hand, which is tapping along to the beat on the table.

"Okay, it's fun, I admit it. I was wrong. You were right."

He swallows a mouthful of sangria, and I'm jealous since the pitchers are empty. Matt slides his glass across the table as if he's read my mind. "You look thirsty."

"Um, thanks." *Super eloquent.* I gratefully take a big chug. It's not like I'm a secret alcoholic or anything, but Matt's even gaze makes me fidget.

"Go on and finish it." He waves to the waitress and orders another pitcher, along with tequila shots.

Huh. Maybe good ol' Matt isn't as boring as I thought. And okay, as he licks the V of his hand between his thumb and first finger to sprinkle salt on his skin, my breath catches and my dick comes to life.

I rip my gaze away and lick my own hand, nearly sending the glass salt shaker flying with clumsy fingers. When I look up, Matt's still just watching me with an unreadable expression that makes me shift anxiously in my chair.

He asks, "Ready?" and holds out his shot glass.

I clink it with mine, pulling my twitchy hand back just enough at the last second to avoid smashing the glasses together and spilling the tequila. We lick our hands, and after the sharp prickle of salt, the tequila burns a path down my throat.

As I shove a slice of lemon in my mouth and suck the tart juice, Matt slaps the table with his palm, grimacing.

He coughs. "Smooth."

Laughter barks out of me, and the stiffness in my spine loosens as we smile together and do two more rounds of shots with sangria chasers. As I'm licking salt remnants from my hand, the tequila going down much more easily, a short, plump older woman appears at our table. "You boys must dance! Come salsa."

I shake my head, but she yanks my arm with surprising strength and drags me onto the dance floor, Matt following, thank God. He shakes his hips like a pro and spins the woman around while I shuffle awkwardly, convinced everyone is watching and thinking about how terrible I am.

Maybe he'll dance with me once the lady gets tired.

I have zero clue where that bizarre thought comes from, but tequila and wine have clearly played a role. Why would I want to dance with Matt? Besides, I've been taking ballet lessons for grace and extension since I was a kid, but salsa is way out of my league.

Suddenly Mylene has hold of my hand, and she pulls me into the group. "Just feel the rhythm," she shouts.

The tequila and wine have done their work, and a warm buzz washes over me as Matt catches my eye and smiles, giving the woman a kiss on the cheek before squeezing into our circle, our arms brushing. My feet are on air, and as I shimmy around the floor, I feel like I'm in my skates, safe on the ice.

PRACTICE ON MONDAY morning comes way too soon. My hangover on Sunday kept me holed up in my tiny apartment instead of my normal grocery shopping, food prep, run, and several hours of stretching. I'm convinced Mrs. C is well aware of exactly how much tequila was consumed Saturday night.

Skate America is in three weeks, and I have to make a strong impression at my first competition of the season. The *Olympic* season. I repeat these words to myself every time I want to take a break.

The Olympic season. The motherfucking *Olympic season.*

What had I been thinking going out on Saturday and getting wasted? I chug from my water bottle sitting on top of the boards and pledge to be more responsible. The Olympics are every four years. Tequila and hot guys will be around anytime.

Yes, I admit it—Matt's hot. Captain Cardboard's an attractive man, and when he smiles at me, I want to please him and make him smile more, especially when he really grins and his eyes crinkle around the edges and—

"Alexander!"

My stomach twists as I realize Mrs. C has apparently called me more than once. "Huh?" Grimacing, I add, "I mean, yes?"

She stares at me from her spot beyond the boards, unamused. "Break time is over. Quad Sal. Now."

Nodding, I do a few quick laps of the rink, gliding out of Annie's way before setting up for my quad and—

Slam. I slide across the ice, pain radiating from my hip.

Mrs. C issues her verdict. "You think of too many things. Think of only the jump." She claps her hands together sharply. "Again."

I do it again with the same result.

"Bad timing. Stop pulling upper body." She dips her knees and motions upward with her hands, palms to the ceiling. "Must come from the ice. Let jumps flow."

As the morning drags on, Mylene and Matt practice one of their lifts that has a blind entry—they're facing different directions as the lift goes up—and three changes of position in the air.

Mylene grins as she soars. They cover the whole length of the ice with this lift, making it look easy as they speed along, Mylene's position shifting until all her weight is balanced on her hip in the palm of Matt's hand and she reaches back to catch her top skate blade with one hand, her back curving into a bow.

I can't think of many teams in the world who lift as well as M&M do. She has incredible balance and flexibility, and Matt is strong and fast. Unlike some of the other guys, when you watch Matt's feet on a lift, his turns are smooth as silk, no snow flying up from his blades.

"Alexander."

I blink back to attention and find Mrs. C gazing at me. "Huh? Oh, sorry."

"You watch handsome boys on own time."

I nearly choke. "What? I'm not watching him." My heart thumps, ears going hot with a full-body flush. Sure, I've accepted that Matt is hot, but it's not like I'm actually *into* him. I'm not into anyone or anything but a gold medal in February.

She ignores me. "Tanner Nielsen has withdrawn from Skate America. Strain in the hamstring."

Staring at her, I open and close my mouth, trying to decide if she'd fuck with me by joking. My pulse zips. "Seriously?"

"Of course serious."

"Holy shit. This means I won't compete against him until Nationals. Assuming he can skate, which I'm sure he will if it's just a strain." I breathe faster, excitement and regret warring. Even if Golden Boy isn't my favorite person on the planet, I wouldn't wish an injury on him.

But I'm not going to complain that he's got one.

I shake my knees, adrenaline sparking. "Do you think I—"

"Short program from footwork. Now. No more thinking about other skaters. *Or boys.*"

Biting back another denial, I speed through my footwork, practically flying. Holy shit, if Tanner's pulling out of Skate America, that means he can't make the Grand Prix Final. Even if he wins at Cup of China, he won't have enough points.

Soaring into a spin, I try to focus. Mrs. C's right. I can't worry about Tanner. And so what if I was admiring Matt and Mylene's lift? We all watch our training mates sometimes and cheer them on. Maybe I wasn't actually cheering out loud, but I was being supportive, that's all. It was nothing.

They whirl by again as I hit my finishing pose, and I pointedly look into the empty stands and visualize a packed crowd watching as I win gold and leave Tanner Nielsen in the dust.

CHAPTER THREE

"PLEASE WELCOME THE next competitor, representing the United States of America."

I take a final sip of water and hand the bottle to Mrs. C as the female announcer continues in an even tone: "Alexander Grady."

The arena thunders, and I nod at Mrs. C before pushing off from the boards with a big competition smile on my face, my arms outstretched. The applause continues as I do a small lap of the rink, grinning at the audience. I may not be Tanner Nielsen, but I do have a lot of fans, and there's nothing better than a home crowd.

There are thousands of eyes on me here in Philly for my short program at Skate America, but I imagine I'm back in Toronto and this is just another day at practice.

I straighten the collar of my costume, which is made to look like a normal button-up white shirt. I'm wearing a dark purple sweater vest over it and gray pants. Really simple and understated compared to my long program. That's when I like to dial up the drama.

As I take my starting position, I roll my shoulders back, breathing through the pounding of my heart, and try to forget about everything else except for the next two minutes and fifty seconds.

My music, a Benny Goodman swing medley, begins. I shoot

off across the rink, trying to get into my knees, keeping them deep and loose. There are required elements in the short program—three jumping passes, a flying spin, camel or sit spin, spin combo, and footwork. There are rules against repeating jumps, or else I'd totally do two triple Axels.

As I leap up forward into the air, everything feels right and I know I've got it. I land perfectly, holding the extension of my free leg and running out the edge of the landing with speed and flow as the crowd roars. There's no time to enjoy it since I'm heading right into my combination: quad toe-triple toe.

Taking a deep breath, I gather speed around the end of the rink with front crossovers before turning back, front, back—toe pick down, up in the air on a bit of an angle, but I get straight for four tight turns with my arms crossed against my chest. Then down, bend into my knees and push off my toe again and up.

I can't quite complete the third rotation in time, and I land short before thrusting my free leg back. Most of the crowd can't tell, but I know the judges will see it on their replay and I'll lose points.

Gotta keep going, can't think about it. *Don't think about it. Stay loose.*

Into the combination spin, with position changes and six revolutions on each foot. The world whooshes by in a blur.

Feeling the rhythm and letting it flow through me, expressing it to the audience, I fly across the ice as they clap in time to the beat. Then I launch into a flying camel spin, trying to take as much speed and energy into it as I can. Eight revolutions can seem like a freaking *lifetime* when you don't have enough speed.

After I skip into my footwork sequence down the length of the rink, it's time for connecting steps that lead into my triple Lutz. *Breathe, breathe.* The music builds. Into my three turn, and then I lift my back leg like a lever and launch off my toe pick. I get too loose in the air, but I muscle out the landing and don't touch my hand down even though my torso dips low.

Final element is the sit spin. The crowd is getting louder, adrenaline pumps, and I mentally scream at myself to focus. Can't mess up the spin—every element in the short program is just as important as the jumps. You can land all your jumps and screw yourself with a bad spin.

Then the last revolution is done, and the crowd is on its feet as I hit my final pose, down on one knee, arms back, chin lifted as the music crescendos and ends.

Hell yes!

First real short program of the Olympic season is done, and aside from the two-foot landing on the second half of my combo, it was solid. My lungs expand and sweet relief flows even as I mentally begin listing the things I could have done better, including the speed on my spins and the extension on my flying camel and—

The crowd cheers, and flowers and stuffed animals rain down on the ice, and I shut off my brain for a minute. In the center of the rink, I bow and wave to all four sides of the arena before skating to the Kiss and Cry, where Mrs. C waits. A few young girls wave teddy bears and call my name, so I skate over, taking the gifts and thanking them with hugs. They tell me they love me, which is always nice to hear.

People often ask what figure skaters do with all the stuffed animals we get. I still have a few back at home in Jersey, but the rest I give away to whatever children's hospital is nearby. It's not that I don't appreciate the fans giving me presents, but what are we supposed to do with thousands of stuffed animals?

I finally get to the Kiss and Cry, which is where we sit with our coaches and hear our marks after we skate. At the door, Mrs. C hands me my skate guards and I slip them over my blades before stepping off the ice.

Then she hugs me, because that's what coaches do in the Kiss and Cry. It's practically a rule. We put our arms around each other and she tells me I did very well. There's a cameraman two feet away, and mics pick up a lot, especially if the TV commentators aren't saying much. I know I'm going to hear about that under-rotated triple toe when we're alone.

But that's her job. She's not *mean* about it, and I don't need my coach to be all warm and fuzzy; I need her to make me the best skater in the world. I need her to make me Olympic champion. My coach before Mrs. C, Sharon, used to give me huge hugs and kisses after my routines, and she did it all the time in practice too. Sharon was great, but I already have a mother.

We walk up a big step onto a riser that holds a bench for us to sit on. In front of us is a camera to film every cheer and sob, and a video monitor where we can see the replays and scores when they come up. I add up my elements in my head, trying to guess my score.

My triple Axel is played in slow motion, and man, it was seriously awesome. Mrs. C gives my knee a pat. "Perfect."

Then it's my combination, and you can clearly see me finish the rotation on the ice on my second landing. "Not perfect," I say.

Mrs. C smiles, which makes me feel even more victorious than I already do. It's taking a while for the marks, which means the technical specialist and the judges are reviewing all the elements carefully to make sure they give me the right scores.

A couple of the little girls who collect the flowers and gifts clomp into the Kiss and Cry on their skates and give me an armful of gifts that I put on the bench beside me. I hug them and say thank you, and they smile shyly before leaving.

My face is wet with sweat, and I dab at my forehead with a tissue. Looking into the camera, I wave and smile and say hi to my family. They'll be here in Philly for the long program on the weekend and the network will only show a couple of the short programs then. Thank God for online streaming.

Network TV coverage for skating sucks ass these days in the States. I guess we need another pretty girl to get whacked in the knee to drum up more interest.

The announcer's voice finally rings out over the arena, stating my results. Total score: 96.55, with technical elements and program components combined. I'm in first place with two skaters left to compete. One of them definitely can't post the scores I can, even on his best day, while the other is a question mark since this is his debut season as a senior.

He's Japanese, and as I watch him take the ice and then nail a quad Sal to open—the bastard—I think Kenny had better watch his back. The men there are so strong that they could probably take the top five spots at the Olympics if countries were allowed to send more than three skaters.

This kid is flying around the rink with no fear, but he splats on his Axel. Still, he's oozing talent, and Japanese Nationals will be like the *Hunger Games*. May the odds be ever in Kenny's favor to bag his first title.

Now that I'm confident I'll be in first place going into the long program, Mrs. C and I head backstage, our arms full of flowers and stuffies before someone from the Federation collects them from us.

In the mixed zone, I talk to the reporters waiting. They ask me the usual questions about how I felt during the program, and I give a stock answer of, "I felt great. I was just having fun out there."

While I did feel good on the ice, it's a dirty lie that I had fun. I've never had *fun* in a competition. I love winning, but competing is way too stressful and important for fun. It's just not possible. However, I'm trying to keep a lid on telling reporters how I really feel after what happened. I'd rather not be on Mrs. C's shit list.

Then come the Olympic questions. How do I like my odds

against the international skaters? How do I think American skaters will stack up overall?

"Do you think you can beat Tanner Nielsen again at Nationals?" a young woman asks.

"Absolutely. I look forward to tough competition, and I think we both push each other to be better. I'm disappointed Tanner couldn't be here this week, and I hope he's healing quickly. He's a great guy, and I can't wait to see him back on the ice." *So I can kick his ass.*

A local reporter who probably hasn't seen a figure skating competition in decades asks how I feel about the 6.0 scoring system being replaced. Considering the IJS—International Judging System—has been in effect since 2004 after the big controversy in the pairs event in Salt Lake City at the 2002 Olympics, I don't even remember the old system.

"I think the judging is much fairer now. For the most part." I could say a *lot* more on the subject, but resist. "It's good for our sport. It makes more sense to add up points instead of deducting from perfect. But there's obviously still room in the component marks and GOEs for judges to reward their favorites." Oops, guess I didn't resist as hard as I could have.

There's a sudden ripple in the air, and the reporters perk up. I smile and add, "But I'm really happy with the judging today!"

Everyone laughs on cue, and I escape to the dressing room to get out of my costume. It's totally true about the judges. They can easily inflate the GOE and PCS—grade of execution and program components score—because it's still basically their opinion on how you skated. They used to call PCS "artistic merit," but now it's skating skills, transitions, performance, composition, and interpretation of the music.

If they like your costume, music, and choreography, it's great. If they don't, not so much. Still though, I wasn't lying to the reporters when I said the new system is fairer than the old one.

As I'm taking off my costume, a kid from the Ukraine shuffles into the dressing room, clearly trying not to cry. I've been there, done that, and I leave him be, letting him lick his wounds in peace.

When the door opens again, Matt's the last person I expect to see. He gives me a big smile, and I can't help but notice how his green hoodie brings out his brown eyes. "Great job out there!"

"Thanks." I return the smile, and Matt's praise shouldn't feel any better than the judges', but butterflies flap in my belly. "Thought you'd be gone by now. You guys had a good skate too?"

He wiggles his hand in the air. "Pretty good. Lost a level on our spins, so we really need to work on that." He heads into the bathroom. "I left my charger in the plug in here."

As Matt disappears, the door flies open. The Ukrainian kid leaps up, stiff as a board as his coach, a mean-looking old guy, storms in and bitches him out in a flood of Russian.

The guy is just laying into this kid, who is probably sixteen at the most. He's practically shivering in fear. I push to my feet. "Hey!"

The man stops mid-yell and turns to stare at me incredulously as the kid's eyes widen. I point to the door. "Skaters only." Fuck this asshole.

The coach's eyes bulge, his craggy face going a shade of red I think might be called "puce." His hands clench into fists, but he leaves, slamming the door behind him like the bag of dicks he is.

I smile at the kid, who quickly wipes his eyes. He says, "Thank you," with a strong accent.

"Anytime." I hand him the box of tissue and squeeze his shoulder. "You'll be okay. You had a bad day at the office. Happens to all of us. You'll be great in the long program."

Smiling tremulously, he blows his nose, nodding. When I pat his back and turn around to finish changing, Matt's in the bathroom entryway watching me with an expression I can't name.

He smiles as he leaves, looking back at me one last time as the door closes.

AT THE HOTEL, I have a shower and think about ordering room service. I'm rooming with a pairs skater from Florida who'll spend almost all his time with his girlfriend, so I'll have a chance for peace and quiet. But weirdly, it feels a little lonely.

After pulling on jeans and a hoodie, I go downstairs to ask the front desk where I can get some food. As I enter the lobby, Mylene's cheery voice rings out. "Alex!"

She's on a couch with a few other Canadian skaters, and I automatically look for Matt. I feel weirdly disappointed that he isn't there, which is stupid. Like I don't see him enough at home? I don't know what's wrong with me.

I go over and say hi to everyone, and Mylene invites me along to dinner. It's barely six o'clock, but we all have to get our sleep during a competition; practices can start at six in the morning depending on the schedule. I'm about to say yes when Matt walks in, all tall and lean and gorgeous in jeans and a black leather jacket.

"Did you guys see Alex's short today? He was great."

For some reason I'm going to hope is hunger, my stomach flip-flops. "Um, thanks," I squeak, as eloquent as ever. "You guys did great too."

Mylene does a little bouncy hop, and her grin is infectious. "We're going to kick so much ass tomorrow."

The group heads out, and we find a chain restaurant down the block. Even though I shouldn't, I order a veggie burger and fries, telling myself I deserve it. Mrs. C frowns on grease, which is strange for a Russian, judging by the time I've spent in Russia at competitions. But sometimes I can't help myself.

We gossip about other skaters, not to mention coaches and judges. As an ice dancer named Todd tells us all about the Russian coach who is dating his barely legal skater, I find myself watching Matt.

I don't even know when it happened, but suddenly I find him really enjoyable to look at. I mean, he always was, but I thought he was so dull, and I don't really know when that changed. Maybe being nice isn't such a bad trait in a guy.

I shouldn't even be wasting my time like this. I have too much skating stuff to focus on instead of the way Matt scratches behind his ear sometimes, or how big his hands are and how long his fingers...

I blink to attention and realize all eyes are on me. "Huh?"

Mylene snaps her fingers playfully. "Earth to Alex! Todd asked you about Mrs. C. What's the dirt? We haven't spent much time with her one-on-one."

"Dirt? On Mrs. C? Uh-uh, not gonna happen. First off, there's nothing to tell. Secondly, I value my life, not to mention my limbs."

"Well, *you're* no fun," Todd's red-headed partner Katrine grumbles. "Since when does Alex Grady keep his mouth shut?"

A few people laugh awkwardly, and anger surges in me like a geyser. "What the fuck does that mean?"

"Okay, okay. Chill," Todd says. "She was just joking."

Katrine's cheeks are pink, and she looks like she wants to say something else, but doesn't. "I didn't mean anything by it. Sorry."

Everyone's staring at me, and I examine the remnants of my burger bun on my plate. "It's fine. Whatever."

"You have to admit you're not always the most...circumspect," Matt says.

The urge to argue is like a jagged rip in my lungs. But I force a breath and a long exhalation. "I guess not." I poke at the bun, and the heat of everyone's stares are heavy on my skin. I imagine the whole restaurant is looking and whispering about me.

Matt leans around Mylene beside me and squeezes my shoulder. "Hey, tell them what Maxim said about Mrs. C's secret addiction."

Matt was there in the gym with us when Maxim laughed delightedly about going into the kitchen late at night and catching Mrs. C with a jar of Nutella, a spoon, and a comically guilty expression. He knows the story as well as I do, but I gulp some fizzy Coke and relay the tale to the rest of the table.

Everyone laughs and theorizes on what will happen to Maxim if Mrs. C. finds out he told. The tension dissipates and I can breathe normally again.

After we finish dinner, Matt says goodbye as we leave the restaurant. "Where are you going?" I ask before I can stop myself.

"It's my first time in Philly, and there's one thing I've got to see."

My mouth opens and out plops, "I want to go with you."

Matt's eyebrows shoot up. "You do?"

"Just don't feel like going back to my room yet." I shrug, my cheeks hot as all eyes land on me again. "But if you want to go by yourself, it's totally fine." Why did I say anything at all?

"No, it's cool." Matt smiles, his eyes crinkling. "Come on."

We turn in the other direction from the hotel after Mylene, who is giggling delightedly for some reason, waves goodbye. Night has fallen and the air has a frosty bite to it that reminds me winter isn't far away, which means the Olympics aren't far away either. We walk along in silence for a bit until I have to say something to break it.

"So, which sight is it?"

Matt zips up his jacket and puts his hands in his pockets. "You can't guess?"

I think about what Philly is famous for. "The Liberty Bell?"

"Nope."

"Some memorial to Ben Franklin?"

"Guess again."

"The cheesesteak museum?"

Matt laughs. "Seriously? They have a cheesesteak museum?"

I laugh too, warmth flowing through me. "I have no idea. If they don't, they should."

We pass a big fountain, walking through a park in the center of a wide, looping street, an imposing building in the distance. As we get closer, it hits me. "Wait, wait. Is this the *Rocky* thing?"

Grinning, Matt nods and points to the building. "Philadelphia Museum of Art, featuring the famous seventy-two steps Rocky Balboa ran up in the movie."

"You a big Stallone fan?" I'm a bit surprised.

"Not really, but who doesn't love that moment? Come on, it's classic."

"I'll give you that."

We keep walking toward the museum, which is lit dramatically. I hardly ever visit any sights when I'm traveling for competitions, so it's a nice change seeing some of Philadelphia. A little voice still nags, saying that I should be resting and getting ready for my long program tomorrow.

Matt says, "My dad loves that movie. We used to watch it together when I was a kid, and it was like... I don't know. Like it helped us relate to each other. He's a plumber from a big conservative Italian family in Richmond Hill—you know, a bit north of the rink? Anyway, we don't really have that much in common. It's tough these days."

He sounds forlorn, and I have to shove my hands in my pockets to keep from reaching out to touch his arm. Maybe things aren't as perfect in Matt's life as I thought.

I clear my throat. "I got lucky with my father. He's always been pretty liberal. He was a hippie or whatever back in the day. We can talk about anything."

"How does he feel about you skating?"

"Aside from not loving how expensive it is, he's all for it."

"My dad didn't like me skating when I was younger. At all. I actually only started to improve my hockey skills, but soon hockey fell by the wayside. I don't know if he's ever forgiven me." Matt's laugh is strained.

"I'm sorry he's not more supportive. That must be so hard."

Looking both ways, we jog across the street to the museum, and Matt shakes his head. "Now that I'm doing so well, I think he's happy. I'm sure he is. Well, I hope so. Besides, he's worked his ass off for years to pay for it, so it's not that he wasn't support-ive in that way. He totally was."

"Totally," I agree. Clearly Matt's got a few conflicting feelings about his dear old dad.

"Still, I think deep down he'd much rather have some stereo-typically macho, hockey-playing son rather than a figure skater."

I'm not sure what to say, so I make an "mmm" noise to show I'm listening. I didn't know Matt could talk this much in a row.

"I just wish he could love me for who I am. I've always tried so hard to make him proud, but I don't know if he'll ever accept a gay son." Matt shakes his head and laughs. "God, sorry. I don't know how this became a therapy session."

"No, it's okay. I don't mind." Wow, Matt Savelli has angst. He always seems so together and unruffled, but perhaps he's not made of cardboard after all. And I knew my trusty gaydar was on the money. It shouldn't send a thrill down my spine to hear Matt confirm it, but…

"You're a surprisingly good listener."

"Thank you? I think?"

His eyes crinkle in the glow of the street lamps. "No, no, I didn't mean it like that. What I meant was… It's been nice getting to know you better."

"Yeah, you too." My stomach somersaults again, my fingers

tingling.

At the middle of the wide, empty stairway we stand at the bottom of the steps, peering up. I whistle. "Wow. That's a lot of stairs."

"Bet I can beat you up there."

I do love a challenge. "No way, no day."

Suddenly, Matt's off and running, and I curse under my breath as I launch after him. He's faster than I thought, and although I close most of the distance, he remains a stride above me as we power our way up the steps. My breath comes in bursts that fog up the chilly air, and I strain to catch up with him. We pass a few people who are coming down, and they applaud as we race by.

I manage to pull up, and we're neck and neck as we take the last steps. We reach the top in stride, and Matt lets out a whoop of joy, raising his arms in the air and dancing in a circle. I join in, because that's what you do when you run up the *Rocky* steps. I've never seen him so animated. Well, except for when he's irritated with me.

We take in the amazing view of the city. Skyscrapers rise in the distance, and before us is the huge oval area we walked across surrounded by the road, with trees and grass and a statue of a guy on a horse I barely noticed passing because Matt was talking.

We jump around like idiots, working up more of a sweat than we did on the stairs, which weren't actually that hard. Matt leans his hands on his knees, and I reach out to give his shoulder a friendly punch, but my palm just rests there instead.

A shock bolts through me, like I've just touched a metal doorknob in winter. We're both breathing a little hard, and Matt gives me this long look that makes me want to throw him down right here and now and do things that would get us arrested and kicked off our national teams.

He stands up straight and my hand falls away as he steps closer. His voice is low. "Thanks for coming up here with me. It was way more fun than doing it by myself."

All I can think of is something else that is way more fun to do with someone else—not that I'd know from personal experience—and I swallow hard, my throat suddenly dry. I manage to get out, "Sure." My pulse thrums in my ears, and it's not because of the running and jumping.

We lean toward each other. I'm staring at his thick lips as he licks them, and I am so turned on right now, imagining what those lips will feel like on mine, and how Matt's hands and body—

"Hurry up!"

Matt and I leap apart as a little boy hurtles over the top of the steps. His parents and a few siblings follow, huffing and puffing from their climb. The parents say hello to us and we reply, and I'm glad it's dark, because I know I'm blushing like crazy.

The father asks us to take their photo, and Matt does, telling them to smile. He gives the phone back, and we stand there awkwardly for a few moments. I clear my throat. "Actually, want to take a pic of me so I can Instagram it?"

"Sure." He takes my phone, and I raise my hands over my head triumphantly with a big competition smile. It's dark, but hopefully there's enough ambient light since a flash will just make it look like shit.

I reach for my phone back, but he says, "Wait a sec." Coming close, he puts a big hand on my shoulder, spinning me to face away from the museum as my heart thumps. He says, "I'll get you from behind."

Of course I practically choke on my tongue, my balls tightening at the thought as I gaze out at the city and try desperately to clear my dirty mind. Matt laughs awkwardly. "Um, you know what I mean."

"Uh-huh." I raise my arms. "Is this good?"

"Yep!" He sounds too cheerful now.

Once he's got the picture, I take a few for him. "I guess we should…" I motion to the steps.

Matt nods. "Yeah, it's getting late."

It's barely eight, but I murmur in agreement and start down. We descend side by side, not talking. It would seem weird to try and kiss him now. Or maybe I should stop overanalyzing and kiss him anyway. But wait, do I really want to kiss Matt? I'm not supposed to kiss anyone right now with the Olympics coming up, especially not Captain Cardboard.

But now that I'm actually talking to him, Matt's different than I thought he was. He's cool, actually. We haven't even argued the whole night, and he wanted me to come out with him.

Well, he didn't argue, and it's not like I gave him a choice. He would have had to be totally rude to stop me from coming, and he's too Canadian for that.

My palms sweat. Maybe he doesn't like me at all. I think he's cool now that I've given him a chance, but what if he thinks I'm a bigger jerk than he did before? *And why should I even care?*

"Is your family coming this weekend?" Matt's voice sounds completely calm and normal. Maybe he didn't really want to kiss me, but was swept up in the whole moment, or something. Or it was all in my imagination and there wasn't a "moment" at all. I need to get a grip.

"Alex?"

I realize he's waiting for an answer. "Yeah. They're driving here tomorrow."

"What does your mom do?"

I tell him about my mom's work as an HR consultant, which I'm sure is fascinating for him. His mom's a teacher, and we talk about that for a while, and before I know it, we're back in the hotel.

In the elevator, Matt presses the eleventh floor. His hand hovers by the bank of buttons, and he looks at me expectantly.

"Fifteen," I answer.

Matt smiles as he steps off on his floor. "See you around to-morrow. Good luck."

"See ya. You too." I'm going for a casual tone and am moder-ately successful.

The doors close, and that's it, like nothing happened. Which I guess is true.

WHEN I WAKE the next morning, it takes a second to remember what happened with Matt. Or what didn't happen, to be more accurate. Embarrassment and horniness flood through me, not to mention confusion. I'm not sure how I ended up crushing on a guy I didn't even like before.

But as I think about Matt and his eye-crinkling smile, my morning wood only gets harder. After licking my palm and spitting, I jerk myself roughly. Now that Matt's confirmed he's gay, I wonder who he's been with.

For all I know, he's got a boyfriend somewhere. Or hook-ups. Maybe he fucked someone last night after we got back. He could have gone on Grindr and found a hot guy to come over. A guy he could have bent over and pounded, a guy who was probably more than happy to drop to his knees and suck Matt's cock, to choke on it—

Groaning, I splay my legs and rub my nipples with my free hand, stroking my dick faster, lifting my hips as I imagine Matt's cock filling my mouth, his long fingers tight in my hair as he comes down my throat.

Muscles tense and my back arching like a bow, I come for real, splashing my belly, legs quivering, pleasure burning bright.

After shuffling to the bathroom to piss and hop in the shower, I scrub shampoo through my short hair. Maybe I should go on

Grindr myself and find someone to fuck. I usually release my pent-up sexual energy with my hand or on the ice, but if I find a guy, I assume I'll stop lusting over Matt.

But the thought of losing it to some random dude sends an uncomfortable pang through me. Not that it has to be some girly romantic moment with candles and a heart-shaped bed, but I want it to be with someone I trust. Someone who won't take secret pictures or gossip about it. Someone who won't laugh at me for being a virgin.

I hadn't meant to put it off this long, but once I got really serious about skating as a teenager and realized I had the potential to go all the way, nothing else mattered. I guess I always thought I'd meet someone at the rink, but it never happened. I was too busy to go looking for it, so…here I am.

At this point it's so lame and embarrassing that I'm not sure I'll even admit I'm a virgin to whoever I end up fucking first, but I still don't want it to be a stranger.

I snap off the shower. Whenever it happens and with whoever, it's going to be after the Olympics anyway, so there's no point in thinking about it now. I've seen too many skaters lose crucial focus thanks to relationship drama. That's not going to be me.

As I eat a banana—not too Freudian or anything—I check the practice schedule, hoping the men aren't right after the pairs today.

I'm in luck, since the women are before us, and I'm in the second practice flight for the men. Matt should be long gone from the arena by the time I get there, back at the hotel preparing for his and Mylene's long program this evening.

That's exactly how it goes down, much to my relief. In practice, I pop my quad Sal, and I know Mrs. C is cursing me in her head because the judges are watching. They're only supposed to judge what you do on the ice during the actual competition, but everyone knows what they see at practice still has an impact. The more consistent and trustworthy a skater is, the higher their marks.

I run through that part of my program again, and this time I can't hold the landing, but at least I don't pop it. I do a couple of textbook triple Axels, hoping that will earn me some points and make a good impression.

The ice is fairly crowded for this practice, and we move around like fish in a tank, bobbing and weaving and coming close to each other but not touching as we speed by. Sometimes we do bump into each other, and as I come around one end of the rink, I'm suddenly face-to-face with a young Swiss skater.

I dodge to my right, but we still clip shoulders, and he tumbles to the ice as I stagger to keep my balance. The sparse crowd of die-hard fans gasps, and I turn to give the guy a hand up. He takes it, and we smile at each other and apologize. No one ever *means* to bang into someone else on the rink—even if you don't like them. No way would you risk injuring yourself.

To prove I'm not shaken up, I practice my quad Sal a few times since it's my hardest element. I actually land two beauties, which I know is being noted by everyone here. The third is pretty wobbly and two-footed, but I'll take it.

A few hours later, I meet Rachel and my parents at the hotel. They're all sharing a room, which has put a big pout on Rachel's face. She's fifteen and at that awkward stage, with a mouthful of metal, gangly limbs that don't quite fit, and zits dotting her chin. She's also cursed with the same mousy blond hair as me, but a smile appears when I give her a big hug and tell her she looks pretty in her new green coat.

My dad pulls me in close before ruffling my hair. I squirm away and complain, as I always do. It's this weirdly comforting little routine we've had for years. Then my mom swoops in on cue, kissing me and telling me I've grown. Apparently she'll still be saying that when I'm forty.

Dad's practically bald now, and his paunch is expanding. My mom is still gorgeous, even if that's weird for me to say since she's my mom. She has long, golden hair and a killer smile, and her regular Pilates keeps her in shape.

The straight guys at the rink in Jersey called her a MILF. She heard once, but I refused to tell her what it meant. I knew she'd google it, but there are some things you're better off not discussing with your mom, thank you very much. *Especially* that guys think she's a mother they'd like to fuck.

After I clean up, we go out for dinner. I eat a big salad with chicken, but I steal a few fries from Rach's plate. We always share two desserts when we go out to dinner as a family, and I let Rachel pick them both since I like everything. She goes for lemon cheesecake and apple crisp, and I'm really tempted to take a piece of cheesecake to go.

I'm back in my room early, and I stretch out on my bed to read my email on my phone. Checking the time, I hop on Twitter to see if M&M have skated yet. It's just friendly curiosity about my training mates. Nothing more.

The scores for the first flight of teams are up, and audience members and people watching online are tweeting comments. The order of skate has Matt and Mylene up first in the second and final flight. I refresh once enough time has gone by for the ice to be resurfaced by the Zamboni and for warm up.

The long program for the pairs is four and a half minutes, give or take ten seconds. I should just go back to my email—even though most of it is probably spam or promo shit—instead of dragging my finger down the screen to refresh the Skate America hashtag.

I read tweets about M&M's gorgeous side-by-side Sals, and I'm so happy for Mylene that she landed hers. Grinning to myself, I refresh every few seconds. Good unison on the spins, Mylene lands a clean throw triple Lutz...

I refresh again, waiting. Then again.

OMG. Bouchard/Savelli go down hard on a lift. She's not moving. #SkateAmerica #praying

My stomach plummets, ice bursting through my veins. Oh my God. Finger shaking, I stab the screen to refresh for tweets from strangers.

Horrible accident at #SkateAmerica. EMTs on the ice with Mylene Bouchard. This is bad.

Holy shit, she went down hard. Can barely watch. #SkateAmerica

You can hear a pin drop in here. Horrific fall. #SkateAmerica #prayers

This is what's happening right now here at #SkateAmerica. So awful.

There's a picture with the last tweet. Matt is on his knees near a motionless Mylene, who is half on her side, half on her stomach near the boards, her purple dress a bright splash of color. An EMT has her hand on Matt's back. Two others huddle around Mylene, blocking her head.

But by their feet, there's blood on the ice.

CHAPTER FOUR

Breathing through a surge of nausea, my shaking thumbs type out a text to Amber Parrish. We know each other from being on the US world team, and she and her partner were in the first flight tonight. She might still be at the arena.

I'm waiting for the three wobbly dots to appear and already jamming my feet into sneakers. She replies:

This is really bad. I can't believe this. We're all in shock.

I want to scream that I don't care about her feelings, but I calmly ask which hospital Mylene's going to. She has to ask someone, but she does find out after what feels like an eternity, and I thank her and tell her to hang in there.

The cab to the hospital probably only takes ten or fifteen minutes, but time has become thick and wrong, like I'm moving underwater or in slo-mo. There's a tear in the fake leather seat, and I poke my finger into it.

I ignore the nurse who tells me I have to stay in the over-lit waiting room crammed with people who are coughing and sneezing and complaining. When she's not looking, I open the door to the ER and stride in like I know where I'm going.

Of course I get busted and herded back into the waiting room, where I'm joined by other skaters, Canadian Federation officials, and Skate America organizers, who must be shitting bricks dealing with this accident.

After pacing in the corner for at least an hour, giving one-word answers to anyone who talks to me, I can't take it anymore and sneak back through the double doors. I know I have no right—I barely know M&M compared to other people in the waiting room, but I just need to see Matt and...I don't know. Tell him it'll be okay.

This time, no one stops me as I sneak down the hall and peek into glass-fronted rooms, my sneakers squeaking softly on the linoleum, disinfectant burning my nose. I make a turn and there's Matt in a quiet hallway. Even though I know it was poor Mylene who was hurt, I'm still relieved to see Matt's okay.

Well, "okay" is a relative term. He's slumped in a plastic chair, staring off into space. As I get closer, I realize there's blood smeared across his hands and white shirt. The shirt has long sleeves and sequins to make it shine on the ice, and Jesus, now it looks like Matt stabbed someone.

I have no idea what to say. "Um, Matt?"

He doesn't respond, and I'm not sure he even heard me. He's still wearing his black costume pants, but his skates are off and he's in his socks. I kneel in front of his chair on the hard floor and sit back on my heels to meet his dazed expression. A streak of blood has dried across his cheek.

I try again. "Hey."

Matt says something so softly that I can't understand it.

"What?"

It's still soft, but this time I can make out the words. "I dropped her."

"It's not your fault." A couple of hospital staff bustle by us down the hall, but they don't say anything to me about not being allowed back here.

"I dropped her," he croaks, his throat working.

"Matt, it was an accident. It'll be okay." I'm looking at the blood on him, and my heart thumps harder. "She'll be okay, right?

I mean, she's not going to…"

The words grate my throat like broken glass. No one's ever *died* from a pairs fall before. There have been some pretty bad accidents, but even Elena Berezhnaya, who had her old partner's skate embedded in her head on a side-by-side spin, survived and went on to win Olympic gold.

He doesn't answer, and now I'm starting to really freak out. On my way to the hospital, I worried it might be a career-ending fall. Getting injured when you're an athlete is a big, big deal. We're all really afraid of it, and it's upsetting when someone is badly hurt. But oh my God, is she okay? I mean, she can't *die*.

Right?

A group of people clustered together down the hall are speaking in low tones. They're Canadian skating officials I recognize from various events. A woman glances at Matt every so often with obvious concern.

"I don't know what happened." Matt isn't really talking to me, his eyes unfocused. "It was the same as always. The lift went up and I was turning and then…we were on the ice. She wouldn't wake up and there was all this blood." He blinks and looks at me. "I don't understand."

"It's okay. Everything will be okay." I'm not sure if it's the truth, but I have to say it anyway.

"I've never dropped her. Not ever. Not even in practice."

God, he looks wrecked, his eyes red and glassy. I reach out and take his trembling hand, but I'm not sure he even notices. "I'm going to find Chantal. I'll be right back."

I can hear activity coming from a room down the hall, and I peek in to see Mylene on the examination table with doctors and nurses working over her. She's still wearing her purple costume, but someone has taken off her skates. There's a tube in her nose and she's hooked up to a heart-rate monitor. Her eyes are closed and blood stains her face and curly hair.

Standing in the corner, Chantal motions me in. "*Où est* Matt?"

I don't speak French, but I can guess what she's asking. "He's sitting out there." I point to the hall.

She nods and takes a shaky breath, rubbing her puffy eyes. I know she's coached Mylene for years and they're really close. I ask, "Is she going to be okay?"

Chantal takes another breath. "Concussion, obviously. But there's pressure in the brain. Bleeding. They might have to operate."

"But she's going to be okay, right?"

"They say the chances are good. If there are no complications." She tries to smile, but I can see this is killing her.

"How did it happen? They're always so strong on the lifts."

She shakes her head. "I think he caught an edge on one of the turns. It was so fast, she came down like…" Chantal gestures, trying to find the words.

"Like a ton of bricks?"

She nods. "*Oui*. Down very hard. No time, and right into the corner by the boards. She couldn't break her fall."

I lean out the door and look at Matt still sitting where I left him, one of the officials there talking to him now while he stares blankly. "Matt's not doing very well."

Chantal's eyes well up and she wipes them quickly. "Can you help me, Alex?"

"Of course."

She leads the way out of the room, and I glance back at Mylene. It's terrifying to see her so pale, lying there so still. Mylene is never still. I gulp heavily over the lump in my throat and whisper a silent prayer.

In the hall, Chantal kisses Matt's head and crouches down beside him while I linger a few feet away. "Alex is going to take you back to the hotel to get cleaned up."

This sparks some life in Matt, and his gaze snaps to Chantal. "I'm not leaving."

"*Mon petit*, Mylene's parents are on their way from Montreal. They cannot see you like this."

"I'm not leaving her!" Matt pushes to his feet, suddenly vibrating with energy.

"Pierre and Fanny *cannot* see you like this." Chantal takes Matt's chin gently in her hand. "Alex will take you back to the hotel to change and clean up. Then he will bring you back. *D'accord?*"

Matt looks down, and it's like he's only seeing the blood on him for the first time. The fight drains away and he nods. Chantal hugs him tightly.

"Are his shoes here?" I ask.

The woman from the Canadian Federation has been listening, and she hands me a gym bag. "We collected his things from the dressing room."

I dig Matt's sneakers out of the bag and Chantal helps him put them on. Then he follows me out of the ER, attracting a lot of stares. I take my jacket off and put it over his shoulders even though it's too small to really hide the blood.

The other Canadian skaters here in Philly are pacing around the waiting room, and they swarm Matt. I don't think he can really handle it right now, so I get myself in-between and relay what Chantal told me. Matt seems to be in a haze of shock again, and I nudge him toward the door. Todd, the ice dancer, tells Matt they'll be waiting when he gets back.

There are a couple of cabs outside the hospital, and I get Matt inside one, maneuvering his long limbs with some difficulty. We don't talk on the way back to the hotel, and once we're there, I take him quickly through the lobby and dig out his key card from his bag while we're in the elevator. He follows me to his room like he's sleepwalking.

Inside, it's quiet in that way hotel rooms usually are, like there's a hush when you close the door behind you, and now you're in a sealed bubble. The curtains are open, and the light from the moon and the street casts the room in a ghostly glow. I go to turn the lights on, but Matt stops me.

"I have a headache. I just want to sit here for a minute." He collapses onto the end of the nearest bed. My coat slides from his shoulders, and I fold it into a ball for lack of anything better to do.

Kneeling, I untie his shoes and tug them off. I'm not sure he notices, but at least he doesn't fight me. When I look up, his eyes are shining, and he hiccups with tears.

"Everything was fine. It felt really good out there tonight. Then my feet weren't under me and I hit the ice and she was... How could that happen? How could I let that happen?"

"It was an accident." Tentatively, I sit beside him, the duvet smooth beneath my fidgeting fingers.

"I'm supposed to protect her! That's my job. The most important thing is to always keep her safe." His face crumples. "She's my best friend."

Tears stream down his cheeks in the pale moonlight, and I'm totally fucking useless. What the hell can I say? "It wasn't your fault. It happens to all of us. We all fall."

Matt swipes his eyes with the back of his hand. "I dropped her!"

"We all trip out there. It just happened at a really, really bad time."

"I should never have let it happen." He chokes on a sob.

I take his hand like I did at the hospital, but this time he clutches my fingers. I keep my voice soothing even though I want to scream at how fucking awful this is. "Matt, sometimes you just catch an edge."

"I've always taken care of her. She's my best friend," he repeats.

I make sure he's looking at me before I say it again. "Sometimes you just catch an edge."

Finally he nods, and I let him cry for a while longer, holding his hand the whole time. He sniffs loudly. "She has to be okay."

"I know. She will be."

He nods again, wiping his face. "I'm sorry. You don't have to be here. You've been really nice, but I'll be fine."

"It's okay. I don't mind." I put my arm around him and he leans into me, shoulders shaking, his head dipping to my shoulder as he folds his big body close.

All I can do is rub his back and let him cry, and it should be weird and awkward, but it feels natural to hold him in a way I can't explain. His tears dampen my neck, and he smells like sweat and something tangy. My stomach churns. It must be blood.

He's warm against me, his breath stuttering, and I rub his back and murmur that it'll be okay. After a little while, his tears and hitching breath slow, and I run my fingers through his thick hair.

"Let's get you cleaned up," I whisper.

Matt doesn't resist as I heave him up and guide him to the bathroom and flick on the light. Blinking, we grimace in the too-bright light on white tile, and Jesus, Matt really looks like shit—his eyes bleary and red, face pale and blood-streaked, his hair standing on end from where I played with it.

I'm strangely embarrassed to see the evidence of touching him, and I drop my gaze and refocus, because this isn't about me.

His hands are shaking too hard, and I circle around to unzip the back of his costume shirt and tug it gently free of his pants. I urge his arms up and lift it free over his head, tossing it into the corner.

In front of him again, I'm face-to-face with his hairy chest, but this is obviously nothing like my furtive, fleeting fantasies. When I run my hand down his arm and squeeze his shivery flesh, he looks at me like he forgot I was there.

After unzipping his black pants, I crouch to peel them down. He obediently lifts one foot and then the other so I can remove his socks. He's still wearing his jockstrap, and he manages to yank it down himself.

Now his thick, uncut dick's in my face, and I shoot to my feet, whirling away to turn on the shower. I wave my hand under the water until it's nice and hot, and pull back the curtain.

"Um, are you…" My heart races. "Do you want help in there?"

Blinking, he shakes his head, and I squeeze out of the way so he can climb into the tub. I grab his clothes and make sure the towels are within reach before escaping to the room, leaving the door open just in case.

After turning on the lamps, I quickly call Chantal for an update. Naturally, her phone goes to voicemail, and I tell her to text me if there's any news. Then I call Amber since I need to talk to someone.

"So you went to the hospital?" she asks.

"Yeah, but I'm at the hotel with Matt now."

"That's really nice of you." Amber's silent for a moment. "I thought you guys didn't get along."

"Who told you that?" Irritation spikes, and I pace the hotel room, scuffing my shoes on the plush, brown and beige-checkered carpet.

"I dunno. I heard it around."

"Well it's not true." At least, I don't think so. Not anymore.

I can hear her smirk. "I guess opposites attract after all."

Embarrassment floods my veins, hot and sticky, and I bark, "Mylene might die you know."

"I know, I'm sorry. I was just… Shit, I'm sorry. God, do you really think she's going to die?" Amber suddenly sounds very young, and guilt joins the murky swirl in my gut.

I soften my tone. "It's possible, but they think she'll make it. It's okay, don't worry." The water in the bathroom shuts off, and I say goodbye to Amber.

I wonder when the Bouchards are arriving and who's picking them up from the airport. Probably someone from the Canadian Federation, and it's not like I have my car here to do it. I resume pacing, wishing I could do *something*. I met Mylene's parents at the end of the summer and they were so nice. They brought us all Montreal bagels and every ounce of the carbs were worth it.

I can hear a towel rustling and try not to think about Matt being wet and naked just around the corner. Now is *so* not the time.

He appears with a towel slung around his hips. "Has Chantal called?"

"No, but I left her a message." I stand over by the desk, playing with a complimentary pen. My phone buzzes, but it's Mrs. C, so I let it go to voicemail. I'm sure she was checking to make sure I'm in bed, and I'll let her think I'm fast asleep.

Matt drops onto the bed and leans against the padded headboard. He's dripping, and I thrust my hands in my pockets to fight the insane urge to push his wet hair off his forehead.

I clear my throat. "Do you want to get some sleep?"

That question seems to snap Matt out of his thoughts, and he gets up and rummages through his suitcase on the floor, his voice steady. "No, I want to go back. I have to check on her."

Then he drops the towel to get dressed, and I spin around and examine the hotel binder very, very closely. Now that he seems more in control and less catatonic, I wonder if I should wait in the hall. Sure, we change around each other in the locker room, but in a hotel by a bed, it feels…intimate. I read the long distance phone rates carefully and take a few deep breaths.

"You don't have to come back with me. Your long program is tomorrow. You should get some sleep."

I risk turning around and find Matt in jeans and a T-shirt. He runs the towel over his damp hair. He's right; I totally, completely should get some sleep. I have practice early tomorrow morning and the competition later in the afternoon.

I shrug. "Nah, I'm not tired."

A tiny smile lifts the corners of Matt's lips for the first time all night.

CHAPTER FIVE

TRUE TO THEIR word, Todd and the other handful of Canadian skaters are still waiting at the hospital. Matt hugs them and he seems a little better now. He's walking and talking normally, at least.

Matt tells them all to go get some rest, and promises to call when he knows anything. Katrine stops as she's leaving and gives me a kind smile. "Alex, are you coming with us?"

"You really should," Matt says.

"You guys go ahead. I'm going to stick around for a while."

No one argues, although Todd gives me an odd look. I ignore it and follow Matt into the ward. The nurse tells us Mylene is in surgery up on the seventh floor, so we take the elevator to find Chantal and a couple of the Canadian officials in a waiting area. Chantal hugs Matt tenderly and he gets emotional again, so she takes him down the hall, where they stand talking.

I pace and try not to watch them. A man who I think is the vice-president of the Canadian Federation nods to me. "I see you're a good friend to your training mates."

Well, don't sound so surprised, dude. "I'm sure they'd do the same for me."

He agrees, and we make uncomfortable small talk while I sneak peeks at Matt and Chantal. She's holding his hands and talking emphatically while he nods. I'm sure she's saying the same thing I did, and it's totally the truth: Sometimes you just catch an edge.

With a soft ping a few hours later, the elevator doors slide open and the Bouchards spill out, the nice Canadian woman who gave me Matt's bag in tow. Matt and Chantal hurry over, and Chantal starts talking to them really fast in French. Mylene's petite mother has clearly been crying a lot, and she grips her hands together. Mylene's dad doesn't say anything, only gazing at Matt with a serious expression.

Shit, I hope he's not mad about the accident. It would really be unfair to blame Matt for what happened. Matt's eyes glisten, and when he says, "I'm so sorry," his voice breaks.

I'm about to jump in and defend him when Mr. Bouchard takes a step and pulls Matt into a big hug. Matt cries and says over and over that he's sorry, but the Bouchards assure him it's not his fault as they take turns hugging him. I exhale in relief, so I can imagine how Matt must feel.

It's long after midnight now and I should really, really get to bed, but I have to wait and hear what the doctors say. We all sit, and there's some quiet talking, but most of it is in French. My eyes get heavy, and I slouch in my hard, plastic chair to doze just for a few minutes…

When I wake, my twisted neck aches, and I bet my back is going to crack big time when I stand. As I straighten, I realize Matt's watching me from a chair across the low coffee table between us. He smiles and points to his chin. "You've got…"

Jesus, I've got *drool* on my face. Yeah, that's always a really attractive look. I bet everyone had a good laugh. I'm wide awake now as I wipe my face with the back of my sleeve. Glancing around, I see we're alone. "Where is everyone?"

"The Federation people went back to the hotel. Chantal and Mylene's parents are with her in the recovery room. I was there, but I came back to wake you up. You were sleeping so soundly I let you have a few more minutes."

So he was just…watching me sleep? And drool? Terrific. "How is she?"

He smiles for real. "She's going to be okay."

"Yeah? A hundred percent?"

"Eventually. They're optimistic."

"What about the Olympics?"

There's a flicker of pain on Matt's face, and then it's gone. He swallows hard. "There's no way. Aside from the head injury, her arm's broken."

"Fuck. I'm sorry." I really am. They've worked their whole lives for this, same as I have.

"I'm just glad she's going to be okay. That's the important thing."

"Totally. I'm really glad to hear it, man. And hey, there's another chance in four years. You guys have plenty of time ahead of you." Still, their season is over. No Olympics in Salzburg. Plus, depending on how Mylene's recovery goes, this could be the end of skating for her. Head injuries can be a real bitch.

"You should get back to the hotel and catch a couple hours in bed."

I pull out my phone and groan softly. It's five o'clock, and practice is in three hours. "Yeah, I'd better."

My neck twinges, and I stretch my arms over my head as I walk to the elevator. Matt walks with me and presses the call button. "Thanks for everything tonight, Alex."

"Sure. It was nothing."

Matt looks at me really intently, and my belly goes all fluttery and weird. "Not to me."

Then he hugs me, and I wrap my arms around his broad back. He smells like minty lemon soap, and his body is so lean and strong, and oh my God, I need to get laid because I'm out of control. Matt's totally traumatized and I'm getting turned on.

The elevator pings, and I break away as the doors open, giving Matt's shoulder a slap. "I'll come by tomorrow after practice."

"See you then." Matt raises his hand in a little wave, watching me with a tiny smile until the doors close.

I DRAG ASS to practice after approximately an hour and a half of restless, shitty sleep. Mrs. C meets me in the arena bowels.

"Did you hear about Mylene?" I ask stupidly.

A sculpted eyebrow arches. "Of course. I went over this morning. Surgery was a success, they say. You were there almost all night."

I'm shocked she didn't come drag me out by the ear, and I brace for the lecture now. But she just gives me a stern look and orders, "After practice, you sleep."

Official practice this morning is forty minutes. There are four other guys in my group, and we each get a turn to run through our long programs with the music playing. Everyone else does their own thing at the same time, and most skaters don't do complete run-throughs, some doing portions of the program, and others doing hardly any of it.

The diehard fans watch in the mostly empty arena. My family is there in the front row by one of the corners, and I give them a smile the first time I go by. After that, though, I don't look at anyone.

It took a while when I was younger to train myself not to focus on anyone past the boards. Sometimes they're only a few feet away, and if I look right at them and make eye contact, it breaks my concentration.

So when we're practicing, most of the time we pretend no one else is there but our coaches. Which doesn't mean we're not well aware of the fans and judges. *Especially* the judges.

I take it easy and manage to make it through the forty minutes without banging into anyone or falling too hard. With a couple minutes left, I wait for the Ukrainian kid from the locker room to take his bow, then do mine, acknowledging the fans, who applaud kindly.

Mrs. C hands me my skate guards and gives the asshole Ukrainian coach major side-eye as we leave to go backstage. Then it's my turn for her glare.

"Sleep now."

"I will. I'm going to breakfast with my folks first."

"No sugar." With a curt nod, she strides off, and I head for the dressing room.

My parents take me and Rachel to a pancake place for breakfast, and I reluctantly order the granola and Greek yogurt bowl while eyeing the maple syrup Rachel drowns her French toast and bacon in. She pushes over her plate so I can snag a piece of bacon. Savoring the sticky sweetness and savory crunch, I grin at her.

"Sweetheart, how are you feeling?" Mom asks, tucking a lock of golden hair behind her ear. "What a terrible accident. We couldn't believe it."

"Okay, I guess. I really need to take a nap but I want to go back to the hospital to check in on them. Not for long, I promise. I should get going, actually."

"*Back* to the hospital?" My dad asks as he finishes his pancake beside me. The wrinkles in his face crease even more.

"I was there last night after the accident."

"Oh, we didn't realize." Mom and Dad share a silent glance. "They said she'll be all right, though? It was all anyone was talking about at the rink."

"Yeah, that's what they said. When I left this morning she was in recovery after the surgery."

"You were there all night?" Mom's spoon pauses in mid-stir as she adds more milk to her coffee.

"Practically, I guess. Matt took it really hard and it didn't feel right leaving him. I got a bit of sleep."

My dad waves to the waitress for more hot water for his tea, then gives me a long look. "I didn't realize you two were so close."

"What? We're not." I scrape my bowl, the spoon clanking porcelain as I scoop up the last bit of fruit and granola. "They're my training mates. Mylene's totally sweet and I was worried about her."

"Oh, of course, of course." Dad nods and scratches his balding head.

Rachel grins with a mouthful of metal. "Alex has the hots for Matt Savelli."

"Shut up! I do not!" I would kick her under the table, but my mom is right across from me and I might get her by accident. "They're my friends. Mylene could have died. And they're out of the Olympics. Who knows when she'll be able to skate again? This could be the end of their career."

Rachel's smile vanishes. "Wow. That really sucks."

"Do you want us to come with you? We can go sightseeing another time." Mom reaches out and rubs my arm.

"No, it's cool. I'm just going to drop by and see how she's doing and then catch some sleep. Where are you guys going?"

"The Liberty Bell, of course, and then we thought we'd go to that museum," Dad says. "You know, where Rocky ran up the stairs."

Naturally this makes me think of Matt and the exhilaration of racing him up the steps, and how we maybe, might have, probably kissed at the top if those damn people hadn't come along. My pulse gallops, and I swallow the last mouthful of breakfast. "Awesome."

Mom asks, "Are you sure you don't want some company at the hospital?"

Returning her smile, I nod. Even though I know he's going

through a terrible time, I'm excited to see Matt again. Maybe we can have a few minutes alone…

Groaning inwardly, I say goodbye to my family and order an Uber on my phone. Aside from friendly concern during this trying time, I shouldn't care about seeing Matt. I'm sure this is just some weird phase or something. Because even if Matt's cool, it doesn't change anything. Until I can win Olympic gold, nothing else matters.

AT THE HOSPITAL, I realize I have no idea which room Mylene is in now. Should I text Matt? If he really wanted me here, he probably would have texted me the room number. Maybe I should just go and leave them in peace. It's not like Matt and I are suddenly BFF or something. Why would he even want to see me? I gave him a hand last night, but I'll be useless today and—

"Alex?" Chantal crosses the lobby and pulls me into a hug, kissing both my cheeks with chapped lips. "Thank you for your help."

"Um, sure. Anytime. How's Mylene?"

Chantal runs a hand through her lank hair, sighing. "She woke up. They don't think there's any brain damage, thank the lord."

My breath catches. "That was a possibility?"

"Of course. Head injury. You never know." She rubs her eyes.

"You look like shit." It pops out before I can stop it, but luckily Chantal laughs throatily.

"Oh, Alex. I do enjoy you. And yes, I'm going to the hotel to sleep for a bit. Maybe you can convince Matt to do the same, hmm? Room five-oh-seven." She kisses my cheeks again and is off.

On the fifth floor, I pass rooms filled with flowers and balloons and realize I didn't bring anything for Mylene. Just as I decide to go back down to the lobby and find the gift store, I reach the right room.

From his chair beside Mylene's bed, Matt turns, and his smile lights up his whole face, sending my heart into palpitations. I find myself smiling back despite my discomfort over not having anything for Mylene.

Of course, she's awake, so I can't run back downstairs. She smiles weakly from the bed and wow, I've never seen her so pale and small and still. Her right arm is in a cast and her head is wrapped in bandages. Her eyes are heavy and I bet she's on a *ton* of drugs right now.

"Hey. Thanks for coming by." Matt stands, and for a second I think he's going to shake my hand, but then he just shoves his hands in his pockets. "She's pretty groggy right now."

"*She's* right here." Mylene's voice is thready, but I'm relieved she hasn't lost her sass.

I smile at her. "How're you feeling?" God, what a stupid question.

"*Comme ci, comme ça.*"

I think that means so-so. "I'm really glad you're going to be okay."

She smiles again weakly, and then her eyes close, and I think she's asleep, just like that. Yep, she's got the good drugs. I look to Matt questioningly.

"She's been in and out like this all morning. They say it's normal." He fidgets, crossing and re-crossing his arms, putting his hands in his pockets, shifting from foot to foot.

"You should sleep."

"Maybe when her parents get back from checking into the hotel. We'll see. I don't want to leave her alone."

"How long is she going to have to stay here?"

"A few days, at least. Then they'll fly her to Montreal. Her parents want her at home while she recovers." He presses his lips together briefly, breathing deeply.

"I guess that makes sense. Are your parents here?"

"No, I told them to stay home. They can't afford to fly down here last minute, and it's not like I'm hurt. I'm fine."

He's very far from fine. I wish I could say something profound and helpful. "You really should get some rest." Oh yes, *very* profound.

"You should get some sleep yourself. You're competing this afternoon." He tries to smile, failing utterly. "I guess I won't have to worry about that for a while."

"You guys will be back before you know it. So you won't make it to Olympics this year. There's always next time. You're totally young enough. Not to mention Worlds every year. This is just a temporary setback. Happens to a lot of skaters."

Matt shrugs, his hands jammed back in his pockets for the moment. "I guess. The specialist said it could be months before she'll even be ready to try skating. And if she ever hit her head again…"

"She won't. Don't worry, you guys will be back on the ice before you know it."

"I don't know." His face creases. His voice is low when he says, "I don't want to hurt her again. I'm not sure it's worth it."

"Of course it is! We've worked our whole lives for this. You're just tired. Don't think about the future right now."

"I guess you're right." He rubs his face. "You should go grab a nap. Thanks for coming by. You know, I underestimated you."

I'm dying to say that I underestimated him too, although I probably shouldn't tell him I initially thought of him as Captain Cardboard. "Are you sure you don't want to come back with me? We could share an Uber or cab or whatever. And we don't have to sleep. We could hang out. Chill."

He looks away from Mylene and meets my gaze with a little hitch of a smile that sends a thrill spiraling through me. "I'd like that. But I won't leave her. Raincheck?"

"Sure. Of course." I'm kind of waiting for him to hug me like he did last night or this morning or whenever it was I left the hospital.

But he sits again. "Good luck this afternoon."

"Yeah. Thanks. I'll see you soon."

Maybe I should give him a hug this time? He probably really needs it. Instead I hover awkwardly by the door before leaving.

Back in my hotel room, at least sleep comes quickly this time, and I dream of an endless run up the Rocky steps, Matt just out of reach.

CHAPTER SIX

B ACK IN TORONTO, practice is the same routine it always is, and we go on like normal. I guess it's the way life is. The world still turns no matter what, and you have to keep up.

My long program at Skate America was…fine. It wasn't a complete disaster, but enough to win since everyone made mistakes. I didn't land the quad Sal, which keeps me up at night even though I know obsessing won't get the jump around cleanly. Only more practice will.

After another day at the rink with no sign of Matt, who's been in Montreal with Mylene, I drive to my apartment in my rattling Honda, restlessly cycling through playlists as the abysmal Toronto traffic inches along.

At least my place isn't far from the rink. It's a nondescript ten-story building close to a strip mall with a grocery store called No Frills, a deli, dry cleaner, and dinky little Chinese buffet. Part of me wishes I could live downtown instead of up here in Thornhill, but it's not practical. I'm not in Toronto to go to cool restaurants and shops. I'm here to win.

My phone lights up on the passenger seat, and I reach for it eagerly at a stop light. It's not Matt, and while it's great to hear from my sister, I really need Matt to respond to my text with more than a two-word lie saying he's okay.

I texted him back more questions, but no reply yet. Which I

know I shouldn't obsess about. That doesn't stop me from checking my phone approximately every thirty seconds.

At home, I resolutely tuck my phone away in my pocket. The mail is all flyers, which I dump on the kitchen counter not far from the front door, just off to the left. It's a narrow galley kitchen with a pass-through over the counter that peers into the living room, and the bathroom and a closet sit across the hall to the right. There's a little bedroom to the right as well, and the living/dining room makes up the rest of my square of a home. It's tiny, but all I do here is sleep anyway. I even have a balcony, which I hardly ever go on.

Sidestepping unpacked boxes, I grab the remote from my futon and click on Apple TV to play the latest Honest Movie Trailer on YouTube as I pick up my dishes from the night before. I should probably decorate the bare white walls, but I'm too tired to do anything but flop at night.

As I chop up veggies for a chicken stir fry, YouTube autoplays a bunch of stuff it thinks I might like. I'm only half listening when I hear the familiar voices of skating commentators and the music for Matt and Mylene's long program to the *Finding Neverland* soundtrack.

Heart in my throat, I abandon dinner and pace by the TV. I've avoided clips of the fall, but now that it's playing, I can't look away. The program's going great until Matt and Mylene do back crossovers around the end of the rink, gaining speed into the first—and in this case last—lift. She goes up as if she's weightless because their timing is perfect and Matt's such a quality lifter.

Mylene changes position as Matt turns, and she has one arm up when his blade catches. They're down in the blink of an eye. Matt still has hold of her right hand, and it's that arm that breaks as Mylene slams into the ice. Her head hits the ice right where it meets the boards, and she's motionless.

Bile rises in my throat, fingers digging into my thighs as I watch.

Matt's clearly in shock as he crawls to Mylene. He looks around frantically for help and you can see a spot of blood widening under Mylene's head in HD glory. The medics are slip-sliding their way across the ice with their gear, and Matt beckons them as if they can't see where to go.

Once they start working on Mylene, the network shows a replay in slow motion. My stomach is all twisted, but I still can't look away. I guess it's like how people are compelled by car wrecks and plane crashes.

I focus on Matt's feet and spot the moment he catches that edge. It's like when you're walking along the street and everything is normal, and all of a sudden you trip out of nowhere. Sometimes you don't even trip on anything in particular. It just happens. Plus, it happens a lot easier when you're on a blade only millimeters thick. The slightest rut in the ice can send us crashing down.

Once his feet go out, there's nothing he can do to stop her from falling. It happens so suddenly that he doesn't have time to catch her, and they're moving so fast across the ice that momentum teams up with gravity, and there isn't a single thing he can do to break her fall as she slams down.

For male pairs skaters, protecting their partner is the number one rule they learn. Even if they take an elbow to the face catching her, it's what they do. I think part of it is instinctive; usually the girl is pretty tiny, so the guy tends to feel protective already. To be a successful pair and have great lifts, throws, and twists, the girl has to totally trust her partner and know he'll be there to catch her.

So I know it's killing Matt that Mylene fell, even though it's completely, one hundred percent not his fault, and the best pairs skater in history couldn't have caught her. That won't help him feel less guilty now.

Pulling out my phone, I re-read the last text I sent him. According to my phone, it was delivered.

I know you must feel like crap, but it really wasn't your fault. Anyway, just hang in there and all that. Let me know how you're doing.

Ugh. I cringe re-reading it. "Let me know how you're doing?" He's doing shitty! I don't blame him for not dignifying my lame-ass message with a response.

I leave the phone on my futon as I go back to finish dinner, and only check it every minute, so it's a step in the right direction.

THE NEXT DAY, I'm leaving the rink just as it's getting dark, which is six o'clock now that winter is fast approaching. My car is at the rear of the country club in a typically deserted part of the parking lot, and as I'm fishing out my keys, Matt comes out a backdoor dressed in his all-black waiter uniform. He's holding two garbage bags and doesn't see me until he's right by the dumpster.

He stops, bags suspended in midair. "Oh. Hey."

I swallow a giddy smile and nod instead, closing the distance between us, hitching up my duffel bag on my shoulder. "Hey, man. When did you get back from Montreal?" *And why didn't you tell me? Not that you owe me anything or that I should even be thinking about you at all.*

"A few days ago."

"Days? You haven't been on the ice." *And you didn't tell me you were back.*

Matt lifts the dumpster lid and tosses the bags inside, closing it with a metallic bang. "I picked up some extra shifts at the restaurant. I don't have anything to train for now."

"But…" I guess he's right, but it feels so wrong not to see him in practice or the gym anymore. "You're not going to just quit skating, right?" The very idea makes my throat go dry.

He shrugs. "We'll see."

"Mylene's going to get better."

"Eventually." He shoves his hands in his pockets, his breath fogging in the cold air. "The fracture in her arm is bad. Then there's her head. It's going to be a while before she can even walk and move around normally. I don't know if she'll still want to skate after all that."

"Of course she will." It's crazy to me that she wouldn't. This is what we do. This is who we are. We're skaters. We skate."

Matt kicks at a stray rock, his gaze on the cement. "Maybe."

"You could always get another partner if—"

"No!" He jerks up his head. "I can't. She's my best friend. I could never skate with anyone else. I can't even imagine it."

God, he's so defeated, and I want to fix it. A light bulb goes off. "Why don't you do singles? You have your routines. You were going to skate in singles at Canadians, weren't you?"

He scoffs. "Just for fun. I'm a pairs skater, Alex. I'm not good enough in singles to really compete."

"Maybe not now, but you could be. If you work a lot on your triple Axel and a quad toe—"

He laughs bitterly. "Do you have a magic wand in that gym bag?"

"If you practice hard, you can do it. I know you can. You won't win, but you could make the team. Montoya and Hamilton will be fighting for the top, but that third spot is totally up for grabs." I bounce on my toes. "You could still go to the Olympics!"

Matt's nostrils flare. "Look, I know you're trying to help, but it's not going to happen. I'm done with skating until Mylene gets better. That's all there is to it. She's my partner. I'm not...leaving her behind." He motions to the building. "I should get back to work."

"But Mylene wouldn't want you to miss out. I know she wouldn't."

Shaking his head, he turns to the door. "She's my partner. I know her best. And anyway, it doesn't matter." He whirls around.

"Sure, fine, yes—she would want me to go for it. But what's the point? My triple Axel is fifty-fifty, and I could get the quad toe consistent if I had a year. It's less than three months now to Nationals. There's no way."

The urge to reach out and shake him has me flexing my fingers. "You don't know that. You don't know until you try. It's the Olympics! Don't you want to give it your all? Rudy Galindo and Kristi Yamaguchi won pairs together before they won singles. It's not impossible. Just try, and that way you won't have to regret what might have been."

Matt shakes his head and huffs out a puff of air. "Why do you even care? Since when do you see beyond the end of your own nose?"

It's like he's slapped me, and I step back, trying to laugh it off. "Good point. You're right, I've got more than enough on my plate. I'll see you around or whatever." Spinning on my heel, I stride toward the car, my eyes burning ridiculously. I shouldn't care what he thinks. I shouldn't care what he does with his life.

"Alex!"

Footsteps jog up behind me, and thank God I'm not actually crying when I turn to face him. "Uh-huh?" I keep my voice steady and cool. "Don't you have to get back to work?"

"I'm sorry. I didn't mean that. I shouldn't take this crappy situation out on you when I know you're just trying to help."

Fiddling with the strap of my duffel over my shoulder, I shrug, my gaze flitting around the parking lot. "It's cool. You're right anyway. I'm a self-involved asshole, so…"

"But are you? I used to think so. Now I think you're full of shit."

I have to look up into his steady gaze. Despite the snowflakes that have begun to sprinkle down and catch in his thick hair, his eyes are warm and kind. My mouth is dry and I croak, "Why's that?"

"You pretend you don't care. You try to act cool so no one can see how afraid you really are. And you do say what's on your mind when you shouldn't, but I like it."

"You do?"

His eyes crinkle with his grin. "I do." He reaches out, and my breath lodges in my throat. His fingers are gentle brushing through my hair. "Snowflakes."

"Right. Uh-huh. Yeah. It's snowing." Oh, Jesus. Kill me now. I sound like the clueless virgin that I am.

But maybe he's not even hitting on me. Maybe this is an ancient Canadian custom of snow removal and he's not leaning in to kiss me, although he steps up right into my personal space, the warm gust of his breath tickling my nose as he bends his head, one big hand cupping my face, his lips parting—

"Savelli! That golden wedding anniversary party just arrived."

Pressing his lips into a thin line, Matt turns and calls, "Okay!"

I back up, the swirl of emotions spinning through me like a quad on acid. "I'll leave you to it."

"I... Alex, I'll talk to you later, okay?" He watches me hopefully.

"Totally. No rush!" I back into my car, laughing like a braying donkey. Throwing my bag over onto the passenger seat, I hop in and peel out before I can humiliate myself any more.

But by nine o'clock, when I should be asleep, I still can't shake off any of it—the snow, the maybe kiss, or the idea of Matt training in singles. After staring at the ceiling for another hour, I give up and tug on my skating clothes.

The drive to the club doesn't take long at all this late in the evening, and I manage to sneak into the back of the restaurant without Matt noticing. There are only a couple tables left. Whispering, I convince one of the waitresses to get me Matt's car keys from the staff room. She's game once I explain my plan.

I'm hoping his skates are in his trunk, and sure enough, there's his equipment bag. I grab my own skates out of my car, and my accomplice tells Matt to go down to the rink on some made-up errand.

The huge overhead lights are out, but the illumination coming through the glass on the second level makes it bright enough. The doors are locked, but I happen to know that one of them doesn't quite latch right, and I'm able to jiggle it open.

Inside, I lace my skates with shaky fingers and hope I'm not making a big mistake and pushing too hard. Breathing deeply, I concentrate on the familiar smell of the rink—clean and cold, stinging my nostrils, crisp and fresh and perfect with possibilities.

A few minutes later, Matt opens the door. "Hello?"

I'm in the shadows at the side of the rink, so I skate into the faint light. "Hey."

The door shuts behind him and Matt loosens his tie as he walks toward the ice. "What are you doing here?"

"Just felt like skating."

He laughs uneasily. "At this time of night? Shouldn't you be in bed?"

"Nah, I'm a big boy."

"Okay. Uh, did you want to talk to me about something?"

I skate over and point to his bag on the bench. "Why don't you put your skates on?"

"What?" Comprehension dawns on his face. "Alex…"

"Yeah?"

"Look, I don't want to skate, okay? It was a busy dinner. I'm tired, and I still have to polish the cutlery." He backs away.

"What, are you afraid or something?" It's childish to call him chicken, but desperate times.

"*No.* I said I'm tired."

"Doesn't look that way to me."

"What should I be afraid of?" he asks sharply.

"Nothing. Absolutely nothing."

He exhales and yanks off his tie, almost strangling himself in the process. "Fine. I'll skate. Even though this is a waste of time."

I wait while he laces his boots and hops up the boards, swinging around to the ice side. But he freezes, just sitting there, his long legs dangling.

"Come on. We'll just have fun. It doesn't have to mean anything." Suddenly I'm not sure exactly what I'm talking about.

He doesn't reply for a minute, and I let the silence stretch out. When he talks, I have to strain to hear. "We've been partners for six years. I don't know how to skate without her anymore. When we started, she was just a baby. Thirteen. I was eighteen and the only thing we had in common was skating and hot chocolate with marshmallows. It's our favorite."

I nod and wait for him to go on.

"She always loved to fly. Lifts and throws and twists—she'd do them all day if Chantal let us. She trusted me right from the start. She was even tinier then, but tough, you know?" He stared into the dark, distant end of the rink. "So tough. And one day I realized she wasn't a little girl anymore. We started talking about more than skating, and we never stopped. We always had a connection on the ice, and then it was off the ice too. And I ruined it."

"You didn't!" My voice echoes in the empty arena, and I take a deep breath. "It was an accident. I know Mylene doesn't blame you. She would never."

He shook his head. "She doesn't, but that doesn't change anything. Doesn't change that I dropped her."

"She's going to be okay. She's a fighter. You have to fight too. It's not too late. You'll never know if you don't try. Come on. Even if you don't want to try for singles, the longer you stay off the ice, the harder it'll be."

"I can't." He looks at me with big, glistening eyes.

"You can."

"It's my fault." His voice cracks. "She's lying in bed for God knows how long, and she's not going to the Olympics, and it's my fault."

I skate closer, stopping a couple feet away. I don't want to crowd him, but I'm not giving up. "Everyone knows you'd take her place if you could. We all know that. No one blames you but *you*." I hold out my hand. "Come on. Just a few steps."

Matt stares at my hand for a long moment, and my heart thumps painfully.

Then he sucks in a breath and drops onto the ice, reaching for me, his fingers warm and palm sweaty. I hold on tight and push off, pulling him along. After a few steps, Matt's skating too, and we circle the silent rink, taking our time like we're in Central Park or something, holding hands and stroking around, our blades whispering on the ice.

I don't say anything, letting him get used to it. It's only been a couple weeks, but that's an eternity for us, especially during training season. He starts to smile, and we go a bit faster around the corners, dipping into the shadows and back out again into the pale light.

I'm not sure why we start racing, but Matt lets go of my hand with a squeeze, and then we're speeding across the ice, keeping pace with each other and cross-cutting around the corners like speed skaters, which isn't as easy to do in figure skates.

"Where's the finish line?" I call.

Matt points to the darker end of the rink, and we both power toward it, laughing as we skid to a stop just before smashing into the boards, snow flying from our blades. We're breathing hard, and I throw my hands in the air like we did at the top of the Rocky steps. Matt laughs, a *real* laugh, and joins in.

After we dance around for a bit, we stand there in the shadows of the end of the rink, catching our breath. I'm just about to say that we should go get some water when I realize Matt is suddenly really close.

"Why are you really doing this?" He runs his palms up my arms and takes hold of my shoulders.

In the dim light, I can see that Matt's staring down at me with that serious expression of his, like there's something so important hidden in me that he wants to read. I force a smile and shrug. "I told you, I felt like skating."

He cups my head gently and leans in even closer, resting our foreheads together, our breath mingling. "Thank you."

Our dry lips barely touch, and fireworks go off behind my closed eyes. Then Matt jerks away and I realize what's happening. We jump apart, blinking rapidly and shielding our eyes from the harsh fluorescents overhead.

"What are you doing? No one's supposed to be in here at this time." A janitor stands by the doors at the other end of the rink, hands on his hips.

I play innocent with a sweet smile. "Oh, sorry. The door was unlocked."

"You're not supposed to be in here," he barks. "Get out."

He huffs impatiently while we take our skates off and shove our feet into our shoes. When we're through the doors into the open hallway, he locks up and shuffles away, grumbling.

He's not the only one pissed off, because Matt was going to kiss me, and we kind of did kiss, and now we're standing here all awkward.

Matt shoulders his bag. "I should go finish my shift."

"Right. Polish the cutlery." My skates dangle in one hand.

"Can we do this again? Skate, I mean? Not necessarily the breaking and entering." He smiles tentatively.

Are we going to do the kissing part again? "Yeah, of course. No B and E required."

"It was fun. I... I had fun." A pinched, guilty expression creases his face, like he's not allowed to do that anymore.

"Me too."

We stand there staring at each other. Okay, maybe I should just grow a pair and kiss him now. Because even though I shouldn't be kissing anyone, and I should be in my bed fast asleep before another long day of training tomorrow, I don't give a shit. Because Matt's right here and I can hardly breathe. I need his hands on me. I need to taste him and make his eyes scrunch and hear him laugh and suck his—

"Matt?" The waitress who helped me earlier is at the end of the corridor. "Sorry, but Manny's wondering where you are. We have side work."

Matt takes a shuddering breath and backs away from me. "Coming. Alex, we'll…"

"Yeah, see you later." I wave my free hand like it's nothing and turn the other way, practically running to the parking lot. Time to get my ass to bed before I turn into a pumpkin. A very confused, horny pumpkin.

CHAPTER SEVEN

CINDERELLA'S WICKED STEPMOTHER didn't have anything on Mrs. C and her pitiless gaze.

I'm only a couple minutes late—seriously, like, *two*—but when I enter the arena, I can sense Mrs. C's supreme displeasure before I've even stepped a foot on the ice.

Passing Annie, Chantal, and a few other skaters, I smile and try to look rested and eager as I skate over to where Mrs. C's standing on the rink in her skates—fur hat, leather coat, and jewels impeccable as ever.

She stares humorlessly. "Late night?"

"Um, not really."

"Mind needs to be *here*." She stabs a finger down toward the ice.

"What? It is."

"Hmm. Last night too. *Here*."

How does she *always* know everything? She probably knows what I was thinking about while jerking off this morning—riding Matt's big cock and coming all over his hairy chest, for the record. I swear she has secret cameras following me around. Or the janitor is on her payroll. I decide to play innocent. "What?"

It's like the temperature instantly drops a few degrees, and now she's really pissed. "No lies, Alexander." Her sharp voice carries, and my skin prickles under the weight of stares from other skaters and a handful of parents in the stands.

Sighing, I give up. "Okay, okay. I'm sorry. It was just a one-time thing. I promise."

"Two weeks is enough."

"Huh?" At her glare, I correct myself. "Pardon?"

"No more distraction. You left head in Philadelphia. Thinking too much about other skaters. Have you forgotten Grand Prix? Going to France tomorrow. You must medal to make final in December. No more games. No more."

The scrambled eggs and avocado I scarfed down for breakfast threaten to reappear. Jesus, she's so right. If I blow it at Trophée de France, I won't go to the Grand Prix Final in Japan in December. I'll lose my momentum. Lose my standing in the judges' minds as one of the very top contenders.

I'll lose everything.

"This is Olympic season." Mrs. C takes my chin in hand. "That is only thought you should have. Yes?"

"Yes," I manage.

She nods curtly and points to center ice. "Start short program."

Everyone else in the arena jerk their heads around and act busy, and humiliation slithers down my spine. I bet they all know I was in here last night with Matt. Although the rink is quiet but for the carve of blades and Rick instructing Kenny on his landing form, I imagine the snickers and derision everyone's holding in. I bet they're wondering what Matt would ever see in me.

And he probably sees nothing. He's probably grateful to me for helping him in Philly, and other than that is just being nice. I mean, what would he even see in me? He's tall and gorgeous and could have any guy he wanted. I'm scrawny in comparison, and mouthy and have zero experience and he—

"Alexander!" Mrs. C's clap echoes like a gunshot. "Focus!"

Shit, fuck, fuck. Everyone's watching again, and I realize I've been skating aimlessly around center ice, not taking my starting position. What's wrong with me? I bet Tanner Nielsen isn't letting Lisa distract him. I hear they barely even see each other when he's training. Jesus, I need to get it together. Forget the Grand Prix—if I blow US Nationals in January, I won't even *get* to the Olympics.

My chest tightens, a hissing boa constrictor wrapped around me as I scramble to hit my mark. Of course I suck, chucking all over the place, my blade catching on the ice, no flow, no smooth edges. And that's when I manage to stay on my feet.

Finally Mrs. C has enough and the music stops. "You will compete like you practice. Must practice better. Now you run." She nods to Rick and skates away from me in disgust, turning her attention to Kenny.

Rick comes over with a long rope, which he loops around my waist, holding on to the ends. Grunting, I take off down the length of the ice, running as I drag Rick behind me. Once I reach the end, it's time to skate backwards while pulling him.

"That's it! Great job!" Rick gives me a thumbs up, playing good cop.

I'm already breathing hard, and after a few more laps, forward and back, Rick feeling a hundred pounds heavier on each one, sweat dampens my neck and forehead. Endorphins kick in, and it's a relief to throw myself into it, not having to think about anything but moving and getting from one end to the other.

My grunts practically become primal screams, and Rick eggs me on for a few more passes before releasing the rope and lifting his hand for a high five. "You got this. Hit the gym and then stretch out."

As I'm slapping his palm, Annie and Chantal erupt in a French screaming match. Maybe it's the stress of Mylene and Matt being gone, or maybe it's the bad energy in the rink, but it seems none of us are having much fun today.

And why should we? Olympics are coming! This isn't about fuck-

ing fun.

Still, I'm relieved to escape to the solitude of the empty gym. Of course my phone buzzes immediately. I should let it go to voicemail, but not this time.

"Mylene? How are you?"

Her lilting voice fills my year. "Every day better than the last."

"I'm glad to hear it. I miss having you around. We all do."

"I miss you guys too."

"So… How's the weather in Montreal?"

She ignores my loser question. "Alex, I need your help." It sounds like *elp*, and makes me smile. Damn, I really have missed her.

"Sure. What's up?"

"You need to convince Matt to keep skating."

Uh-oh. "Um, I don't think he'll listen to me."

"You're wrong. He'll listen to you more than anyone."

My heart beats faster, and I start pacing a circle around the empty gym. "Why's that?"

"You know why."

Yeah, except Mrs. C's right and this is no time for romance.

After my silence, she says, "I can't go to the Olympics this year. Matt can. He's good enough to make the team in singles if he works very hard. I don't want him sitting around waiting for me. He loves skating. It's… Like a fish needs water. You know?"

Do I ever. "Yes, but if he won't listen to you…"

"Annie says you broke into the rink and got him to skate."

"Glad to hear the gossip pipeline is still reaching you. But that was just… It didn't mean anything. I can't help him. I've been too distracted already. I have my own skating to worry about."

"I'm too far away. I'm stuck. You can make him listen. I know you can."

"I wish I could help. I really do." I need to focus on myself. I don't have time for this.

"Please? Just try. For me?"

I imagine her lying in bed, her Olympic dream over, at least for now. "I'll try, but I can't promise anything."

"*Merci*! I knew I was right about you."

"Wait, what?"

"*Au revoir*, Alex. Good luck in France. You can do it!"

In the silence of the gym after she hangs up, my mind spins her words over and over. I really do want to help Matt, and the idea that he'd listen to me because he likes me shoots little thrills down my spine despite my best efforts to stop feeling anything for him but casual friendship.

Wearing jeans and a hoodie, Matt walks in as I'm lying back doing leg presses, and his eyes crinkle as he smiles. Lust, affection, and happiness battle in me with frustration, guilt, and the bone-chilling terror that I'm going to fuck up everything I've worked so hard for.

Matt says, "Hey," and he's still smiling and looking as stupidly handsome as ever. An image from my morning fantasy flits across my mind, and my dick twitches.

But Mrs. C's lecture rings in my ears, and I resolutely turn my gaze back to the ceiling. "Hi." I count out another five presses, thighs straining as I push the weighted platform upwards. I'll talk to him about skating singles, but maybe not right this second. Maybe I'll call him later. Keep my promise to Mylene while still putting distance between me and Matt.

"I have the lunch shift today, but I thought maybe we could do something tonight?"

Remember the Olympics. Tanner Nielsen. *Focus.* "Sorry, I can't. I really need an early night." I stare at the ceiling, Matt hovering in my peripheral vision.

"Oh." The happy energy in his voice has dissipated. "Sure, I understand. What about tomorrow? Or the weekend?"

I keep on shoving the weight up with my legs, even though

my quads are burning and I've done my reps. "Can't. Have too much training. No time." It's the truth, at least.

"Can you stop that for a minute?" Matt reaches out and touches my thigh, which promptly tingles traitorously, and I lower the weights back into the resting position, grunting softly. As I sit up, he hands me my towel. "I know you've got a hard training schedule, but—"

"But nothing." I wipe my forehead and sling the towel around my neck. "I've been way too distracted lately. I need to focus, okay?"

"Right. I just thought..." He smiles tentatively. "You can't train all the time."

"I'm going to France tomorrow. Obviously I need to medal." I take a swig of water and imagine myself winning in Bordeaux. "Look, it's nothing personal."

Matt's smile evaporates. "I guess it isn't. My mistake."

Guilt tugs at me, low and insistent. "Olympics are in, like, three months—"

"I know when the fucking Olympics are."

I jump to my feet. "Good! Then you know I don't have time to dick around since I'm actually still going."

"You're an asshole, you know that? I thought maybe we were..." He clenches his jaw. "I don't know what I thought. Temporary insanity."

"Whatever. Maybe the Olympics don't matter to you anymore—"

"Of course it matters!" He steps right up to me, fists clenched, his usual calm evaporated.

"Then why are you being such a coward? Why don't you at least try singles?"

"*I'm* being a coward? What about you?"

I shout, "What about me?"

"This!" He waves a hand between us, his knuckles hitting my

chest. "What are you so afraid of?"

"Nothing!"

To prove it, I lunge for his mouth, our teeth clacking and lips mashing together. I have no clue what I'm doing, but I go for it, kissing him like he's the air I need to breathe, digging my fingers into his arms.

When I actually *do* need to breathe, we break apart, chests heaving, staring at each other. Then Matt backs me up against the wall of mirrors, his hands strong on my shoulders as he dips his head.

This time, his tongue pushes inside, and I open my mouth wider on a low moan, because holy shit, kissing Matt is *nothing* like what I imagine it would be like kissing a girl. His stubble scrapes my face, and the rough contrast to the wet, dirty slide of his tongue has my dick hard in about three seconds.

The mirror against my back shudders as Matt runs his hands down my sides and thrusts our hips together. Memories of the glimpse I had in Philly of his thick, uncut cock explode, and I hitch one leg up around his hip, panting and desperate.

His tongue commands my mouth, and I push back against it with my own. With a groan rumbling in his chest, he ruts against me harder, holding my hips in place, the rock-hard bulge of his cock pressing against the fly of his jeans.

I might come right here, right now, and I mumble that as I gasp for air. With a positively feral grin that darkens his blown pupils another shade, Matt glances around and tugs me into the single unisex bathroom in the corner of the gym.

Inside, he flips on the fluorescent overheads and pushes me back against the locked door. In the harsh, white light that probably makes me look pasty and red-blotched, he's fucking beautiful, and I reach to trace my fingers along his prickly jaw.

"Oh, Alex." He licks his red, parted lips. "The things I want to do to you."

Gulping, I ask, "Like what?"

Matt kisses me, whispering against my mouth, "I don't know where to start."

"At the beginning?"

With a low chuckle, he sucks on the juncture of my neck and shoulder before lifting his lips to my ear. "First time I jerked off thinking of you, I imagined shoving you to your knees and fucking that big mouth of yours."

Holy. Shit. I can only whimper and cling to him, his breath tickling my ear, shivers rippling through me.

"Want to fill your mouth with my cock. See your lips stretch around it until your eyes water and all you can do is moan."

My knees smack on the tile when I drop, but I ignore the flare of pain. Staring up at him, I reach for his fly before I lose my nerve.

Matt threads his fingers through my hair, his chest rising and falling. "Are you sure?"

"Yes." It's hoarse, but I mean it. I've never even touched another man's dick before, but if I don't get Matt's in my mouth ASAP, I might actually die. And then I wouldn't win Olympic gold anyway, so what's the sense in denying myself now?

Because oh my God, as I suck hard on the tip, it's *everything*. My blood's on fire, the musky, sweaty scent filling my nose and salty tang on my tongue perfect. I stroke the base of his dick while sucking the head, pushing back the foreskin. He's hard and hot and it feels like mine, but it's not. I'm actually doing this—I'm blowing another guy for real.

Matt moans, gripping my head as I lick and suck almost frantically, a strange panic spurring my pulse, fear that this is going to be taken away from me before I can really experience it.

I tug Matt's jeans and boxer-briefs down his powerful thighs, burying my face in his groin, his trimmed pubes scratching my cheeks as I lap at his heavy balls. His fingers tighten on my head, but he's letting me lead right now, letting me explore. I take one testicle and then the other into my mouth gently so I don't hurt him, my lips spit-wet.

When I move back to his cock, the frantic drumbeat returns, my heart slamming against my ribs. I suck him desperately, trying not to choke, willing myself on past the coughs that scratch my throat, looking up to his flushed face, desperate for approval.

Now Matt leans over me, bracing a palm on the door, the other coming around to the back of my head, his fingers digging into my skull. "So good."

Pleasure flows through me, and it has nothing to do with my dick, although that's certainly begging for attention. I press the heel of my hand against it as I open my mouth as far as I can and try to relax my throat, fighting my gag reflex.

Matt takes over now, setting the rhythm as he fucks my mouth. I want it all. I want him to climb inside me until there's nothing else—no fear, no judges, no gold medals.

His eyes are locked with mine, and as he thrusts, his hand cushions my head so it doesn't bash into the door. My eyes are watering and spit dribbles from my lips, the wet smacking sound filling the bathroom positively porny, especially combined with Matt's panting and my little moans.

My cock is going to explode, still trapped in my jock in my tight Lycra pants. I rub against it with my hand, and it's like I'm in a tug-of-war, the mounting pressure of pleasure in my dick and balls competing for attention with Matt's cock fucking my mouth, overwhelming my senses.

His balls practically slapping my chin, Matt suddenly stiffens, biting back a cry as he comes. I can't swallow fast enough, and now I'm choking and coughing, and he pulls out, spurting onto my cheek and chin instead, his mouth open and body shaking.

Gasping, I try to catch my breath. My lips feel puffy and my jaw sore, but I'm smiling up at Matt, elation flowing in my veins.

He pulls me to my feet and holds my face in his hands, licking his cum from my skin before feeding it to me on his tongue, kissing me long and deep.

Then he drops to his knees and tugs down my pants and soft jock strap, holding my hips as he swallows me almost to the root. I can't hold in my shout, and it only takes two long pulls of his mouth before my orgasm crashes through me.

If not for Matt holding me up, I think my knees would give, the burn of pure bliss hollowing me out in the best possible way as he swallows every drop, sucking until it's too much and I whimper, "Enough, enough."

He pushes to his feet and gathers me close, nuzzling my head and kissing my cheek. "Alex, that was…"

A wave of doubt roars in, and I go stiff. "Sorry, I'm sure you've had better. I don't really know… I could use a lot of practice, I bet." *Practice. Shit, I need to get back soon. What am I doing? I've lost my damn mind.*

Pushing away the thoughts of skating, I wriggle from his arms and pull up my pants, heading for the sink.

"Alex. Look at me."

When I turn back, he's standing there with his jeans and underwear halfway down his thighs, his spent cock still hanging out. "Uh-huh?" I resist the insane urge to giggle.

I just did that. This is a thing that happened. In real life.

"You've…" Matt's brow furrows. "You've done that before. Right?" He pulls up his pants, zipping them as he watches me with concern.

Keeping my head low as I turn and wash my hands, I shrug. "Nope. I'm a total loser, I know."

Matt's hands on my shoulders are gentle as he turns me around. He gazes down at me intently. "You're a virgin?"

I try to laugh, my cheeks going hot under his scrutiny. "I guess not anymore, although I suppose it depends on your definition of 'sex.' It sure felt like it to me, but obviously I'm no expert. I've barely kissed anyone before."

"Shit, why didn't you tell me? I wouldn't have been rough like that!" His brow creases as he runs his thumb over my swollen lips. "Was it too much?"

"*No*. I wanted it. I mean, in case that wasn't obvious. I really wanted it. I've never... There's never been anyone I've even considered it with." My hands are wet, and I wipe them on my pants, dropping my head. "Anyway, I hope it was okay, and I should get back out there."

"Don't run away." Matt nudges up my chin, but I keep my gaze on his neck. "Alex, that wasn't 'okay.' That was the hottest sex I've ever had."

My heart skips as I meet his eyes. "Seriously?"

"Absolutely." He kisses me, licking into my mouth, slow and deep.

Winding my arms around his shoulders, the sink against my ass, I kiss him back, smoldering, quivering lust ready to blaze.

Matt leans back, breathing hard against my mouth, murmuring, "I want to do everything with you. God, I want to fuck you. Do you want that? Do you want to take my cock?"

"*Yes*. Please. I'll do it right now. Need it. Need you. I want it to be you."

Groaning, he wraps his arms around me. "You're going to be the end of me, Alex Grady, surprise virgin. Surprise *everything*. But I'm going to be late for work, and you need to get back to the rink."

Turning my face into his neck and inhaling the vague scent of mint, it's my turn to groan. "Can't we call in sick?"

He laughs, trailing his fingers up and down my spine. "I think with Mrs. C, you'd have to call in dead. Besides, I don't want your first time to be in a bathroom. I mean, I realize it just was, but there are other firsts, and you deserve a better place."

I lift my head. "You won't change your mind?"

"Remember that part where this was the hottest sex in my life? No, I will not change my mind."

"You could come over tonight. I can buy whatever we need on the way home."

He bites his kiss-swollen lip. "What time's your flight tomorrow?"

Crap. "Uh, crack of dawn. But it's fine, we can fit it in!"

"That's what she said."

The burst of laughter is warm in my chest, and Matt's shoulders shake. I add, "So to speak."

"Let's not rush. I want to take my time with you." He pulls me flush and runs a palm over my ass. "You're worth it."

I blurt, "Am I?" before I can engage my filter.

"Yes. Absolutely." He kisses me softly. "Positively." Another kiss. "Worth." Kiss. "It." Kiss and nuzzle this time.

"What if the plane crashes?"

Laughing, he takes my face in his hands. "The plane's not going to crash." He glances around the white-tiled bathroom, then leans over to bump his knuckles on the roll of toilet paper. "Knock on wood. Paper used to be wood, so it counts. And you're going to do great over there."

I kiss him and rub our noses together. With a deep breath, I think of Mylene's pleas and sigh internally. I don't want to break the magic of the connection I feel, like I'm a magnet slapped to Matt's fridge door. But I promised her, and I want what's best for him. If he doesn't even try, I think he'll always regret it.

"Have you thought any more about skating singles?" I guess blurting it out is better than not saying it at all.

"What?" Matt's smile slips, and yep, tension fills the growing space between us as he steps away from me. "I told you, I'm not skating without Mylene."

"Even if you're miserable not being out there on the ice? Even if that's what she wants?"

"How do you know what she wants?"

"I... I mean, I'm sure she would want you to keep competing."

"Did she put you up to this?" Matt's voice suddenly echoes too loudly in the confines of the bathroom.

"No! I talked to you about this before, remember?"

"So how do you know what Mylene wants?"

Rolling my shoulders, I confess. "Okay, busted. She called me, and I talked to her. If that makes me an asshole, I guess I'm an asshole."

Matt exhales a long breath and fiddles with the zip of his hoodie. "You're not an asshole."

A million thoughts are running through my brain, and my filter doesn't work very well at the best of times, so I just spit out the truth as I see it. "You love skating, and you're being a martyr by giving it up. The accident wasn't your fault. Get over it and start training again. You're an idiot if you don't at least try. You're not doing Mylene any good being depressed and missing skating. Suck it up already and *try*. No one wants to be at your pity party anymore."

For a few moments, Matt stares at me. Then he barks out a laugh. "Tell me how you really feel, Alex."

"I just—"

"It's okay. I like it." He comes near again and runs his hands up and down my arms.

I lean into him. "You do?"

"Yeah." He laughs again. "Okay. Yes. I'll talk to Chantal and see what she thinks. You're right, I do miss it. I hate that Mylene's hurt, and I'd give anything to change it. But I can't. Trying singles is something I can do."

"You totally can." Excitement zips through me. "I know you can do it."

From the gym, Rick calls out, "Alex? Are you in there? You're late."

Matt scrunches up his face. "Say hi to Mrs. C."

I should be *running* back to the rink, but all I want to do is kiss Matt one more time, so I do. After the second and third kisses, he shoves me out the door, grinning.

I should run, but there's no need since I'm floating.

CHAPTER EIGHT

I HATE FRANCE.

Okay, not really, but right now all the croissants and Brie and charming cobblestone streets in the world can't make up for the fact that I just lost the Trophée de France by *one* damn point. Even less than that! Two tenths of a point to be exact.

But the crowd is applauding my score, and I'm waving to them from the Kiss and Cry with a big smile on my face, pretending I'm not upset. I tug my ear for everyone at home and say hi to my family.

Mrs. C helps me with my toys and flowers, and I go backstage to talk to the media. Blah, blah, it'll be the usual routine. I already know they're going to ask about my rivalry with Tanner and about who will win at Nationals in January. I have my answer prepared, not to mention approved by Mrs. C.

I pass the winner, Oleg Sokolov, and we shake hands and I pretend I'm not mentally replaying my program in excruciating detail to figure out where I lost two tenths and how easy it would have been to just extend my leg a little straighter or emote just a fraction more or carry the flow out of my quad toe a few inches farther.

And of course if I'd landed my damn quad Sal, I would have won comfortably. Not only did I go down, but I got dinged with an under-rotation. I tried to shake it off and not let it affect the rest of the program, but I know it did.

Sue Stabler, a sleek, middle-aged woman with short red hair from the Federation, watches me talk to the reporters. After I'm done, she gives me a smile and a nod, and at least I'm not in the Feds' bad books today.

Before the medal ceremony, I go to the dressing room to take a quick bathroom break and check my phone. My stomach flip-flops ridiculously as I see the text from Matt.

We've texted back and forth a few times daily since I've been here in France, and I've been tempted to call him at least once an hour. But I don't want to seem... I don't know. Needy? Whenever he texts me first, my heart soars ludicrously.

Less than a point! Ugh. I feel your pain. But stop obsessing about it and enjoy the fact that you've made the GP final! Congrats. You deserve it.

My thumbs fly and I respond:

Me, obsess?

My breath comes fast and shallow as I wait for his reply.

LOL, never. Btw, I ran through my LP today. I think you were right.

Even though I know I'll be holding up the ceremony in a minute if I don't get my ass back out there, I quickly tap out a message.

I'm always right! Get used to it.

Hmm. Should I use an emoticon there at the end? Smiley face? Heart? No, not heart. I should wink, but is that too...something? Maybe I should rewrite the text. Or put in another exclamation point at the end? Is that too teenage girl? Is it clear that I'm joking?

I should rewrite it. But if he's looking at his phone, he can see the dots that show I'm typing, so if I don't send it soon, he'll wonder what took so long. Although I don't know if he's looking, and I should send the best text I can, shouldn't I?

"Alex? The ceremony is about to start!" Sue calls from outside the door.

Fuck it. After hitting send, I hustle to rink-side, where everyone is indeed waiting for me. Mrs. C arches a disapproving eyebrow, which practically disappears under her mink hat. I pretend not to notice and start chatting with the bronze medal winner from Germany, Hans Gerber, not to be confused with Hans Gruber from *Die Hard*, my family's favorite Christmas movie.

I once made a joke to Hans about shooting the glass, and he had zero idea what I was talking about. Everyone in the locker room had stared at me like I'd grown a new head and it'd just performed a quad. One of the many reasons I shouldn't make jokes. I rarely say the right thing unless it's scripted.

Medal ceremonies are way more fun when you win, but it's still nice being applauded and getting another piece of hardware for my bedroom wall at home. Oleg, Hans, and I shake hands and hug in turn as we take our places on the podium, and as I watch the flags go up, I visualize the Stars and Stripes in the middle.

Then we all stand on the top of the podium together and smile for a zillion pictures with our arms around each other, holding our medals. The lap around the rink to shake hands with fans and take selfies is fun, and someone gives me a US flag to drape around my shoulders like a cape.

I talk to a couple loyal fans who go to as many competitions as they can. They're plump, middle-aged soccer moms from the Midwest who are so sweet.

One of them, Rose, hugs me and kisses my cheek. "Don't worry, you'll have that quad down cold by Boston."

"I hope so!" I smile and lean over the boards to hug Rose's friend Mary. "I missed you guys at Skate America. I can't believe you came all the way to France!"

Rose grins. "Philadelphia doesn't quite have the allure that France does! We splurged."

Mary pats my back. "Your footwork was the strongest it's been this season! Sokolov was way over-marked. All he does is flail his arms around and pretend it's artistry."

This is the part where I have to pretend I don't completely agree with her since I don't want to be a bad loser. I just don't address her comments about Oleg. "Well, I tried my best."

"You always do, Alex." Rose beams and holds up her camera, and I lean in backwards to take a selfie with them before moving on around the rink.

In the dressing room, the first thing I do is check my phone, but the only new texts are from my mom and Rachel. Which is really nice, obviously. But now I'm staring at what I wrote Matt. Was it too cocky? Should I have used a stupid winky face? Or maybe a bitmoji or a gif. Why didn't I think of that?

I guess the bright side is that now I'm not obsessing over my skate.

THE GENTLE VIBRATION might as well be a fire alarm the way I shoot up in bed and snatch my phone off the side table, blinking at the screen.

Sorry, work was crazy. Huge bar mitzvah party that took over the whole restaurant. Just got home. But yes, ha ha, I'll try to get used to your epic rightness. ;)

Pulse zooming, I reply:

Whoa, late night. It's just past two, right? Jet lag has me all messed up. Japan in a couple weeks is really going to throw me for a loop.

After a few seconds, the three wobbly dots appear. I scratch my bare chest and tug a loose string on my plaid boxer shorts.

Did I wake you? Sorry. You don't have to be up early today, do you?

That he knows my schedule makes me stupidly happy. Never mind that he knows it because he's competed at these competitions. The last day is gala practice, gala, and then the closing banquet, where we all dress up and smile and try not to eat too much. I lie and respond:

Np. I was already up. Jet lag and all that. I guess you should get to sleep?

As I wait, I will him to say no and talk to me more.

Too wired. Need to unwind. Knowing you, I bet you do too. Have you unclenched yet about not winning?

I laugh to myself in the stillness of my single room, the black-out curtains drawn over the sunrise, which peeks in around the edges. At some competitions I share with another American skater, but it was only me and Sabrina Pang here in France, and the Feds weren't about to room us together. Not that anyone who knows me would think little Sabrina and her virtue have anything to worry about.

I don't ever unclench, lol.

After a few moments, the phone vibrates in my hand, a FaceTime call coming in. Heart pounding, I answer and smile at Matt. His hair's damp on his forehead, as if he recently washed his face, and it doesn't look like he's wearing a shirt judging by his bare collar bones.

"Hey!" I squeak, before clearing my throat.

"Hey. I can barely see you. Can you turn on a light?"

Leaning over, I flip the switch on a lamp. "Better?"

"Much." He smiles and repeats, "Hey. I've missed you this week."

"Me too. Missed you, I mean." I laugh too loudly.

"So, on a scale of one to ten, how much are you obsessing about your quad Sal?"

I sit back against the padded headboard, holding the phone up so my face is in frame. Ugh, I have total bedhead and a zit growing on my chin. "Um, about a six hundred and twenty? Give or take. Don't remind me."

Matt smiles sympathetically. "Sorry. You know, we really need to work on the unclenching thing."

"Well, if you were here, we could." Wait, did that sound

porny? "I mean, um…"

He licks his lips. "Oh yeah? I can still help you out from here. If you want."

"Like…on the phone?"

He smiles. "You're a sexting virgin too?"

I shift uncomfortably and roll my eyes. "This isn't dick pics and texts. This is, like, real time. But yeah, I've never done any of it. I know, it's pathetic."

His smile vanishes. "Not at all. It's hot, actually."

"Hot?" I scoff. "Come on."

"Truth is, it really turns me on."

My cheeks flush so warm that I must be beet red, and I have to look away.

His brow furrows. "Is this too much right now? I don't want to make you uncomfortable or pressure you."

As embarrassed as I am, my dick's springing to attention. "No, don't stop." I look at the screen again. "It's not like I haven't watched a shit-ton of porn. And I want to do things. I want to do everything with you. But talking about it's hard."

"I can do the talking." He grins. "If people only knew how shy tough, cocky Alex Grady really is. Fuck, you make my dick hard just thinking about the things I want to do with you."

My throat's so dry I can barely whisper, "Yeah?"

"Want to see?"

Nodding is the only answer I have right now. I hold my breath as his phone shakes, fabric rustling. He's sitting up in bed too, the edges of a framed poster behind him, some kind of art that might be Monet. Then the camera's moving, and holy shit.

The angle's tilted, but there's Matt's cock filling the screen. It's half erect, and I wish I could suck it and feel it grow in my mouth.

"Nnnngh," I mutter.

His laugh echoes. "Like what you see?" He moves the phone

105

to his left hand and starts touching himself, spreading his legs and giving me a show. He eases back his foreskin and plays with the head. "Wish you were here. Your mouth is amazing, Alex. You did so good. I want you to suck my balls again. Want you to lick my ass."

I gulp in a sharp breath and reach into my boxers with my right hand to jerk my dick, switching the phone to my left. I've seen rimming in porn and the thought of doing it to Matt—or him doing it to me, Jesus Christ, is almost too much.

"You want to do that, Alex?"

"Yes," I gasp. "And I want…"

"What, baby? Want me to do it to you? Want me to spread your ass and eat you out? It'll feel so good when I lick you and open you up."

I moan and blurt, "Will you spit on my hole?"

He inhales deeply, jerking his dick harder on screen, the tip dark red now. "Oh, yeah. Get you so wet. Get you ready for my cock. You want that? Are you hard thinking about it?

"Uh-huh." I spit in my hand and pull back my foreskin as I stroke.

"Let me see. Please?"

Taking a deep breath, I kick off my boxers and spread my legs, lifting my hips as I jerk. I lower the camera, not sure how close to get, but apparently it's good enough since Matt groans.

"Fuck, you're beautiful. Tell me what you want. If I was there and we could do anything, what would it be?"

I'm burning, lust building, the pressure so intense it feels like it's pushing against every pore. Before I can second guess, I tell him, "I want to be on top. Want to ride you. Want to slam down on your cock and take it so deep I'll feel it for days. Want to be…free. Want to come on you."

"Yes," he pants. "Keep going. Fuck, Alex. Tell me."

"Want to come on your hairy chest. Rub it in."

"Yeah. And I'm going to come so hard inside you. Fill you up until it drips out. You want that? Want to take my cum?"

My hand flies on my dick, and I dig my heels into the mattress, arching up my hips, the thought of Matt's cum leaking from my ass mind-blowing and I don't even know why. But fuck yes, I want that. "*Please.*"

"You want it? Want to be my cum slut?"

With a cry, I'm coming, closing my eyes and banging my skull back on the headboard, my back arching.

"Let me see!" Matt's voice is muffled, and through the haze of pleasure I realize I dropped the phone, my limbs twitching. Milking myself, I hold up the camera again.

"Oh yeah. That's it. Get it all."

When every drop is splashed on my belly, my legs go lax and I lift the phone to my face. Matt's lips are parted and he's breathing hard, the camera shaking, sounds of skin slapping filling the air.

He licks his wet lips, eyes dark. "Swipe it up with your finger. Eat it for me."

With a moan, I do as I'm told, reaching down and running my index finger over a long splash. My eyes locked with Matt's on the screen, I lick my finger clean, sucking it into my mouth with wet pops.

His breathy little pants are like the sweetest music, and I gather more cum, relishing the salty taste. I've tried my jizz before out of curiosity, but never gotten off on it. But as Matt moans and I lick it off my finger, an aftershock ripples through me and I gasp.

Now it's Matt's turn to cry out, and I open my eyes to watch him come, his skin flushed red down his neck, the camera shaking. When he opens his eyes, a lazy smile lights up his face. "Thank you."

"I...anytime."

We both laugh then, and I'd give anything to be with him right now, to feel his body against mine and kiss his fevered skin.

"When are you coming home?" he asks.

"How about I skip the gala? Be home by tonight." The yearning to see him again is an ache that goes far beyond my bruised hip and sore muscles.

"And get fined by the ISU for not appearing? As much as I want you here, you probably shouldn't. It's an Olympic season, in case you haven't heard."

"Olympics? Never heard of them."

We laugh some more, and when it's past time for Matt to go to bed, I fall back asleep, as unclenched as I think I've ever been in my life.

CHAPTER NINE

MY FIRST DAY back at the rink in Toronto begins like any other training day. Up at the ass crack of dawn, get on the ice, skate around and do the same elements a million times, perfecting every little detail.

Matt's not here and hasn't texted me since last night after I got home. My flight was delayed and I had to get to bed since Mrs. C doesn't believe in jet lag. I'm itching to text him, but what if he gets sick of me?

Kenny and I jog together in the gym after a TRX suspension training session with our trainer, and Kenny keeps up a running commentary on everything and anything that pops into his head. I don't mind, since all I have to do is nod and make the right noises so it seems like I'm listening and not thinking about Matt.

Because I'm not. Because that would be pathetic. He's not my boyfriend.

Is he?

We've only hooked up once in person, and haven't talked at all about a relationship or commitment. For all I know, he's FaceTiming right now and jerking off while some dude eats his own jizz.

A flash of lust bursts through me, and I swipe at my face with a towel. Focus. I need to focus. I don't even want a boyfriend! This is why I've never dated. I don't have time for this shit.

So why do I keep obsessing about it all through lunch? When I head back down to the rink, I give my head a mental shake, because Mrs. C will have my balls in her borscht if she doesn't think I'm putting every ounce of energy into training.

I put my skates back on, ready to concentrate on the task at hand. Then I get rink side and Matt speeds by me before going into a gorgeous triple Salchow-triple toe combination. The various people scattered around the arena clap for him, and I join in. Matt smiles as he passes by again, and seeing him in person makes me shivery and hot all at the same time.

When I skate over to Mrs. C, she stares at me with zero amusement before I realize that I'm grinning like a complete idiot. I wipe the smile from my face and ask her what we're working on this afternoon.

I try to focus. I really do. But I can't stop watching Matt out of the corner of my eye. He and Chantal talk a lot, and he works on his jumps for a bit. As happy as I am that he's really considering going for it in singles this season, it actually is incredibly weird to see him skating without Mylene. I can only imagine how it is for him.

My mind races as I go through the middle section of my long program, a couple spins and a slower choreographic sequence where I catch my breath before my next round of jumps with the ten percent bonus in the second half of the program.

Shit, did I even ask about her when we talked on the weekend? Well, *talking* was only part of it, and nope, I don't think I did due to the mutual masturbation. I really should have.

Although maybe not, if this is just going to be…what? Hooking up? Friends with benefits? Maybe Matt doesn't really want to *talk* to me. Although he did text after my long program, and that wasn't about sex, and—

Slam.

Fuck me. Down hard on my second quad toe, the jolt practically shaking my teeth.

"Alexander!" Mrs. C stares daggers as my music dies. "Again. Mind here."

The afternoon drags on with more Mrs. C yelling and me sucking, and I'm dying to get the chance to talk to Matt alone. Finally, it's time to go. I linger by the boards, taking forever to put my guards on my blades, hoping Matt will finish up too. But he and Chantal are talking intently on the other side of the rink, and I'm starting to look like a stalker.

Kenny and Maxim are in the locker room, and I change into street clothes and do the nodding and smiling thing while Kenny stresses about Japanese Nationals at the end of December, and how he's certain he won't even make the Olympic team if he makes more than one mistake.

When Matt walks in, Kenny gets up to hug him and says, "Very happy to have you back! You will compete?"

Matt smiles. "Yeah, I've been convinced I should give it a shot."

I clear my throat and go for a casual tone. "Glad to hear it, man."

Maxim asks, "How's Mylene?"

"Improving. She's been on my case every day about doing singles, and she said it'll help her get better knowing I'm not sitting around moping."

I smile so he knows I'm just kidding. "Well, we certainly haven't noticed any moping."

"I know, I've been hiding it *really* well." Matt laughs, and Kenny and Maxim join in, and *why are they still here?*

As I mentally scream at them to GTFO, Matt says, "It's great to be back on the ice. Thanks, guys. See you tomorrow." Then he's gone.

Wait, that's it? We don't even get to talk alone? Matt is acting like... Well, I don't know what he's acting like. Like we're just friends, I guess. God, maybe what happened between us really didn't mean anything. Maybe it was only sex.

And maybe I should stop acting like a sixteen-year-old girl. I shove my feet into sneakers and fight the laces. So what if it was just sex? Why should that bother me? I'm a guy. I shouldn't care. I should be stoked! Sex with no strings—perfect.

I toss the rest of my crap in my gym bag. Yes, this is perfect. I didn't have time for Matt anyway. Time to go home and get my head together. *This is the Olympic season. Olympic season. Olympic season.*

I wave to Kenny and Maxim and march down the hallway to the back door to the parking lot. *Olympic season. Olympic season.* I don't give a damn about anything else but gold.

Suddenly, I'm being tugged into what might be a broom closet, although I'm not sure because it's dark—and who gives a shit because Matt's kissing me.

My bag drops to the floor with a thud and I kiss him back, my tongue diving into his mouth. As we keep on kissing, Matt's hands wander all over me, and he backs me up into the wall.

There's something with a handle jabbing my kidneys, but he's doing a wet, rolling thing with his tongue and his thigh is jammed between my legs, and everything else fades away but his mouth and hands and body.

We're panting when he pulls back and rests his forehead against mine. "I really do have to go to work."

Groaning, I slip my hands under his shirt, digging fingers into his flesh. "Sorry. Not letting you go."

He chuckles. "I don't think my boss will accept that as a valid excuse." He nuzzles my cheek in the darkness. "Good thing the plane didn't crash."

"Mmm." My dick strains against the fly of my jeans, and I nudge my hips against Matt's answering hardness. "Good thing."

He kisses me again. "Alex, you're…surprising."

"*Me?* I never thought mild-mannered, clean-cut Canadian Matt Savelli was the type to drag boys into broom closets." *Or fuck my mouth in a bathroom or jerk off with me across an ocean.*

His arms steal around my back, and he nips my earlobe, dragging his teeth before whispering, "Oh, you'd be surprised what I can do."

Suffice it to say, I can't wait to find out.

THE NEXT TWO days are a blur of training and sneaking time with Matt anywhere we can get it. Neither of us wants to tell anyone that we're—what, dating? Between training, early nights, and his work schedule, we still haven't had time to put a name on it yet.

We end up alone in the gym one morning, and are in full make-out mode on the weight bench when Kenny's voice chirps from the hallway. I leap off Matt and make it to the treadmill just as Kenny comes in, Annie hot on his heels. Matt and I are both breathing heavily, but at least in a gym we have a good excuse.

Kenny seems oblivious, but Annie eyes us shrewdly, and I can imagine what she'll be reporting back to Mylene.

My mom calls Thursday night just as I'm half-heartedly rinsing a stack of dishes in the sink. I stopped and picked up Thai food, which is a fat and sodium bomb I shouldn't eat while I'm training, but I just couldn't face leftover stir fry again.

"Hey, hon."

I tense immediately. "What's wrong?" I can tell from her voice.

She sighs. "I don't want you to worry, but…"

"Mom, I'm worrying."

"Your father lost his job."

The greasy food in my stomach roils. "What? How? Why? When?"

"It's the economy, sweetheart. They laid off a dozen people. Last in, first out."

Guilt stabs. My family only moved to Trenton so I could train with Mrs. C. If we hadn't, my dad would still have his old job in Colorado—where we'd only moved so I could train. "Is he okay?"

"Well, no one ever likes losing their job, but he's adjusting."

"Already?" Bile creeps up my throat. "Mom, when did this happen?"

There's a pause before she says, "Last week."

"Last *week*? Why didn't you tell me!"

"You were in France. We didn't want to worry you when you were focusing on a competition. You needed to do well to make the Grand Prix Final. And you did, and we're so proud of you, Alex. We know how important this is."

"I've been back since Monday. Why did you wait until now to tell me?"

"We were hoping we'd have some good news, but a job lead didn't pan out. Don't worry, your dad will find something soon."

I think about how much money my parents have spent on my skating. They wouldn't have huge debts if it weren't for me. "Do you have enough money? I can talk to my agent about getting me another endorsement. I don't care what it is. I'll do an infomercial hawking a blender that also cuts your hair and sharpens skates."

She laughs. "No, no. We're fine. Honey, just concentrate on yourself and training."

"Are you sure?"

"Yes! Alex, of course I'm sure. The Grand Prix Final is weeks away. You concentrate on *you*." Her tone indicates that it's settled. "Now, shouldn't you be getting ready for bed? Did you eat a good dinner?"

We say goodnight and I abandon the dirty dishes that have piled up in my kitchen all week and go sit out on my tiny balcony to brood. Summer is long over, and I don't even have any folding chairs, but I throw a blanket down and huddle on the cold concrete, staring up at what I can see of the night sky, only a few bright stars that are probably satellites penetrating the city's haze.

I really want to call Matt to talk about this. About how shitty I feel right now. But he's at work because he's not rolling in money either. And with Mylene sidelined, no more prize money's coming in. No, Matt has enough to deal with.

The next morning, a black cloud follows me to the rink. Mrs. C gives me a hard time about my GOE on the landing of my Lutz, and I don't even come close to doing the quad Sal. My hip freaking hurts like hell from landing on it over and over, making the same mistake again and again.

Yet she doesn't seem to care, watching me splayed out on the ice from her favorite spot by the boards. "Again."

I push up to my feet and circle the rink, thinking about my dad stuck at home with no job, thinking about how he probably doesn't even want to talk to me because it's my fault, and for what?

Gaining speed before I go into the three turn, I grit my teeth. *I'm going to land this quad. I'm going to land this quad. I'm going to—*

I crash back down on the ice, feet tangled since I didn't come close to completing the fourth rotation. I can't do it. I hate this jump. I fucking hate it.

Mrs. C's dispassionate voice rings out right on cue. "Again."

"Would you give me a fucking break?"

The words scream out of my chest, soaring into the arena and reverberating off the rafters. Everything goes in slow motion as the skaters, other coaches, and parents pivot toward us as one, eyes wide. Matt's nearby, and he reaches toward me, warning under his breath, "Alex, don't."

I jump to my feet, anger and frustration boiling over as I speed toward my coach, skidding to a stop in front of her, snow flying.

"I'm so fucking sick of you telling me what to do. If it wasn't for you, I wouldn't have made my whole family move to New Jersey, and my Dad wouldn't have had to get a new job, which he just lost. And for what? We were barely in Jersey for a year before you up and moved to *Canada* of all places. What, was Trenton not cold enough for you? Figured you needed some more Siberian temperatures? Or maybe you just wanted to make my life even more difficult because you're a total *bitch*."

My shoulders shudder with my exhalation, and I'm suddenly out of venom and words. Mrs. C's face is carved from granite. The seconds tick by like minutes.

Finally she raises a hand, her rings catching the light. Her finger extends toward the main door. "Out."

Then she turns her back, strides to the other end of the rink, and begins coaching a shell-shocked Maxim and Oksana as if nothing happened. The rage that was flowing so freely moments ago drains away completely, cold, clammy fear replacing it.

Oh God. What did I just do?

I consider going after her, but I think she'll throw me under the Zamboni if I get within ten feet. With dozens of eyes on me, I flee the ice and jam my guards on my blades before escaping to the locker room.

I've only just collapsed on the bench before Matt is there, standing over me with wide eyes. "Alex. What the hell?"

"I don't know." I try to think of an explanation, but there's nothing. "I don't know."

His face softens, and he tries to hug me, but I squirm away, getting up to pace, my skates clomping on the tile floor. Holy shit, I've really done it now. I need Mrs. C. She may not be the warmest and fuzziest, but she's the best coach I've ever had.

"Your dad lost his job?"

I keep on pacing, not looking at Matt because I can't bear to. "Last week."

"I'm really sorry."

"Yeah. Thanks."

"I totally understand why you're upset, but... Geez, Alex. You know it's not her fault, right?"

I spin around to face him, worked up all over again in a blink. "I know! You think I don't know that? I'm pissed off and tired and stressed, and sometimes words just come out and I can't stop them."

Matt raises his hands defensively. "Okay, okay. Don't take it out on me too."

Dropping back down, I shake my head, elbows on my knees, the burst of fury draining away. "I'm sorry. I don't know what's the matter with me. I know it's not her fault. Or yours."

He sits and rubs my back softly, and I lean into his touch gratefully. "We're all under a lot of pressure," he murmurs. "It's okay. You're okay."

Staring at the floor, I take a deep breath. "I need to win. My family has given so much so I can win."

"It's not all about winning."

He can't possibly believe that. Of *course* it is. I manage to chuckle. "Sure, keep telling yourself that."

"I'm serious, Alex."

"So am I! I need to win!" I groan loudly. "Did I seriously just call Elena Cheremisinova a bitch?"

"I believe your exact words were 'total bitch.'"

I bury my face in my hands. "Oh God. I'm dead. I'll end up in a Siberian gulag, digging shallow graves in the frozen ground."

Matt barks out a laugh, and I can't help but laugh too, giggling helplessly and slightly hysterically when Kenny comes in and stares in shock. "You are laughing?"

"It's either that or weep," I tell him.

Kenny's clearly disappointed in me. "Such disrespect. Very shameful."

My laughter trails off pathetically, humiliation and guilt back in full force. "I'll apologize."

Unfortunately, something tells me *apologize* isn't a strong enough word. I think *grovel* may be more like it.

Maxim walks in and shakes his head gravely. "You said terrible things."

"Tell me something I don't already know." I rub my flushed face wearily. "Sometimes she just gets to me. I don't know how you and Oksana can be with her all the time. I'd go insane."

Maxim stares, his forehead creased. "Mrs. Cheremisinova is very kind. Rink in Latvia was awful. Bad ice. No money. She brings Oksana and me to Canada and gives us free place to live. She helps us in every way. Cooks meals, gives us lessons. We would not be skating without her."

Wow. I didn't realize Mrs. C was letting them stay with her for free. That really is nice. Plus, she drives them every day, and I bet she's not charging them as much for coaching as she's charging me. She might not be charging them at all by the sound of it. Which is fine, because compared to them, I can afford it.

Maxim goes on. "Mrs. Cheremisinova is lonely sometimes without her husband. But she cooks us nice Russian food, and helps us with English and takes us places on weekend. She is good woman. Best coach."

I nod to acknowledge Maxim's statement, and sigh, defeated. How do I always manage to screw up so badly?

Matt squeezes my shoulder, but there's nothing he can say or do. I need to make this right on my own.

WHEN I ARRIVE at the rink earlier than usual the next morning, I'm the first person there other than the janitor who unlocks the doors. Mrs. C arrives with Oksana and Maxim in tow, and they quickly disappear down the hall to the locker rooms. Mrs. C goes to stand at her favorite spot by the boards, sipping a paper cup of Tim Horton's coffee and ignoring my presence.

"Mrs. C?"

Her reply is an icy glare, red lips pressed into a thin line.

"I'm really sorry about yesterday. About what I said, and how I acted. I was totally wrong."

She leaves me hanging for a good ten seconds, which is a long time when you're waiting for someone to reply to your apology. "I try to make you best skater I can, Alexander."

"I know."

"I'm not mother, or best friend. Skating is hard. Going to Olympics is hard. Sacrifices must be made."

I nod. "You're absolutely right."

"I am sorry to hear about father's job. But you asked me to coach. You and your family made choice."

"You're right. It's not your fault at all. You're the best coach I've ever had."

She takes off her Hermes scarf and folds it into a perfect square. "Maybe not right coach for you."

Oh please no. Please don't kick me out. "No, you are!" I'm about to get down on my knees if that's what it takes. "You've made me the best skater I can be, and I know you'll help me be my best in Salzburg. I need you. *Please.* I didn't mean what I said. It'll never happen again."

One thin eyebrow arches. "Never."

"*Never.* I didn't mean it."

"Alexander, you always mean what you say. You just usually shouldn't say it."

She's got me there. "I'm sorry. I'm really sorry."

With a glance at her gold watch, she says, "Time for practice. Short program run-through." She turns on her heel, and I'm dismissed.

Relief courses through me as I run to put on my skates, desperate to get on the ice and please her. Matt arrives ten minutes later while Mrs. C is picking apart my transitions between the first two jumping passes.

As Matt glides by on a warm-up lap of the rink, he smiles encouragingly, and even though I'm supposed to be paying attention to my coach and my skating and the goddamn Olympics, I can't help but smile back, just for a second.

CHAPTER TEN

M Y ALARM BLARES, and fuck. It hurts to swallow, and my head feels two sizes too big.

Fuck.

I can barely breathe, and all I want to do is stay in bed and sleep for days. Of course, I can't. I *won't*. I do want to call my mom and whine, but it's five a.m. and I'm not that much of a dick. Although Matt should be up, and I long to hear the low, reassuring timbre of his voice. Still, he arrived back late the night before.

He's been in Montreal for a week working with a jump specialist and visiting Mylene. We've been sexting every night, although no FaceTiming since Matt didn't feel comfortable doing it in the Bouchards' guest room. I've been dying to see him again, but sex is the last thing on my mind this morning. I just want him to wrap me in his strong arms and make this go away.

Which is ridiculous, because since when do I need babying? I need to get my shit together.

Muttering, "Olympic season," I force myself into my little bathroom. Usually I don't shower in the morning since I'm just going out in the dark to the rink to get sweaty, but I run the water as hot as I can take it and hope the steam will help.

I blow my nose for what seems like five minutes after dragging myself out of the shower. I'd love to chug some DayQuil, but skaters have to be so careful with cold medication. Athletes have been screwed before by over-the-counter remedies. No way that's happening to me.

Wincing, I gargle with warm salt water, which is as disgusting as it sounds. Gargle and spit, gargle and spit. Tipping my head back, breathing through my nose, I swish the water around my aching throat, but I took a bit too big of a mouthful and almost swallow some.

Retching, I brace myself on the sink and spit the rest out, my stomach seizing. *Ugh.* Okay, smaller mouthfuls next time.

Usually I'd eat breakfast, but I'm not hungry at all—a dire warning sign that something in my body is not right. In the car, I force a few bites of a power bar. I don't even taste the coffee I wash it down with, but it's hot, so I keep drinking.

The Grand Prix Final in Tokyo is next week, and I have an eighteen-hour flight to get through in four days. I cannot be sick. Jet lag is bad enough; throw a bad cold on top of it and I might as well stay home.

To make matters worse, Vladimir Sidorov *and* the Canadian champ, Chris Montoya, had to pull out of the final. So that means Tanner Nielsen is in since he was able to compete in China and win.

I can't back out of competing against him. I have to beat him now to send a message before Nationals.

Mrs. C takes one look at me when I arrive late and barks an order at Maxim in Russian. He scurries off to her office and returns with a bag full of pill bottles. Mrs. C gives me a bottle of water and five different pills to swallow, each of them huge.

At my skeptical and slightly terrified expression, she says, "Herbs. All legal." After the meldonium scandal with Russian athletes, I know she's extra careful, so I force them down.

I really hope her ancient Russian secrets or whatever work, because there's no way I can skate at the final next week like this.

Since I'm in no shape to do program run-throughs, Mrs. C has me work on my edges and expression in the slow part of my long program. It feels colder than usual in the rink, and the other skaters and coaches give me a wide berth, except for one.

Even though I've only been on the ice for half an hour, I need to sit and take a break. Matt skates over and sits beside me in the stands as Mrs. C gives her attention to Oksana and Maxim's death spiral.

Matt reaches for my shoulder, but I lean away. "Careful. Don't get too close."

"Alex, you should be in bed."

"I know, but..."

"But *nothing*. You're shivering."

"I can't just spend the day in bed not training at all." Leaning over, I rest my head on my knees. "I'll be fine in a minute."

Matt makes a sputtering noise, then shouts, "He needs to go home!"

"Yes." I look up in surprise when I hear Mrs. C's voice already close. She gives Matt an appraising look. "You will take him?"

"What?" I shake my head. "No, he has to train. I'm fine. Just give me a minute."

"I can take a break, Alex. I worked my ass off in Montreal." He grasps under my arm and tugs me up firmly, yet his hands are gentle. "You shouldn't drive yourself. You shouldn't have even gotten out of bed."

Mrs. C ignores any further protest on my part and hands Matt the bag of pill bottles. "One of each. Three times. Twice more today." She places the back of her hand against my forehead. "Acetaminophen too."

"But..." I can't just *go home*. "This is the—"

"Olympic season," Matt finishes for me. "We know. And you're not going to win by turning a cold you can nip in the bud into pneumonia or something. We're going." Matt leads me to the locker room and sits me down. I have to admit that it's a relief being out of the frigid rink air. Matt kneels and unlaces my skates with quick fingers before getting my shoes on.

"You're good at this."

He glances up as he makes the final bow on my right sneaker. "I have four younger brothers and sisters. This is nothing." He smiles and quickly changes into his own shoes.

He insists on driving my car home for me, even though that means he has to Uber or cab it back. He parks in my underground spot and it occurs to me in the elevator that my apartment is a mess. As I fumble with my key in the door, I tell him, "I haven't cleaned up lately."

"Alex, it doesn't matter."

I open the door and kick a box of kitchen stuff aside. I really need to unpack that.

Matt peers around at the sparse furniture, unpacked boxes, and bare walls, and I cringe as I take off my coat and toss it toward the open closet. "I know, it's not exactly…"

"Lived in?" Matt finishes for me. "You've been here since the summer, haven't you?"

Wow, I guess I have. "Yeah. I just haven't been… Well, I've been busy. I'm sure your place is way better."

He shrugs. "I live in my old room at home. It's fine. But Mylene and I trained in Montreal for a few years, and now here I am back with my family. Not that I don't love them, but my parents still treat me like a kid sometimes. I guess it's pretty typical these days, people still living at home. I always thought at twenty-four I'd have my own place, but it's stupid to spend the money on it right now. At least I decluttered and tried to make my room more grown-up. Got rid of most of my school stuff. Don't even have paper books anymore. They're all on Kobo."

As I'm wondering when he has time to *read*, I'm seized by a coughing fit, and Matt gets me a glass of water. "Come on, you need to take something for that fever and get to bed."

I nod and point him to the bathroom as I go into the bed-room. Aside from my bed, there's a little table with my alarm clock and a lamp from IKEA. At least I have curtains on the window now and not a tacked-up sheet.

After changing into my boxers, I sit on the side of the bed feeling outside myself, like this feverish shaking is happening to someone else but I'm trapped, watching.

"Here." Matt is suddenly there with water and two white tablets. I swallow the acetaminophen, which grates my swollen throat, and get under the covers.

Matt sits on the edge of the bed and pulls the duvet up to my chin. I have to admit, having him here to take care of me makes me feel warm and fuzzy. Being alone and sick really, really sucks. But he can't just give up a whole day of training.

"I'll be fine. You should get back to the arena. You haven't missed too much."

"Alex, I'm not leaving you alone."

"I'm just going to sleep anyway." As if to punctuate my sentence, my eyes begin to feel heavy. I wonder what was in those herbs? "Take some money out of my wallet for the cab, okay?"

"No. I'm staying here."

"Please? It's bad enough I'm missing training. I won't be able to sleep knowing you are too because of me." It's not true that I won't be able to sleep, but the guilt will churn my stomach.

Matt sighs. "Okay, I'll do another session. But I'm coming back in a few hours. I'll take your key and lock up for you. Just sleep. Don't worry about skating or anything else."

The battle to keep my eyes open is lost, and I murmur a response. The mattress shifts as he stands, and I wait to hear the front door closing. Instead, his lips brush my forehead, his fingers gentle in my hair as I go under.

I THINK IT'S the smell that wakes me. As I open my eyes, I'm shocked to see that it's dark once again. Blinking, I try to focus on the clock. It's after six, and I've been in and out of a feverish sleep all day. My throat is swollen sandpaper, and I gingerly sip a glass of tepid water.

Matt's been back since early afternoon, and a band of light shines from beneath my bedroom door. As I stumble out into the living room, my heart contracts and soars to see him in my kitchen, affection flowing as freely as the snot from my nose.

He turns from the stove top, where he's stirring something that smells amazing even with my stuffed-up sinuses. "Feeling any better?" he asks.

"Maybe," I croak.

"Sit down or you'll tire yourself out." Matt walks around and pulls out one of the stools tucked under the counter separating the kitchen from the living room. "It's time for more pills. I have them ready for you."

I nod and manage to get on the stool. Swallowing the pills isn't easy, but I get the job done. "What is that?" I indicate the pot on the stove.

"Nonna's famous Italian chicken soup."

"Italians are famous for chicken soup?"

Matt laughs. "No, but my nonna is. She taught me to make this when I was a kid. We always have it when we're sick."

"You can cook?" Way to state the obvious.

He smiles and adds perfectly chopped celery to the pot. "You'll have to tell me whether I can or not."

Soon, he makes me go back to bed, and after a while he comes in with a tray. I sit up against the pillows and taste the soup. Even with my diminished taste buds, it's incredible.

"Can't believe you made this." I take another sip, enjoying the warmth.

Matt perches on the side of the bed. "Glad you like it. I'm telling you, it's worked miracles in my family for generations. Or so Nonna says."

I swallow another mouthful. It's weird how comfortable I feel with Matt seeing me so…pathetic. Normally my mother is the only one I'd allow to witness my shame.

Even though I've only been awake less than an hour, I'm tired already. I finish half the bowl of soup, and Matt goes to clean up the kitchen. I tell him to leave it, but he ignores me and I'm too weak to go after him. Instead, I flop down and listen to him doing the dishes. A while later he comes back and sits on my bed again.

"You should go. I don't want you to get sick."

"I'll take my chances. I'm washing my hands like a maniac— it'll be fine. Besides, I already told my mom I won't be home. Unless you want to be alone."

"No!" Okay, that came out a little needier than I intended. "But I don't want you to get sick."

"I'll sleep on the couch. Do you have an extra toothbrush?"

"Under the sink." Not exactly how I imagined the first time Matt sleeping over.

A smile lifts his lips. "No, not exactly what I pictured."

Wait, did I say that out loud?

He brushes the hair back from my forehead. "We've got plenty of time for fun sleepovers. Get some rest. If you wake up in the night, take more acetaminophen. I'll leave it here beside you with water, but if you need help, wake me up, okay?"

I think I say okay, but I'm falling asleep again, and I seriously think Mrs. C's Russian magic herbs include sedatives.

The fever wreaks havoc on my dreams, and I toss and turn in an endless nightmare where I fall down on the ice and no matter how hard I try, I can't stand up again. Millions of people around the world watch as I struggle to my feet, always crashing back down, pulled by some unseen and all-powerful force. I guess it's gravity.

I'm not sure what time it is when I wake enough to realize Matt's there. He lifts my head, and I swallow the pills and water he brings to my lips, coughing and whimpering.

Then there's more darkness, and I sink into it.

The next thing I know, an insanely loud noise blares. As I try to think of what it could be and how to make it stop for the love of God, it suddenly goes silent.

"Jesus! Your alarm could wake the dead."

Prying my eyes open, I make out Matt standing beside my bed in the dark, shirtless in his boxer-briefs, holding my alarm clock.

"How're you feeling?" Matt switches the lamp on low and touches my forehead with the back of his hand. His hair sticks up adorably, and I wish I had the energy to reach up and smooth it down. "You're not as hot as before."

As I shake off the dopiness of sleep, I realize that I definitely feel better than yesterday. Not a hundred percent, but it's an improvement. I joke, "You don't think I'm hot anymore?"

He frowns and rests his hand against my forehead again. "No, I think the fever's down." The other shoe drops, and he rolls his eyes with a grin. "Well, maybe you're still a little bit hot."

"Just a little?"

"In a few days, I'll show you exactly how hot I think you are."

See, now this bug is really affecting my life. Missing training was bad enough. Now I have Matt practically naked and adjacent to my bed, and I can't even kiss him. Life is supremely unfair sometimes.

"I guess I should get up, or we'll be late."

Matt laughs. "We? You're not going anywhere near that ice rink today."

"Of course I am. I'm better." My throat still feels like I've swallowed razor blades and I'm supremely stuffed-up, but...

"That doesn't mean you're well enough to skate today. You need to rest. Eat more soup. Sleep. Watch TV."

"Watch TV. All day?"

"Yes! You say that like I just told you to eat worms."

"The Grand Prix Final is next week. This isn't the time to be lazing around." I push away the covers.

With a laugh, Matt pulls them back over me. "Have you ever taken a day off in your life?"

"Of course! Maybe. There was one time. But not right before a major competition in an Olympic season."

"I swear, I'm going to charge you a dollar every time you say the words 'Olympic season.' You need to take a break so you can be at your best next week when it counts."

"Mrs. C will—"

"Mrs. C will agree with me. Now rest. I'll be back as soon as I can. I'll put some more soup on the stove, and when you're hungry, just turn it on medium-low and it'll heat up in a few minutes."

As I lie there, I try to mount an argument, but the truth is that it feels good to be in bed and not driving over to the rink. Matt leaves after a few more orders for me to rest, and I go back to sleep.

When I wake, the sun streams through the windows. After a long, steamy shower, I pull on a T-shirt and track pants and heat the soup. I also choke down more vitamin pills, which is as unpleasant as ever. Then I get comfortable on the couch and watch a bunch of stupid talk shows, putting my feet up. I should probably ice my knees and hips, but I'm wrapped in a blanket and don't want to move.

Of course I'm totally bored after a couple of hours. How some people can sit around all day watching TV and doing nothing is beyond me. Even on my Sundays off, I still go for a run and stretch and do errands and get out of the apartment. I'm still really tired, and my throat is sore and I'm coughing, but I loathe sitting around. There must be something I can do to work on my skating while I'm couch-bound.

I consider watching some of my competitors' recent skates, but...no. That'll just wind me up. I have to be the best I can be and not worry about what they're doing. I totally worry anyway, but watching their programs on YouTube is a bad idea.

Matt comes back mid-afternoon, which is earlier than I'm expecting. Right away I can tell something's wrong as he asks if I'm feeling better. His voice is strained and too cheerful.

"Yeah, a little better. What happened?"

"Hmm? Nothing." Matt puts my keys on the kitchen counter and looks everywhere but at me.

"Um, there's clearly something." I push myself up straight on the couch. "What's going on?"

Matt sighs as he opens the fridge, his back to me. "It's nothing. I'm just being...whatever. In my own head."

"Tell me." I'm going to get up and force him to look at me, but he comes over and sits beside me on the couch. I realize with a jolt that he's been crying, the faint redness visible now that he's close. "What happened?"

"I went to the shrink. The sports psychologist."

"Oh. Well, it's a good idea, isn't it? After what happened?" It's standard, actually. I've talked to quite a few over the years. I Skyped with my last one in Trenton just the other week. I want to touch Matt and pull him close, but ugh, germs.

"Chantal thinks so. So does Mylene. She's been seeing someone in Montreal, and she's been bugging me about it. So I finally went today at lunch." Matt stares at the floor, his hands in fists on his thighs. "He made me watch the fall. All the different angles and slow motion. Over and over again."

"Shit. He thinks that'll help? Torturing you?" I want to hunt down this shrink and rip him a new one for making Matt look so small and defeated.

"He says it will 'desensitize' me to the fall and help me accept what happened and move on."

"I'm going to go out on a limb and guess that it's not working."

"The past couple of weeks, training again and focusing on my singles programs, it's been great. Having something else to think about, you know?" He looks at me, and I hate seeing the pain in his eyes. "Watching it again, it's like reliving it. How Mylene laid there, not moving. Bleeding. I've never been so scared in my life. It was the worst feeling, knowing she was hurt because of me. Because I failed."

Fuck germs. I put my hand on his leg, rubbing lightly in what I hope is a reassuring way. "It wasn't your fault."

Matt shakes his head. "You keep saying that. Everyone keeps saying that. But it was! Of course it was my fault! Who else's was it?"

"No one's. It was an *accident*."

"Only three teams skated in the first flight before us. The ice was still clear; there was nothing to trip on."

"You don't know that. Maybe one of the other teams put a rut in the ice on warm-up. Maybe the kids missed a spot and didn't fill it in enough before the Zamboni went around." Volunteers with buckets of icy snow filled in any gouges.

"I shouldn't have fallen. I should never have dropped her." He squeezes his eyes shut, and I know he's trying not to cry again.

"You just caught an edge. It happens to all of us."

He suddenly jumps to his feet and begins pacing. "Why did it have to happen? We should be getting ready for the Olympics, and instead she's stuck at home in Montreal with a broken arm and a concussion, and I'm wasting my time trying to be a singles skater."

"You're not wasting your time." I stand and put my hands on

his shoulders, waiting until he looks at me. "You're not. And it happened because life sucks sometimes. Because unfair, crappy things happen."

After a few seconds, he nods, and I pull him into a hug. We drop down to the futon, and he curves around me, lowering his head onto my shoulder. God, it feels wonderful to have him warm and safe in my arms as I rub his back. I want to take him to bed and crawl under the covers and just hold him, but I'm still a snotty mess.

We curl up on the couch and watch dumb TV, eating the rest of the soup for dinner. I'm drowsy and ready for bed by seven, but Matt's arm feels so good around my shoulders.

Finally, I blurt, "Are you going to stay over again?" Maybe I'm being too needy. "You don't have to."

"Do you want me to?"

"Do you want to?"

Matt chuckles. "We could go back and forth all night, but yeah. I do."

"Me too." My laugh morphs into a hacking cough, and I bury my face in the crook of my arm while Matt pulls out his cell.

"Hey, Mom. Yeah, he's still sick, and he doesn't have any family here." There's a pause. "Right. Alex Grady. Yeah, the American champion."

Since my fame precedes me, I hope Matt's mother isn't a Tanner Nielsen fan. He says goodbye, and I ask, "Your parents okay with it?"

"Yeah, they're fine."

"Do they know about us? I mean, that we're…" I wave my hand back and forth.

Maybe it's my imagination, but tension zaps up Matt's spine and he looks away, shrugging. "We don't usually talk about that kind of stuff."

Should I be upset? That I'm "stuff"? I'm not sure, and I don't currently have the brain function to deal with it. Since I haven't really mentioned Matt to my family either and we haven't even established what we're doing here aside from hanging out, I let it go. We watch more TV, but my eyes are drooping. "Do you want to sleep in there?" I motion vaguely toward my room. "I'm still sick, but... It's up to you. If you want to stick to the futon, no worries."

"I'll sleep with you. Thanks."

Sleep with me. In our underwear in the bedroom, we climb under the covers, and even though we've had each other's dicks in our mouths and everything, this feels far more intimate.

In the darkness, I curl on my side. After a minute, Matt's strong arms move around me, and he pulls my back against his chest. "Is this okay?" he whispers.

Nodding, I settle against him. It's way more than okay. I'm sniffly and achy, and I have to fly halfway around the world for a major competition in days, but as Matt holds me and I drift off to sleep, nothing else matters but the gentle tickle of his breath on my neck and the warmth of his arms.

CHAPTER ELEVEN

TOTAL DISASTER.

The Grand Prix Final hasn't even started yet, and it's a total, utter disaster. I'm in Tokyo. My skates are not. Where are they? Good question, for which I have no answer. Neither does the airline that lost my suitcase.

Competition starts in three days, and I have no skates or costumes. I don't have any underwear or clothes either, but I can buy more of those. That's not the problem.

The problem is that my skates, which cost a hell of a lot of money and, more importantly, took months to break in and get just right, are lost. And my costumes, designed and tailored specifically for me and these programs, are lost. Everything that matters is *lost*!

The airline assures me it's doing everything it can. I remain unassured. I don't even think that's a word, but it's how I feel. Mrs. C says she's on it, and maybe the Russian mafia can pull some strings, but until my suitcase is here, I can't unclench.

Fuck, I wish Matt were here to talk me down, but it's too late to call him.

As I'm pacing back and forth in my hotel room, there's a knock. I mutter a prayer that it's someone with my luggage and run to jerk open the door. Kenny stands there with a grin. "Ready for lunch?"

Shit, I totally forgot we'd made plans. "I won't be very good company. The stupid airline lost my skates. Not to mention my costumes. Everything."

Kenny's face pales and his smile vanishes. "No."

At least he understands what a huge deal this is. You'd think it would be incredibly obvious, but the people at the airline don't seem to get it. "Yes. For all I know, my skates are in Timbuktu. They just say they're looking. I wish I spoke Japanese. I worry stuff is being lost in translation."

"You have phone number?"

I hand over a piece of paper, and Kenny whips out his cell phone. Soon he's talking in Japanese at an extremely rapid clip. The only thing I make out is his name and mine. In a minute, he hangs up and grins. "Baggage will be here by morning. No problems."

"What?" I'm flooded with relief. "They found my suitcase?"

"Not yet. But they will. It is guarantee."

The relief evaporates. "What if they don't, though?"

"It is guarantee. It would bring dishonor if they did not. I have been promised."

I have to laugh at Kenny's super-serious expression. "Okay. I really hope my suitcase gets here and no one has to commit hari-kari in the morning."

"Now lunch?" he asks hopefully.

Well, I have to eat, so I temporarily forgo pacing and driving myself crazy with worry. My cold's finally cleared up, and the last thing I need is to get sick again because I'm not eating.

Kenny wears a Yankees cap, but of course it doesn't fool any of the crazy-yet-sweet fangirls. They literally *scream* when we walk out the hotel door, and although many ask for my autograph too, it's Kenny who is the rock star here.

Then Hiro Kurosawa, who is an even bigger star and the reigning Olympic champion, comes out, and we're able to fight our way into a waiting car, security guards herding the fans.

We're actually only going down the street, but walking would take about three hours and thousands of autographs. It's all rather intense in Japan. The fans are so polite and respectful, but also very…dedicated.

Kenny takes me to a sushi restaurant where we get our own private room. Over the best eel rolls I've ever had, we talk about what else? Skating. Kenny barely managed to qualify for the Grand Prix Final, and since it's being held in his home country, the pressure is intense, to say the least. The poor guy is stressed. He wants to beat Hiro so badly at Japanese Nationals in December. Suffice it to say, I can relate.

All of a sudden, I realize Kenny's mother isn't around. Outside the gym, it's so rare to see him without her in the background. I almost expect her to be standing guard outside our little room, lurking by our shoes. We sit on cushions on the floor, and even though chopsticks are not my friend, I do pretty well getting most of the food in my mouth instead of on my shirt, which I might be wearing for days.

At the thought of my lost luggage, I feel sick to my stomach all over again. I really hope it's not the sushi, because food poisoning would just be the icing on the cake right now.

"Where's your mom?"

Kenny glances up from the green tea he is slurping. "I tell her I want to go out with my friend alone."

"She didn't mind?"

His face flushes, which is all the answer I really need. "She still thinks I'm little boy."

"Yeah, she's a bit… I mean, she's always…" This is the part where I'd usually just blurt out that she's a controlling stage mom who needs to get her own life. "Um, she's always around," I finish lamely. "You're not a kid."

"Your parents, they do not go with you everywhere?"

As if we could afford it. Especially now. My dad hasn't found a job yet, and here I am off in Japan. "No, they have to work. They're there for all the major competitions. They're definitely coming to the Olympics. Bought the tickets and paid for the flight/hotel package ages ago."

Assuming *I'm* going to be there. God, what if I fuck it up? What if I don't come top three and I don't even make the team? That thought sours my stomach further, and I gingerly sip on my tea after checking my phone for messages.

We manage to sneak into the service entrance of the hotel after lunch, and the red light on the hotel phone in my room is cruelly dark, dashing my hope that the airline had miraculously called. After flopping down on my bed, I turn on the TV and try not to fall asleep. Traveling to Asia sends my internal clock haywire, and I'm exhausted.

After my second shower of the day, I pull out my cell and hit Matt's number. He should be getting ready to go to practice now.

His sleepy voice answers. "Alex?"

"Hey. Aren't you up yet?"

"No. It's four-thirty. I still have forty-five minutes."

"Crap. I fucked up the time. Sorry."

"You'd better be. You know how important those last forty-five minutes are."

I can hear the teasing in his tone, but seriously, I do know how important they are. "I'm really sorry. Go back to sleep and we'll talk later."

"No, no. I'm awake now. What're you doing?"

"Lying here in my hotel room, trying not to fall asleep before dinner."

"What're you wearing?"

"Nothing."

"Mmm. This could be a *very* good wake-up call after all."

While I'm tempted to take the edge off, I'm too stressed for phone sex. "Unfortunately, I'm wearing nothing because they lost my baggage and the only clothes I have are hanging up in the bathroom. I'm hoping the steam from the shower will make them slightly less gross. I need to go shopping in a bit."

"Wait, what? They lost your suitcase?" Suddenly he's wide awake, his voice sharp. "Skates? Costumes?"

"All of it. I only had my iPad and a travel pillow with me. I'm an idiot, I know. Skates and costumes are going carry-on from this day forward."

"Shit. What did they say? They have to find it. Right?"

"I sure hope so."

"Or you're fucked."

"Totally fucked."

"Don't worry, you'll get them back."

"It's not even just the Grand Prix. What about Nationals? If I have to go back to old boots, or break in new ones…" The thought quickens my pulse, my throat going bone dry.

"Just breathe. You won't," Matt soothes.

"Promise?"

"If you think it'll help."

We both laugh, and even though I saw Matt yesterday—or was it the day before now?—I miss him already. It's totally insane how much I wish he were here. Still, I should get moving so I don't fall asleep. "I need to go shopping. Have a great day at the rink. Your Axel's looking fantastic. I told you that, right?"

"You did. Thank you. Try not to worry."

I really want to tell Matt I miss him, and while usually anything that crosses my mind has no problem tumbling out of my mouth, I pause. Is it too much? We're still not official or anything. It occurs that I don't actually know how people become an official couple. Do they talk about it, or just change their Facebook status and call it a day?

"Alex? You still there?"

Fuck it. "I miss you."

I can imagine his smile as he says, "Me too."

After I hang up, I lie there naked on my bed, thinking of him and grinning to the empty room. Matt misses me. Maybe my AWOL skates aren't such a big deal after all.

OF COURSE MY missing skates are a *huge* freaking deal, no matter how many cute, awesome guys miss me. By morning, I'm losing it. Naturally, I call my mother.

I know that when you turn eighteen you're supposed to magically be a grown-up, and that at twenty I should be totally able to handle problems on my own, but... When I'm really stressed, I just want to call my mom and have her fix everything in that way moms do.

"What's wrong, sweetie?"

I guess my voice isn't as calm and collected as I'd hoped. "The airline lost my suitcase. Skates, costumes, everything."

She gasps softly. "Have you called them this morning to follow up?"

"Yes, and they said my claim is being processed. What does that even mean?"

"Do you want me to call them?"

This is the part where I have to be an adult, and besides, Kenny already called for me. "No, it's fine."

"Don't worry, sweetheart. This happens all the time, and I'm sure they'll find them."

"That's what Matt said, but I have practice in a few hours. What am I supposed to do? Mrs. C told me she's coming up with a plan, but..."

There's a pause. "Matt?"

It hits me that I don't talk about these things with my mother, mostly because I've never really dated anyone and there's been nothing to talk about. I attempt to play it cool. "You know, Matt Savelli."

"I didn't realize he was there. I thought his poor partner was out for the season?"

"Oh, she is. He's skating singles for now."

"But he wasn't on the list of six men for the final, was he? How would he have gotten the points?"

"No, no, he's not here at the final. He's at home. I mean, in Toronto. I was just talking to him."

"On the phone?"

"Yes, mother, on the telephone. It's this amazing new invention. Alexander Graham Bell, I believe."

"So you two have become good friends, I see. That's a very long distance call."

"Mom, I know what you're doing, and it was a free call through WhatsApp, just like this one to you."

Her tone is playful. "What? What am I doing?"

"Look, we're just… I don't know. Hanging out."

"But you like him?"

For some stupid reason, I find myself blushing. "Yeah, I like him. He likes me too, it seems."

"Of course he does. You're wonderful."

I snort. "Says my mother! *Many* would disagree."

"Well, they're wrong. And I'm delighted to hear about you and Matt. We'd love to meet him."

That will definitely make it feel like an official relationship. With a capital R. But I find myself smiling. "That would be cool. Not sure when since we've got a lot going on obviously, and you're in Jersey and we're in Toronto. But yeah, he's cool. I think you'd like him." I realize I'm babbling and stop.

Mom chuckles. "I think we will too, sweetie. I know you boys have a lot on your plate, and I'm so glad you can help each other."

"You don't think it's dumb of me to be getting involved with someone right before the Olympics?"

"I don't think there's ever a wrong time to welcome love into our lives."

"Okay, let's not get carried away, Mom!" I laugh awkwardly as my belly flutters. *Love.* It's clearly too strong a word to describe what's going on with me and Matt. Right? "It's been, like, five minutes."

"Well, my point remains. Alex, you've worked incredibly hard since you were a little boy. And you deserve all the love and friendship and happiness in the world."

Shit, now my throat's thick and my eyes burn. I cough a few times. "Thanks, Mom. I should go. Say hi to Dad and Rach. Love you."

"Say hi to Matt! Love you too, hon."

As I'm sitting there smiling and trying not to cry, there's a rap at the door. An extremely apologetic man bows and rolls in my missing suitcase before bowing again a few more times.

Thank you Jesus, Mary, Joseph, and whoever the fuck else. I unzip open my bag and find everything just as I packed it—skates, costumes, and all. I take a picture and post it on Instagram, thanking the universe and the strings rock-star Kenny pulled.

THE AIRLINE MUST have sprinkled some magic dust on my skates after finding them, because I wind up in first place after the short program a couple days later. I resist the urge to tell perfectly blond Tanner Nielsen to suck it as I pass him backstage. Instead we smile and pretend we don't hate each other.

A thrilled Kenny is in third place behind Tanner. He chatters excitedly in the dressing room, and although his mother clearly disapproves, Kenny and I go out to a Karaoke bar. We don't drink, and there's no way in hell I'm singing anything in public except "The Star Spangled Banner" on top of the podium, but it's fun to listen to everyone else. I'm still in bed by nine, though. Which feels like morning, but I manage to sleep.

The next day in practice, I land my quad Sal three times. Granted, I splat more times than that, so the ratio still isn't good. I hate falling in front of the judges and photographers and fans so freaking much. Not to mention Tanner and my other competitors.

The day of the long program, I wake feeling invincible. I know I'm going to land all my quads today. I just know it. I'm skating last, and after the warm-up for the final flight of skaters, I hide out with my iPod backstage so I can't hear the crowd or any of the scores. I'm deep in my bubble.

Tanner's right before me, and as he skates to the Kiss and Cry and I step onto the ice, I can tell from the way the arena is throbbing with applause that he did well. Possibly fantastic. I've trained myself well over the years not to listen to things I don't want to hear, and Mrs. C loudly gives me last minute instructions as the scores are announced. I don't catch them, but the crowd roars.

After my name is called, I skate a lap around the rink, breathing deeply, keeping an eye on the timer counting down on the scoreboard. My simple costume of black pants and a slightly bedazzled green shirt feels like a second skin. Everything is in place. Everything is *right*.

As I take my starting position with plenty of time to spare, adrenaline is a bullet train in my veins. All eyes are on me, and I have to do this. I can do it.

Pavarotti starts singing, and I'm off. I land my quad toe combo. Check. Triple Axel. Check. Now time for the quad Sal. In the split second as I take off, I know I'm going down. My blade slips as I'm going up, and I don't get the height I need or the rotation.

Pushing up off my ass and back into the program, my mind whirls a mile a minute. I'm going to land that quad. I have a triple Lutz combination next, but I change the choreography and go after the quad Sal again, this time squeaking it out.

The crowd roars, and my heart pumps. As I'm whirling in a sit spin, I think about the next jumping pass and how I can get the most points to make up for that first quad Sal without breaking any of the jump rules.

I throw in the Lutz now, and it's a beauty, but shit, I need another combination, and I have to make sure I turn my planned triple Sal later in the program to a double so I don't repeat it too many times and get zero points.

For the rest of the four and a half minutes, I'm constantly thinking a step ahead of the choreography and changing it when I need to. When the program finishes, I'm triumphant, and the audience is cheering. There's no way Tanner beat that. No way.

After my bows, I practically skip into the Kiss and Cry. Mrs. C puts her arms around me and grips, and for a second I'm not sure if she's hugging me or possibly about to strangle me.

Sweat drips down my face, and I blot it with a tissue before waving to the camera and saying hi. I hope Matt is watching. Feeling giddy, I blow a kiss to him without saying his name.

The technical score comes up, and it's big. The crowd cheers. Then the second mark is announced, and it's...not as big. The crowd is still clapping, but I'm staring at the final result in shock.

Pl	Name	Nation	Points	SP	FS
1.	Tanner Nielsen	USA	295.71	2	2
2.	Hiro Kurosawa	JPN	294.67	4	1
3.	Alexander Grady	USA	294.23	1	3

I'm third in the free skate. Third overall. I lost. What. The. Fuck. How is this possible?

With a massive effort, I force a smile and wave for the crowd, then follow Mrs. C backstage and pretend it's not killing me to finish behind Tanner. Not to mention losing silver by tenths of a point.

I march toward the dressing room, but before I get there, Mrs. C takes my arm and gives it a sharp tug, yanking me into an empty room. She closes the door, and I suddenly realize with a sinking feeling that she's not happy. At all.

"It's not fair!" I blurt.

She regards me coolly. "Is very fair."

"How? I landed my quads!"

"By ripping apart program. Taking pieces and making them like jigsaw puzzle."

"Okay, so I shifted a few things around. It's not a big deal."

"This is why you lose." She points a manicured finger very close to my face. "No artistry. You were just thinking, thinking, thinking. Changing everything. No heart. No soul. Never in the moment. This is why you lose."

"But… But I landed the quad Sal! I did it! Yes, I fell on it first, but the second time I did it."

"Quads are important, Alexander. Yes. But you have to skate program as designed."

I guess she has a point, considering I just lost. Still. "But I—"

She holds up her hand. "Never change choreography again."

"What if—"

"Never, Alexander. Understand?"

The way she's staring daggers, I think my life is possibly on the line here. Looking at my feet, I nod.

"Important lesson to learn."

With that, she leaves, and I stay behind to feel sorry for myself until I know they'll be looking for me to start the stupid medal presentation. I go out there and smile and wave, and shake hands with Hiro and Tanner, who seems to tower over me more than usual up there on the top step of the podium. I've only beaten him the one time, and it feels like I never will again.

And now I'll have to Instagram a podium pic and be all gracious and write a caption saying it was a great learning experience and I can't wait to compete again, and blah, blah, blah. At least I'll get a bunch of supportive comments from fans. I can't complain about that.

The flags go up, and I while I have nothing against Hiro, I wish it was Kenny with silver. That would at least be a sliver of consolation for having to listen to Tanner sing our anthem in a clear, confident voice that's better than mine will ever be.

CHAPTER TWELVE

I'VE BEEN ON a plane for a bazillion hours and I'm sure I stink, but I need to see Matt's smile. We've texted, but our time zones have been all messed up. I know he's at the rink, and even though I'm supposed to go home and sleep, I give the cab driver the address of the club.

Closing my eyes, I lean back and imagine all the ways Matt might greet me. His hands, his mouth… Mmm, that mouth. He'll kiss everything better. His lips are so—

"Turn here?"

Blinking, I look around. "Yeah, make a left."

I expect to find practice as usual going on at the rink since it's late afternoon, but instead the skaters and coaches are clustered together in the stands. Their backs are to me, and I can't see what they're looking at. Leaving my suitcase by the door, I make my way over.

Annie notices me and grins. "Alex! Look who's visiting!"

The crowd parts, and there's Mylene. She's sitting on the bleachers with Matt beside her, her arm still in a cast and sling. She waves to me with her good hand. "Alex! Welcome home."

For a moment, I'm completely, irrationally, *awfully* jealous. So much for *my* reunion with Matt. He's beaming at Mylene, his arm snug around her waist. I don't think he'll be ditching her to run off to the locker room with me. M&M are reunited, and I should be delighted for them, but I want to punch something or possibly cry, and I'm not sure which is more pathetic.

Everyone's watching, and I know I'm being stupid and selfish, so I smile and try to sound genuinely happy to see her, which I should be. "Hey! Welcome home to you too." I kiss both her cheeks. "How are you feeling?"

"Better. Still not all the way, but closer."

Matt's beaming at her like she's the most amazing thing he's ever seen. "You'll get there. Look how far you've come already!" He kisses her cheek. "Amazing!"

Everyone voices their agreement, and I nod and make the right noises. It's true, Mylene looks great considering what she's been through. She's wearing a really cute little cap over her chestnut curls, probably to cover the scar from surgery. God, she had *brain surgery*. I need to stop being such a pissy bitch.

"It's awesome to see you," I tell her, and mean it this time.

"You did great in Japan, congratulations."

Ugh, the last thing I want to talk about, but everyone chimes in and tells me how close it was. Like I don't already know. I remind myself that they mean well and that I just decided ten seconds ago to stop being such a baby.

So we talk about Japan and I tell the tale of my lost skates. Then I realize I really am tired and need to get some sleep. My eyes linger on Matt as I say goodbye, and I can tell from Mylene's smile that she knows exactly what's going on. She's thinner and a bit frail, but that firecracker grin hasn't changed.

Hell, the whole rink probably knows, but the only thing I want to think about now is a shower and sleep.

At home, I've just gotten under the covers when my phone rings. A spark of energy ignites when I see that it's Matt.

Clearing my throat, I go for casual. "Hey."

"Sorry, were you asleep already?"

"No, it's okay."

"Sorry we couldn't really talk. Mylene showed up at lunch to surprise me. Her parents drove her down now that the doctors say she's okay to be out of bed. She has to go back in a few days, though."

"It was really great to see her. She's doing so well."

"Oh my God, she's incredible. They think she'll be able to skate again by next spring or summer, so we can start training again. I can't wait. She's so supportive of me doing singles. I lucked out hard when our old coaches put us together back in the day. She's the best partner I could ever ask for."

Stupid, ugly jealousy roars back with a vengeance. "Sounds like it."

There's a pause. "Are you okay?"

"Yeah, I'm just tired."

"Are you still upset about the long program?"

"No. We already talked about it. It's fine."

Matt says, "We texted about it. Not the same thing. I'm really glad you're back. I was hoping we could have some alone time, but with Mylene here…"

"It's okay. I totally understand."

We say goodbye, and I try to sleep and not replay my free skate from Japan for the thousandth time. The minutes become hours as I toss and turn. I just need some time alone with Matt. I'll feel better then.

GETTING MATT ALONE turns out to be really easy, because as soon as our first practice session is over in the morning, he asks me to help him get a cake from the restaurant fridge. He had the chef do up some fancy design for Mylene, and he's surprising her with it at lunch. Which is really sweet and makes me smile at him in a totally goofy way, and at least I'm not resenting her today, since she doesn't deserve that.

The walk-in fridge door is barely shut before Matt is all over me. Oh God, it's good to kiss him again. We're all hands and lips and tongues and friction, and you'd think it would be impossible to get so hot in a refrigerator, but that's figure skaters for you.

"I want to fuck you so bad," Matt breathes in my ear, his hands gripping my ass. "I missed you."

"Uh-huh. Let's do that. Let's fuck." My cock is tenting my Lycra pants, and even if I get frostbite, I want Matt to drill me right here, right now. When he's touching me, there's nothing else—no skating or judges or third place or Tanner Nielsen's blindingly perfect teeth. It all melts away, and I can be in the moment in a way I've never been able to.

Voices rumble from outside the fridge, and we spring apart before one of the cockblocking cooks opens the door and blinks in surprise.

"Cake!" Matt practically shouts before lowering his voice. "Just getting the cake."

It really does take two of us to carry it. The chocolate slab, featuring the words "Get well soon" as if they've just been written by a skate blade, is surprisingly heavy, and it's a bit of a struggle to maneuver it to a private room on the second floor where we're holding a lunch for Mylene.

"Stop that," Matt hisses as we make our way down the hall with the cake between us.

"Huh?"

"Stop looking so horny. It's very distracting." He grins.

"Sorry. There's this guy here who really turns me on. Hot bod, killer smile. Can do amazing things with his tongue."

"Wow, I should really look him up."

I balance my side of the cake in one hand as I open the meeting room door. "If you hang out in the broom closet or the walk-in fridge long enough, you're bound to run into him."

Matt laughs as we set down the cake on a table. "Broom closet, you say? Hmm. Sounds warmer than the fridge. I'll have to check it out."

Running my finger down his chest, I lean in close. "Maybe I can show you."

"Matthew?"

Matt leaps away from me like I'm strapped with a nuclear bomb and addresses the two people in the doorway. "Mom? Dad? What are you doing here?"

Matt's parents walk in and his mom smiles stiffly. She's a little dowdy and dresses like it's the eighties, with big hair and glasses, but she's pretty in a mom-like way.

She says, "We thought it would be nice to take the afternoon off work and surprise you and be here for Mylene."

"Oh, cool. You guys recognize Alex from TV, right? He was just helping me with the cake." Matt's talking really fast and his voice is hitting this weirdly high pitch. Whoa. That's all I am? The cake helper? Apparently the broom *closet* may be a good place for Matt after all.

Putting on my competition smile, I shake his parents' hands. "So nice to meet you." His father doesn't smile and his grip almost makes me squeak.

A couple of restaurant staff members arrive with carts full of sandwiches and salads, and I'm rescued from having to make small talk by helping them spread everything out on the table. One of them gives me an odd look, but hello, I'm not that much of a diva that I can't help put out napkins and plates.

Matt and his parents talk by the window overlooking the rink, and every so often, I catch Mr. Savelli eyeing me with an expression that can only be described as deeply suspicious. Bordering on hostile.

Terrific.

All the skaters, coaches, trainers, and any parents around come for lunch. Mylene is thrilled by the attention, and her parents beam proudly. I can't help but notice that Matt appears to be avoiding me like the plague, and I sit with Oksana, Maxim, and Mrs. C. They carry on a long conversation in Russian, which is totally fine by me because I'm not in the mood for chit-chat.

Mr. Savelli seems totally out of his element. Matt's dad is short, has a beer belly, and looks like he finishes every sentence with "bada boom, bada bing," which is ridiculously stereotypical and offensive, but it keeps running through my mind despite my best efforts. He and Matt couldn't be more different aside from their dark hair and eyes.

When I escape near the end of lunch, Matt doesn't even look over as I leave. Anger grows in my gut with jagged edges of hurt. I can't help but think of my mom and how cool and excited she was when I told her about Matt.

She asks about him now on the regular, and my dad emailed and said they'd been YouTubing Matt and Mylene's old programs and how much they enjoyed them, etc., etc. Meanwhile, Matt's apparently ashamed of me.

Mrs. C has me working on my triple Axel-single loop-triple Salchow sequence, and I nail it over and over. It occurs to me that I'm trying to impress Matt's parents, which is *ridiculous* for all the obvious reasons.

But I can't help it, and when Matt goes down on a triple Axel, I feel a sick, petty swell of victory. I shouldn't want to see my— well, I guess I shouldn't call him my *boyfriend*—fall. Yet today, I find it darkly satisfying.

I leave without acknowledging him at the end of the day and drive home in a red fog of resentment, screaming at other drivers as traffic creeps along.

The knock at my door comes a few hours later as I'm toweling my damp hair after a long bath in Epsom salts for my muscles, and staring balefully at a pile of dirty dishes. I tug on sweatpants and sling the towel around my neck before yanking the door open.

Matt stands there in the hallway in jeans and his black leather coat, his face pinched and expressive eyes sorrowful. It makes my chest ache to see him like that, but I remind myself that I'm pissed.

"Are you sure it's safe to be here?" I snap. "We wouldn't want anyone to get the wrong idea."

"Alex, I'm sorry. Can I come in? Please?"

Sighing heavily, I stand back and close the door once he's inside. Standing just inside the living room, he opens his mouth, but I don't give him a chance. "Look, I don't exactly want to make out on Snapchat or spray paint *Alex+Matt 4-eva* on the rink boards. I want killer endorsements after I win the Olympics, so I haven't come out publicly to the world. But what the hell was that?"

Matt steps closer, his eyes beseeching. "I know. I'm sorry. It was just such a surprise that they showed up, and it's not something we talk about. Ever."

"About me?"

"About *me*."

"Wait, what?" Blinking, I stare at him. "They know, though. Right? That you're gay?"

"Yeah. I mean, I think so. They must have figured it out by now. They're not stupid."

Whoa. "You've never *told* them? You've never said anything about it? Ever?"

"Alex, you don't talk about something like this in my family. Everyone might suspect it, just like we all think my cousin Rita went to visit our aunt in Naples for six months because she was having a baby, but we don't talk about it."

"Don't they ever ask if you're seeing anyone?"

He barks out a laugh. "Are you kidding? I think my father would rather eat glass. Your parents don't ask about your love life, do they? They don't know about me, right?"

"Uh, yeah. They do."

His eyebrows almost disappear into his thick hair. "Seriously? You told them?"

"Yeah. I know we're not broadcasting it at the club, but I didn't think it was a dirty little secret. There's never been anything to tell before you, but they're totally cool."

He shakes his head, clearly trying to process. "It doesn't bother them at all? Wow." He rubs his face. "It's not like that with my parents. Look, they're great for the most part, and I love them, but... They're old-fashioned."

"A.k.a. homophobic."

He sighs, nodding. "They don't talk badly about gay people or anything, but... Well, they don't talk about gay people at all. It was never mentioned once when I was growing up. It made me feel...invisible. Like I had to hide. There was no other option."

My heart clenches at the thought of little Matt and his secret. I want to say the right thing, but he goes on.

"When Mylene and I trained in Montreal, I had a boyfriend named Jean-Paul. I tried telling my mom about him a few times, but she just said she was glad I made friends and changed the subject as soon as I brought him up." He shrugs, a sad little jerk of his shoulders. "They don't want to know, so I don't tell them."

Jesus. I inhale deeply and blow it out. "Okay, I get that. In Philly you talked about your dad a bit, but I didn't realize it was like this. Still, the way you acted when they walked in. It was like..." Like he was deeply ashamed of me. The hurt hung on stubbornly.

"I'm so sorry." They took me by surprise. I guess I have some hang-ups of my own when it comes to them. I don't know. There's a lot of repressed Catholic guilt in my family. I've tried to get past it, and in a lot of ways I have."

My anger's fading. I hate seeing him so sad and upset. "Like with sex?" I smile tentatively. "Because if that's you being repressed…"

His lips twitch as his cheeks flush pink. "I've definitely worked through my repression in that department. It was part of accepting who I am. Accepting my desires. Embracing them."

"Right. That makes sense. But I'm sorry things are like this with your parents. I wish I'd known."

"I should have told you."

"So you're not embarrassed to be with me?" Saying it out loud makes me feel like I'm having a dream where I'm naked on the ice and the audience is dressed.

"Oh my God, no." In a rush, Matt has his arm around me and he cups the back of my head with his other hand. He gazes down with pure sincerity. "It's not about you. Wait, that didn't sound right. I mean that my issues with my parents are completely about me."

"Yeah?" I want to believe him, and the way he's looking at me and holding me close, caressing my damp skin, makes my knees actually tremble. "I suppose you just seemed so confident that I never thought…"

"I guess we both have our insecurities." He brushes a thumb over my lips. "I've never felt this way about anyone before. God, that sounds like such a line, but it's true." He stops and swallows hard. "It's true," he repeats, then kisses me softly.

I melt into him, opening my mouth, eager for his tongue, eager for all of him. The towel's twisted around my neck, and I pull it loose and toss it aside. "I want you to fuck me. No more waiting." To hammer my point home, I bend and strip off my sweatpants. Then I'm standing there naked, my dick already at attention, lust burning my veins.

Matt takes me in from head to toe, licking his lips. "Fuck, you're gorgeous." He steps right against me, his hands roving over my bare back and ass, pressing me against him and kissing my neck.

He's still fully dressed, and the sensation of leather and denim ignites sparks on my bare, bath-reddened skin. That I'm naked and he's not makes me feel vulnerable while still inspiring a tingling thrill a moment later.

"Can I suck you like this?" The words spill out before I can think twice.

His head snaps up. "Fuck yes." He kisses me hard and wet. "Want to get on your knees for me?"

Nodding, I drop to the parquet floor, which is hard and cold, but who gives a shit when Matt's dick is about to fill my mouth?

"Get the towel." He runs a hand through my drying hair. "It's right there."

Apparently Matt gives a shit, and my chest tightens as I reach for the towel, shoving the damp material under my knees. Matt waits, letting me undo his jeans and free his cock, letting me take the lead.

And *fuck*, the taste of him—sweaty and earthy and male— makes my head spin as I lick and suck.

"Mmm, that's it. Your mouth was made for this," he mutters.

I hold his thighs, denim under my hands as I lick the underside of his cock, tonguing a long ridge and making him gasp.

"Oh fuck. Have to stop soon. Going to come in your ass this time. You want that?"

Moaning, I suck harder and resist reaching down to jack my straining cock. Matt's fingers tighten in my hair, and he pulls out of my mouth. A long strand of spit hangs from his dick to my parted lips, and he groans.

"Fuck, look at you." He lifts me to my feet and dives for my mouth, our tongues winding together. When he tears away to breathe, he murmurs, "So gorgeous, Alex."

Breathing hard, I want to believe it, but I can't stop myself from blurting, "But my teeth could be better. Couldn't afford full veneers. And I highlight my hair. It's not really this blond. I use Miss Clairol. How lame is that? And—"

"*Stop.*" He strokes my back, slowing his touch. "Alex, you're gorgeous. Okay?" Nuzzling my cheek, he presses kisses down my neck and behind my ear, his hands calming on my body, big and warm and steady. "Okay?"

"Okay," I whisper as my pulse eases and I relax into him again, his leather jacket soft against my bare skin.

Matt kisses me, meeting my tongue with a slow, slick slide, and we stand for a minute just kissing and pressing together. I want him naked now, but I can't seem to tear away from his lips.

"It's so hot that this is your first time," Matt murmurs against my mouth.

A horrible thought blooms in my mind, and I go stiff as it expands, inky tendrils snaking down my spine.

Frowning, Matt leans back. "Hey. What is it?"

The words scrape out of my dry throat. "Do you... Is that why you're so into me? Because I was a virgin? Because I'm, like...a novelty?"

He sucks in a breath, his eyes widening. "No! Alex, no." Cupping my cheek, he looks so earnestly horrified that he might be a cartoon Mountie after all. "I'm into you because of *you*. Yeah, it's exciting that you're doing all this stuff for the first time with me. It's..." He laughs softly. "This sounds so corny, but it's an honor. It makes me feel good that you trust me. That you want me too. That you want me to be your first. But it's much more than that."

"It is?" I want to believe him, and have no reason not to. "But I'm..." I wave my hand. "I'm a damn good skater, but not much else."

His brows draw together as he makes a sad little sound in his throat. "Do you really believe that? Alex, you're smart and funny and kind and the hardest worker I've ever met. You hide behind this cocky attitude that isn't even real. You're so much more than just a skater. And I'm lucky to know you."

It's amazing how he can be dirty-talking and bossy one minute and utterly sincere and sweet the next. My heart skips and soars like I just landed a perfect quad combo. "Yeah?"

"Yeah." He kisses me soundly, firm and confident. But when he draws back, he frowns again. "Am I pressuring you? We can slow down. We don't have to try everything right now."

I shake my head vigorously. "No, I want to fuck. I do. I'm sorry, I'm ruining this, aren't I? My stupid head. My stupid mouth."

"No. Nothing's ruined." He smiles. "If we miss a jump, we get up and keep going. Don't let it affect the rest of the program."

Chuckling, I nod. "Still more jumps to come. Gotta keep our focus."

"Mmm-hmm. Right back on track." He kisses me lightly.

"I want you inside me. I'm ready. Because I do, you know. Trust you? I do. I want the first time to be with you." *First, middle, last.* "You need to be naked now."

His laughter lights up his eyes. "I really do." He steps back and unzips his jacket, then pulls his wallet from his pocket and removes a condom and little pack of lube, and shit just got real. I'm going to have anal. I'm going to have a dick in my ass, and not just any dick. Matt's.

My cock had softened during my minor freak-outs, and now it springs back fully to life, and I can't resist giving it a few tugs as Matt finishes stripping.

By my bed in my tiny room, Matt flicks on the lamp and pulls my back to his chest, his breath hot on my ear. "You want to get on your stomach? Put a pillow under your hips."

"But…"

He squeezes my shoulders. "What? You can tell me anything. If you want to stop, or do something else?"

"I want to see your face when you fuck me."

"Oh, you will." He licks the shell of my outer ear, and the shiver goes straight to my balls. "You're going to ride me, just like you fantasized about. You're going to come all over my chest."

I can only gasp and nod, almost smacking his forehead.

"But first, I'm going to eat your ass. Going to lick you and fuck you with my tongue. Open up your tight hole. Yes?"

Scrambling onto the bed, I shove a pillow under me, rutting against it with a moan as I spread my legs and Matt climbs between them. He doesn't waste any time in parting my cheeks, and I wait anxiously for the wetness of his mouth. But he teases first, dipping his thumbs along my crease, barely skimming over my hole.

"Come on," I whine, craning my neck to see.

Laughing, he bends over and presses sloppy kisses to my ass cheeks, moving closer and closer to where I want him. Fuck, where I'm *dying* to have him.

When he finally flicks his tongue over my hole, my cry echoes off the bare walls. He licks fully up and down my crack, and it seems to spur him on when I'm loud, so I moan and whimper.

"Such a pretty little slut for it, aren't you?"

"Yes!" I push my butt back, closing my eyes and rubbing my face against the sheets, my feet jiggling. "Please, Matt."

He buries his face in my ass, stubble scraping my sensitive flesh, his tongue soothing the burn. "So good," he mumbles against me, nibbling the edges of my hole.

Jesus, being rimmed is better than I'd even imagined, and I've imagined it quite a bit. Being exposed with Matt right there—his face and mouth and hands coaxing me open—is breathtakingly intimate, even more than blow jobs.

He inches in a slick finger while he licks around my stretched rim. "That's it. You're doing so good, baby."

The burning in my ass grows, and by the time he's got two fingers inside me, it's hard to breathe. It hurts, but I like it at the same time, pain and pleasure indistinguishable.

"You've never played with your ass? You're so tight."

"Not much," I gasp. "Just the tip of my finger. This is…" Groaning, I can't find words for once.

Matt's fingers push and ease in a slow little rhythm. His hairy chest brushes my back as he kisses the nape of my neck. "You like it? You want more? Want my cock in you? You're going to come so hard all over me."

I'm moaning and muttering "yes" and "please" and "Matt," and as he eases out his fingers and fucks me with the point of his tongue, I have to rut the pillow, my cock leaking. Then he's suddenly gone, and I'm alone and whimpering. "Matt?"

"I'm right here." There's the sound of foil tearing, then he stretches out beside me on his back and lifts me right up and over him like I don't weigh a thing, which is so sexy I can hardly stand it.

Straddling his hips, I lean my palms on his chest, rubbing against the thick hair scattered there. He's breathing hard too, his red lips parted as he rubs up and down my flanks.

"Ready?" he asks.

"So fucking ready."

Matt laughs delightedly, and I join in and lean down to kiss him. I can taste something ripe and new, and the fact that it's my ass should be gross, but only makes me lick into his mouth deeper.

He passes me the open packet of lube. "Get the rest on my dick."

I do as I'm told, reaching back for his long, thick shaft. It feels bigger than ever in my hand, and excitement and trepidation skip through me at the thought of it inside me. But fuck fear, because I want it. Want him.

I shift back and hold him steady, pressing my hole down on the wide head of his dick. "Holy shit, it feels like a baseball bat!"

Matt's shoulders shake as he laughs. "You do have a way with words, sweetheart." He smooths his palms up and down my thighs. "Now's definitely a time to unclench. Go slow. That's it. It's all up to you how deep you want to go."

"All the way. I'm going to do it. It's just like the quad. No hesitation. Have to go for it." Bearing down, I grit my teeth and push past the head.

We both cry out, and Matt smiles joyfully. "You're one of a kind. Oh my God. That's it. Ready to ride me?"

"Fuck yes." I breathe hard through the pain, rising up and down, going lower and lower, Matt's cock stretching me impossibly, his hands tight on my hips, helping.

Circling my hips, I rub against just the right spot, and I swear to God there are actual fireworks behind my eyes as I whip my head back, panting.

"That's it," Matt mutters. "You found it. You're doing so good. So tight. Fuck."

Flexing my thighs, I lower myself until Matt's buried to the hilt. My ass is incredibly full, and my cock stands out from my bush, flushed and dark red. With fingers still slippery with lube, I take hold of myself, groaning.

"Yeah, baby." Matt tightens his fingers on my hips. "Jerk yourself. Jerk it all over me."

He starts thrusting up with his hips, and my body strains and stretches to the breaking point, fire in my tight balls licking out through my veins. I half expect to see sparks shooting out my dick as I stroke and watch Matt's flushed, beautiful face.

When he rocks up and hits my prostate, the fireworks return, and after a few hard, fast jerks of my dick, my fantasy is complete and I come, squeezing his cock with my ass and spraying his chest with jizz, even getting a splash on his chin as I quiver, mouth open on a silent scream.

"Oh yeah, fuck. Like that." He pumps his hips up into me, the muscles in his neck straining. He comes, his head tipped back.

"Fuck, Alex!"

I wish I could feel his cum inside me, but I imagine it's dripping out of my ass as I lean over and rub my face against his chest, smearing my jizz in his hair and on my cheeks and nose.

Matt runs his fingers up and down my spine, his chest heaving. "Holy shit. How do you feel?"

"My ass throbs and my muscles are cramping and I think I broke my dick coming so hard." I lift my head. "I feel fucking amazing."

He laughs. "Me too, baby. Me too."

Then he licks the cum off my face, and we kiss and kiss and kiss, and I want to stay right here forever.

CHAPTER THIRTEEN

T HE NEXT FEW days are practice, practice, practice. Out of nowhere, I get a massive blister on my left heel and have to see a doctor to take care of it. It sets my teeth on edge. I cannot afford to have any problems with my feet. Nationals are coming.

Mylene and her parents end up staying the whole week, which is great for Matt since Mylene's his best friend and I know he feels better having her here, cheering him on. It's less great for my newfound sex life, but I should be focusing on skating anyway.

On Mylene's last day before going back to Montreal, she calls me over to sit with her in the stands after I finish afternoon practice.

"So, Alex." Her eyes dance.

"So, Mylene." I nudge her shoulder lightly with mine.

"You and Matt are getting along very well now."

"I guess we are." My ass isn't tender anymore, but I imagine I can still feel Matt deep inside me, a thrill skittering across my skin, my cheeks going hot.

She grins, and it's impossible not to join her. "I knew from the first day you came here. He kept telling me how much he didn't like you."

I have to laugh. "Well, I didn't like him either!"

"I know. You two are perfect. All it took was me getting dropped on my head for you to figure it out."

The laughter dies in my throat. "I'm so glad you're going to be okay. It was really scary there at first."

She touches my arm. "I'm glad you were there for Matt. I know he still blames himself, no matter what he says. Thank you for helping get him back on the ice."

"You'll get back on it too."

"How do I say… Ah: you bet your ass."

"Exactly like that!" I raise my palm, and she high fives it with her good hand.

"I miss it so much." Her smile fades.

"I can only imagine. You worked all these years, and you're so close to the Olympics and then this happens. It's not fair."

Mylene looks at me with a little crease between her brows. "Yes, the Olympics are important, but it's just one competition. I miss *skating*." She waves her hand at the skaters on the rink. "I miss being here. I miss flying. I can't wait to get on the ice, and soar through the air with Matt beneath me. There's no other feeling like it."

I decide not to press about the Olympics. Since she can't go, it makes sense she's downplaying it as just one competition when obviously it's *everything*. "You're not afraid? After what happened?"

"I trust Matt. It's worth the risk. What happened was a fluke. I could never be afraid of doing something I love so much." She peers at me intently. "Do you love it, Alex?"

"Of course." What kind of question is that? I mean, I wouldn't be doing this if I didn't. I'm a competitor. It's who I am. "I'm going to win in Austria. I'm going to be Olympic champion."

She leans over and kisses both my cheeks. "I hope so. And if not, I hope you still love it."

Before I can respond, Matt joins us and gulps from a bottle of water. "God, I'm tired. I wish I didn't have to work tonight."

"Shouldn't you cut back on your shifts?" I ask.

Mylene answers for him, since Matt is still chugging. "He has, but he needs the extra money. Nationals are in Vancouver, and he wants to bring his family."

Matt crushes his now-empty plastic bottle. "The restaurant is busy with the holidays, so it's good money. Hey, when are you flying home for Christmas?" This question is for me.

"I'm not."

Mylene and Matt stare at me like I've suddenly grown three extra heads. "You're not?" They exclaim this in perfect unison, which makes them giggle.

"No way. Can't miss that much training."

"But it's Christmas. Alex, you need to catch your breath. Recharge the batteries," Matt says.

"Nationals are the second week of January. I don't have time for eggnog and Santa."

"Is your family coming here to be with you?" Mylene asks.

"Can't afford it. My dad lost his job." I try not to think about it most of the time, and when I remember, my gut clenches and sweat prickles my neck. I know it's not my fault, but all the money they've spent on me over the years…

"What are you doing for Christmas?" Mylene looks so sad that I almost want to laugh. Geez, it's not that big a deal.

I wave my arm grandly around the rink. "You're looking at it. The club's open, and Mrs. C and I will be here."

"Mylene!" Mr. Bouchard's voice carries up from rink side. He calls something else in French that I think means it's time to go, and Matt gets a lump in his throat and gives Mylene a kiss. Everyone gathers around as we say goodbye.

When I go back after she's gone to get my hoodie from where we were sitting, Matt follows. He stares out into the distance, deep in thought, and I sit beside him.

Glancing around to make sure no one's watching, I smooth

my palm over Matt's thigh. "She'll be back before you know it." I really hope it's the truth.

"Yeah. I was just thinking about… I don't know. Everything. It's been a whirlwind lately." He takes a deep breath and blows it out. "I'm going to talk to my parents. See if they'd be okay with you coming to dinner on Christmas."

Oh great. A pity invite. "Don't worry about it. I don't want to intrude and make things weird. It's one day. It doesn't mean anything." Despite myself, memories of tinsel and lights and stockings and hugs and way too much food fill my mind.

"You wouldn't be. I mean, you're my friend. Of course you're welcome."

"Right, as your *friend*."

"I don't want to upset them at the holidays. It would be so complicated." He runs a hand over his face and really does look exhausted. I guess I shouldn't expect everyone to be as open with their parents as I am. I know it has to be the right time for him to come out. It still hurts, though.

I rub his leg. "Seriously, don't worry about it. I'm going to stuff myself with Chinese food and watch Netflix after training. Total relaxation." Well, I'll order steamed rice and one dish—garlic chicken, maybe—then maybe watch *Die Hard* if I can stay awake. "It'll be awesome. And I'll see you the next day, right?"

"Yeah, I'm coming in on Boxing Day."

I laugh. "On *what?*"

"Boxing Day. It's the sacred celebration of an extra day off and big sales. Kind of like the Canadian Black Friday."

"I thought maybe you got to punch the person who gave you the worst Christmas present."

He grins, and God, I love his smile. "Oh right, that too. Although we often don't wait until Boxing Day. We just lay them out right there by the tree on Christmas morning."

"You Canadians are hard core."

We're both laughing, and I really wish he didn't have to work tonight, and that he could come home with me and sleep over. Well, the sleep would come after way more sex.

"I should go." He sighs. "I need to get a coffee or something before my shift."

I'm still thinking about what we'd be doing if Matt slept over. "Or something."

He picks up on my tone right away and raises an eyebrow. "Think anyone's in the locker room?"

"Maybe. But I *know* no one's in the broom closet. And I know blowing you will put a spring in your step."

Matt ends up being ten minutes late for work, but it's totally worth it.

TORONTO GETS ITS first big dump of snow a couple days before Christmas. My street hasn't been plowed yet, and I leave earlier than normal and barely make it to the main road. I really need to get some snow tires on my car.

When I get to the rink I'm not expecting Matt to be there yet, since he's coming from farther north, and I bet the snow is even worse. Yet here he is, practicing his quad toe, which is still two-foot but getting closer. We're the only ones who've made it in so far, and when I applaud an almost-clean landing, Matt whirls.

"Alex! You scared me."

"Sorry. Thought you heard me come in." Instead of going to the locker room first, I put on my skates and leave my crap on a bench. "Didn't think you'd make it in for a while."

"I left at four-thirty and got lucky. They'd just cleared and salted the roads in my neighborhood."

"Cool. So I guess it's just us for now." Skating is pretty much the last thing on my mind at the moment even though we're on the rink.

He smiles slyly and tugs me close. "Guess so."

But then my stupid brain decides to ask, "What are we?"

Matt pauses where he's leaning down to kiss me. "Is this an existential question? It's a little early for me."

"No, I mean... Are we hooking up? Friends with benefits? Dating? Or...boyfriends?"

His gloved hands settle around the small of my back. "What do you want us to be?"

Great question. "Well, I always said I don't have time for a boyfriend."

His Adam's apple bobs as he swallows, and his voice is serious. "Right. And I get that."

"But now I'm like, fuck it, you know? Because I really like you, and I'm assuming you like me. But maybe you want to see other people and keep it casual, which would be... It would suck donkey balls."

His eyes light up as he laughs. "We barely have time to see each other, let alone anyone else. Besides, I don't want anyone but you." He does lean down and kiss me now, soft and slow. "So will you be my boyfriend, Alex Grady?"

My heart thumps as I nod and grab him into a fiercer kiss, all tongues and clutching hands, our blades slipping on the ice. Holy shit, Matt's my *boyfriend*.

Naturally Mrs. C chooses this moment to barge through the arena doors, Oksana and Maxim in her wake as always. Matt and I untangle and skate away from each other immediately, but I know we're busted. I should have guessed nothing would keep her from being on time. She's like the post office. Through rain, sleet or snow, Mrs. C will be at the boards with coffee in hand.

She ignores us thoroughly.

Morning practice is quiet. Kenny's gone home to Japan for Nationals, and Rick went with him. Annie and Chantal are driving to Quebec to visit their families for the holidays. Mid-morning, when I usually go to the gym, Mrs. C takes me aside and we go up to the café.

She stares at me and guzzles a black coffee as if it's not even hot. Apparently her lack of feeling extends to her mouth too.

I clear my throat when the silence becomes unbearable. "Look, I know you saw me and Matt this morning."

She's still silent for an insanely long time. "You should be concentrating on training."

"I am! Aren't I here every day but Sunday at the ass-crack of dawn?"

"There is time for romance, and time for work. You and that boy—"

"What, is that the problem? That he's a boy? Would it be okay if I was kissing Oksana?"

Mrs. C's expression pinches even tighter, if possible. "You think I am…" Her nostrils flare. "What is the word?"

I'm terrified to answer, but I don't have a choice. "Um, a homophobe?"

"Yes. You think that is problem?"

Truthfully? No. I know that's not the problem. I know the problem is that I switched up the choreography in Japan on the fly, and that I think about Matt when I should be concentrating on technique and a hundred other things that aren't him. "Maybe."

She sees right through me. "No, that is not difficulty, and you know it. Matthew is very nice young man. But kissing doesn't get you to Olympics."

"I know that, but—"

"Alexander. There can be no 'but.'" She finishes her coffee. "You want victory?"

"Of course!"

"You must work harder. When you are here on ice, there is no boyfriend. Vladimir Sidorov is in Moscow right now doing dozens of perfect quads every day. He's planning two in short program. Five in free skate. Plus he has artistry and transitions, and listens to coaches. He is not distracted."

Honestly, it wouldn't shock me if she had secret cameras planted in his rink, and *Jesus fucking Christ,* if he does that many quads, it's game over. She's right that he's got the rest of the skills as well and isn't just a jumping machine. I put on a cocky face and wave my hand dismissively. "I can beat him. He didn't even make it to the Grand Prix Final."

"Because of food poisoning. Do not underestimate opponents, Alexander."

Now my stomach's queasy.

"Tanner Nielsen is not distracted by romance. You must work harder than your competitors. You must work hardest."

Ugh, Tanner. She knows just which buttons to push, and I shove back my chair. "Let's go practice."

Mrs. C nods in approval, and we return to the ice. Matt's by the boards when I take off my skate guards, but I don't even look at him. He can't be my boyfriend here at the rink.

Kissing doesn't get you to the Olympics.

CHAPTER FOURTEEN

"ALEXANDER THE GREAT!"

I roll my eyes, but can't help smiling as I slow my evening run to a walk and hold up the mouthpiece on my earbuds. "Hey, Benny. What's shaking?" With my agent, it's always something.

"You're doing an interview. The reporter's calling tomorrow at seven o'clock. You'll be home by then? I want you paying attention, not giving half-assed answers as you drive."

"When have I ever done that?" I cross over to another quiet suburban street and walk toward a park.

"You haven't yet and there'd better not be a first time. I have enough problems with these football players. They'll be the goddamn death of me."

"So, back to me." Once Benny starts complaining about his football clients, he can go for hours. "Who am I talking to?"

"Chick named Elizabeth something."

"And where does Ms. Something work?"

There's a slight pause. "Great paper. Big distribution numbers. Tons of hits on their site."

"Uh-huh. What's it called, Benny?"

"I can't really think of the name offhand; I'll get back to you."

"Benny!" I sidestep a dude picking up his dog's shit at the edge of the sidewalk. "Just tell me already."

"The *Boston Community Reporter*."

Groaning, I shake my head. "Is that even a real paper?"

"Of course!"

"That people pay money for?"

"So it's free. Hey, more people read free papers these days, and it'll be online. Online's what matters. Nationals are in Boston and we can use all the publicity we can get."

Benny loved talking about *we*. "Is that the best you can get me? I'm defending national champion, remember?"

"You know how it goes, kid. Win that gold medal in Salzburg and I guarantee I'll get you in *People* magazine. Your federation's doing a bunch of press, and it's tough to get any bites on an article that's only about you. Everyone's talking about Nielsen or that little Pang girl who'll probably win Nationals and be too young to go to Austria."

Poor Sabrina. Four years is a long way away for a teenaged girl about to grow into hips and boobs that will totally throw off her jump technique.

Benny goes on. "Now listen. You're not gonna run your mouth off to this woman, right?"

I don't bother denying that I've done that before. "No. I promise."

"She'll ask about your love life. You'd better know going in what you're going to say."

A wave of uneasiness washes over me. "What love life? Unless you mean the deep and meaningful relationship I have with the blisters on my left heel."

Benny snorts. "Uh-huh. Nice try. I mean the hot and heavy thing you have with that Canadian kid who dropped the pretty little girl on her head."

I'm momentarily speechless for once. "How did you find out?" I sputter. "And that accident wasn't his fault!"

"Down, boy. Duly noted. And I have my sources." Benny

snorts. "Besides, subtle isn't exactly in your repertoire. You'd better tone it down in Austria or the internet's going to have a fucking field day."

I'm not ashamed of Matt or being gay. But what we have is…special. The thought of people online gossiping and talking about it makes me want to puke. They'd probably wonder what the hell Matt sees in me.

"Now, that could be a great angle to work—how you've helped mend his shattered spirit and selflessly got him back on the ice even though he could be your competitor in Austria, etc., etc. It could be heartwarming as shit."

Rolling my rigid shoulders, I turn down another dark suburban street. "Right, but I'd also be coming out. Obviously."

"Indeed you would. Frankly, I don't think it's a good idea. The world's come a long way, but there's been some backsliding of late. You want to appeal to the broadest possible audience to nail down more endorsements."

My dad had been the second choice for a job opportunity he'd been excited about, and the thought of my parents' dwindling bank account makes the back of my skull throb. "Yeah, I need all the income I can get. I owe it to my family."

"Exactly. Rumors are one thing, but admitting it to a reporter, making it official—that's not what you need right before the two biggest competitions of your life. If she asks, *don't tell*."

"I won't. Going to play it smart."

Ugh. It feels shitty and gross, but I've gone this long without coming out to the public. I can go a little longer. Besides, Matt's not even out to his folks. No way would he be down for me telling the world, and I have to respect that.

"Smart as always. You're Alexander the Great, right?"

"Right." Benny's only scored me that one local endorsement in New Jersey for subs, but he's always good for an ego boost, which I need after not landing my quad Sal at *all* today.

"You be a good boy and don't talk shit about any of the other skaters. Especially your pal Tanner. You hear me?"

"Don't worry, I'm on it."

WHEN I TAP my phone a few day later as I'm icing my hip in the locker room, my stomach clenches with dread. Eleven messages this early in the morning can't be good news. And not just texts—actual voicemails.

I call my mom immediately without listening to any. "Mom? Is someone dead? What's going on?" My heart thumps.

"What? No, nothing like that."

"Oh, thank God." Shifting on the wooden bench, I wince and adjust my ice pack. "So what's up?"

She has a longsuffering tone to her voice. "Oh, honey. Did you have to be so…"

"Huh?"

"That interview online this morning. It came up in my Google Alert."

The dread returns like a ton of bricks. "Wait, what? Mom, I have no idea what I said that was bad."

"I know you and Tanner aren't the best of friends, but insulting Lisa was uncalled for. She's a gold medalist, Alex. She deserves respect. What did she ever do to you?"

I wrack my brain trying to remember what I said about Lisa Ackles. "We barely talked about her! I said she seemed like a really supportive girlfriend. What's wrong with that?"

"Alex, you said it must be nice to have nothing else to do but fly around the world going to Tanner's competitions."

"It *would* be nice! Mom, I didn't mean it in a bad way. Then I said Lisa was a great champion and I hoped Tanner and I would be able to follow her example and be ambassadors for the sport.

I'm guessing that bitch reporter didn't put that part in, huh?"

"Watch your language, young man." Her tone is razor sharp.

I want to scream, or maybe crawl into a hole. My skin prickles, bile rising in my throat. "What else is in there?"

"That, and I quote: 'Kenny Tanaka doesn't have a chance to win in Austria.'"

The pit in my stomach drops another mile. "What about the rest of it?" Jesus, I'm going to strangle that reporter. "She asked me who I think the medal contenders will be, and I gave her a few names, including Kenny. I said if Vladimir Sidorov does two quads in his short and five in his free skate like he claims he will, *none* of us will stand a chance! Not just Kenny! I said me and Tanner and Hiro too! Why the fuck would she zero in on Kenny?"

Mom sighs. "Maybe because he beat Hiro at Japanese Nationals and has the momentum now. It was a huge upset and he's getting a ton of press."

"I swear I didn't single him out!"

"Sweetheart, I believe you, but you know you have to be careful with the media. They can spin anything to make you look bad or create controversy. I've gotten phone calls already today, so I think it's working."

I jump as the locker room door bangs open and Kenny's tiny mother marches in. I've never really spoken to her before—she's usually only a silent presence in the rink, hovering near Kenny, but always in the periphery. Now she's in the men's locker room, bold as anything, looking about ready to rip my balls off and shove them down my throat.

"Um, Mom? I'll call you back later." I leap to my feet. "Mrs. Tanaka, let me explain."

She shakes her head sharply. "You are supposed to be friend to Kenjiro."

"I am! Listen, I was misquoted. It was taken out of context! What I said was—"

"You are not friend."

Then she turns on her heel, and my cheeks flush hot in shame, even though I know I didn't mean to throw Kenny under the bus. I quickly lace my running shoes and hurry out to the rink. Kenny has apparently been told, because he won't even *look* at me as he marches by to go to the gym.

Worse yet, Mrs. C is silently fuming as she takes Oksana and Maxim through their paces. Other people might not be able to tell, but I'd know her simmering anger anywhere. Can't wait for that fucking lecture.

But the very worst part is that Matt and Chantal have arrived, and Matt looks at me with such disappointment. He hasn't even let me explain, and he's judging me already—and that slices so deep that the hurt sparks into my anger and it all explodes.

"Fine, don't even hear my side!" I yell, my near-screech echoing in the rafters. Everyone in the arena turns to stare, the skaters on the rink skidding to a stop. The tango music for Oksana and Maxim's short program plays on as I stalk out, slamming the door behind me.

I can't go to the gym because Kenny's there, so I stomp outside through the main doors of the club, slipping on the icy steps and barely catching myself on the railing. I'm almost to my car when I realize I don't have my keys, which turns up the internal volume on my rage to an ear-splitting level, my whole body shaking as I scream silently.

After kicking my front tire a few times, I lean against the side of the car, even though the metal is freezing through my T-shirt. Crossing my arms, I take deep breaths, my exhalations clouding around my face in the wintry air.

I'm being a massive suck, and as the fury recedes, humiliation takes up the slack. Did I really just have a hissy fit in front of everyone? Fuck me.

But I hate that people are thinking I'm a bag of dicks when

I've tried so hard not to be. I hate that Kenny's feelings are undoubtedly hurt because he's the sweetest kid in the world and I value his friendship. I hate that Mrs. C is mad at me yet again. I hate that countless people online who don't even know me will be tweeting and posting and blogging about what a douchebag Alex Grady is.

And most of all, I hate that Matt looked at me like that.

"It's a little cold to be out here without a jacket, isn't it?"

Even though he's interrupting my pity party, I sigh in relief as Matt approaches. At least he's not too disgusted to talk to me. He hands me my coat, which I put on gratefully, then unlocks his ancient Ford Fiesta a few rows away, and we climb in.

It's freezing, so Matt turns on the engine. I cross my arms again, still cold and angry and hurt. "I'm surprised you're willing to be seen with me."

"It's okay. No one can see us this far back in the lot."

He's clearly joking, but fuck my life, my eyes fill with tears.

"Hey, hey." He pulls me close and caresses my cheek with his free hand. "I'm sorry. I was trying to lighten the mood."

I can only nod because I might sob if I try to talk, and he thankfully only holds me tighter. I tuck my face in his neck. He strokes my hair, and I close my eyes, clinging to him.

We don't say anything for a while. The heat comes on and soon the car is nice and toasty. I could just stay here all day, away from everyone staring and judging.

His chest rumbles when he speaks softly. "Don't worry. It'll blow over."

The warm, safe little bubble evaporates, and I bolt up. "But I didn't say those things! At least, not like that. The reporter totally twisted my words. I know I have a big mouth, but seriously, I wasn't bagging on Lisa or Kenny. I *really* wasn't."

"I know you didn't mean to. Sometimes you just don't think before you talk."

I shift away, my back to the passenger door. "No, seriously. That reporter twisted my words and left out whole chunks of what I was saying. She totally screwed me over."

"It's okay, I believe you."

"No! Don't placate me. Because here's what I actually said." I lay out the answers I gave, counting on my fingers forcefully. "So you see? I can understand how what I said about Lisa could be misconstrued. But not Kenny. That was total bullshit."

Matt opens and closes his mouth. "Well shit. This really does suck." He snags my hand. "I'm sorry. I should have known better. I should have trusted you."

Squeezing his fingers, I try to smile. "It's okay. I've said so much stupid shit over the years that I can't blame you."

"Yeah, but I know you now." He tugs me closer and kisses me tenderly. Leaning our foreheads together, he says, "I know the real you that no one else gets to see. And I'm sorry I didn't give you the benefit of the doubt."

"Can we run away and go somewhere with no reporters and no ice and no judges and no Olympics?"

Leaning back, he laughs softly and kisses my forehead. "You wouldn't even last a day, baby."

I have to laugh too. "Accurate." Pressing our lips together, I slide my tongue into his mouth, and he moans softly and tilts his head.

I still can't believe Matt likes me and wants to kiss me—*me!*—and I'm kind of waiting for him to laugh and say it's all been a big joke, even after everything we've done together and how sweet he's been.

My mind whirls, but I don't pull away and demand reassurance that he really does like me. His tongue's in my mouth—clearly he likes me. Right?

Yes, he likes me. He says he does, and why shouldn't I believe him? Sure, I'm a fuck-up sometimes, but if he didn't want to be my boyfriend anymore, he'd—

Matt pulls back and peers at me intently, brushing back my hair. "What's going on in there?"

Breathing deeply, I try to banish the stupid worry. "Sorry. Just my brain. It doesn't want to shut up sometimes. Similar to my mouth, come to think of it."

He smiles, gazing at me with such tenderness that my heart squeezes. "I wish we had time for me to distract you properly." He waggles a thick eyebrow.

Glancing at the time on the stereo, I groan. "My next session's about to start. Mrs. C's already going to be pissed without me being late."

"Everything's going to be fine. You'll explain, and they'll believe you. Okay?" He kisses me soundly. "Now let's go land some jumps."

The great thing is that we do, and even Mrs. C has to smile when I channel my frustration into nailing a gorgeous quad Sal.

After lunch, I manage to catch Kenny alone in the bathroom at the sink. Not like I'm stalking him, but I kind of am since his mother is still shooting me death stares across the rink.

"Kenny, I didn't say what was in that article."

He won't look at me, scrubbing his hands under the water as if he was disinfecting to perform surgery. So I explain what happened and hope for the best.

"Seriously, I wasn't putting you down." I tentatively rest my hand on his shoulder, and he doesn't shake me off. "You're an amazing skater. And you're my friend. I care about you."

Kenny nods and smiles, which fills me with relief. "I believe you, Alex." He does that little bow, and I bow back, which makes him giggle. Then we hug it out, and I ask him to explain to his mother so she doesn't slash my tires or "accidentally" push me down the stairs.

When I finally get a chance to read the article myself, I'm

pissed off all over again. Mrs. C seems to accept my explanation, but she's still not happy. I know it's partly my fault for running my mouth off in the past. I don't exactly have a shining track record. Gosh, seeing Tanner and Lisa at Nationals should be more fun than usual.

The other part of the article that sticks in my craw as I drive home is that even though I insisted I'm too busy to date right now, the reporter heavily implied I'm afraid to come out. She didn't actually say it in those words, but the meaning is clear to anyone with two brain cells to rub together.

It shouldn't bug me since it's my choice to not come out right now. But I'm not *afraid*. I'm practical. There's a difference.

Matt's working, and I'm tempted to go wait for him outside the restaurant so I can get a hug. Which is insane, because I've gotten by just fine on my own for years without a boyfriend holding my hand.

I need to be a big boy and deal with this on my own. Although I feel better when my dad calls, the guilt and worry of his unemployment tugs at me.

I'm desperately trying to fall asleep at eight-thirty and end this shit-tastic day when Benny calls from New York. Being Benny, he's thrilled, because the Associated Press picked up the article and now it's everywhere, because *of course* it is.

I need to never speak again. Or at least not until after I win Nationals, Olympics, and throw Worlds in for the cherry on top.

CHAPTER FIFTEEN

D *EEP BREATHS. DEEP BREATHS.*

*D*EEP BREATHS. DEEP BREATHS.
        The Olympic issue of *Time* magazine just came out, and guess who's on the cover? Big hint: a top US male figure skater and it's not me. Golden Boy Tanner Nielsen, Mr. Perfect. Mr. I Have an Ideal Girlfriend and There's Nothing Homosexually Threatening About Me.

Because of course.

Women's skating has always been the big seller in the US, but with Sabrina too young, our women aren't podium contenders. So instead of the latest ingénue gracing the cover of the magazine in a group shot with a few other American athletes, it's Tanner.

Tanner, with his perfect, blindingly white teeth and chiseled jaw. I haven't brought myself to read the interview yet, but I'm sure it's nauseating. I glanced at the pictures online, and there's one of him and Lisa looking disgustingly cute and in love.

Since I don't want to be seen buying it, I make my sister go down to the hotel store and bring it back up to my room. I could read it online, but for some reason I want to hold it in my hands and stew in my impotent resentment.

Rachel sits on my roommate Sam's bed, watching me fume. Sam's an ice dancer from Detroit I've roomed with before at competitions, and his flight is still fogged in, unfortunately for him. Rachel asks, "Why does Tanner bug you so much?"

"Duh. Why do you think?"

"You beat him last year. Why do you still let him get to you?"

For a fifteen-year-old, Rachel can be surprisingly rational. I hold up the magazine. "Yeah, I beat him, and I'm the reigning national champion. But *he's* on the cover of *Time*. I won bronze at Worlds and he was fifth. I rest my case."

"People on Tumblr think you're totally in love with him."

Sputtering, I pace by the bed, gripping the magazine. "What? That's insane!"

"There's a bunch of hate-sex fic about you two."

Sweet Jesus. "Okay, number one? I can't believe my baby sister just said 'hate-sex.' Number two, please tell me you haven't read any."

She squishes up her face. "Eww. No, I don't read about my brother getting laid. But seriously, what did Tanner ever do to you? Was there some douchey incident I don't know about?"

"No. We're always civil. He just…"

She picks at her braces. "Exists?"

"Yes. No!" I roll and unroll the magazine. "He's everything I'm not. He says the perfect things and has perfect looks and is perfectly hetero."

"I really don't think anyone else compares you guys as relentlessly as you do."

"Come on. You know the Feds like him better. He's doing way more press this week than I am." I brandish the now-tattered magazine. "He's on the cover of *Time*! I rest my case."

Rachel rolls her eyes. "Okay, so maybe he's their fave. But you shouldn't let it get to you. You're your own worst enemy, Alex." She clicks on the TV and starts watching movie trailers on the pay-per-view channel.

The thing is, I know she's right. I'm not stupid. I shouldn't let it bother me, but it does. After tossing the magazine in the trash, I lean back on my pillows and try to relax.

I last through two trailers about shit blowing up before I'm pacing around the room. It's the short program tomorrow, and I'm second in the final flight of skaters. Tanner's last, because of course he is. The plan is to throw down a perfect skate and set the bar nice and high.

Matt's in Vancouver for Canadian Nationals, and I check my phone again to find no texts. He's at practice, and I'm hoping it goes better for him than his session yesterday. He was really down about not landing his quad toes, but the fact that he's even gotten it half consistent in a few months is amazing.

"You're supposed to be resting," Rachel says, not looking away from a rom-com trailer about a clumsy girl who moves to the big city and gets a job in fashion even though she's—wait for it—not fashionable at all.

I flop back on my bed. "There. I'm resting."

"Want me to send you links to some Tanex fic? Should be good for a laugh since you're obsessing about him anyway."

"*Tanex*? We have a shipper name?"

"Duh, of course."

"Is there fic about me and…anyone else?"

Rachel's smile is sly. "Gee, anyone in particular? Matt Savelli, for example?"

I groan. "Mom and Dad told you?"

She rolls her eyes again. "Dude, people have been gossiping about you since Skate America. You both Instragrammed pics from the Rocky steps that were clearly taken at the same time." Turning to me eagerly, she asks, "So, are you two together? What's he like? Do you love him? Mom and Dad hardly know anything. Spill!"

There's a knock on the door, and I hop up to let my parents in, muttering, "Saved by the bell." Having a boyfriend is one thing. Discussing it with my family in detail and having them get all *involved* is another. After the Olympics, sure. But I don't want to deal with the questions now. There's already too much going on in my stupid head.

At dinner, I pick at my lobster salad at the seafood place Rachel picked and try not to worry too much about tomorrow. In the silence after Rachel has finished telling us in detail about what she's going to wear to some chick's sweet sixteen party, my mom turns to me with an innocent expression that immediately raises my guard.

"How's Matt? We're hoping for the best for him in Vancouver."

Dad and Rach give me similarly faux-innocent looks, and I sigh heavily. "I'm amazed you held out this long before asking."

"Well, if we didn't ask, you wouldn't tell us anything, now would you?" Dad says. "So? How are things going? Are you two officially an item now?"

"Things are going fine, and yes. I guess we're 'an item,' as you would say if this were the eighties or something."

Mom laughs. "Please don't talk about the eighties like they were the fifties." Then she frowns. "Although I guess the eighties *are* to you what the fifties were to us. My God. How is that possible?"

Dad grimaces. "We're old, hon. That's how."

Rachel's braces gleam as she grins, ignoring our parents and addressing me. "Are you guys totally in love?"

"Now, now. Let's not pry too much," Mom says while looking at me expectantly.

"Ha!" I take a bite of lemony salad. "That's rich coming from you, Mother."

"Don't talk with your mouth full, and is it wrong to be interested in my son's life?"

"Okay, okay." I groan. "Please don't go into your martyr routine, Mom. I can't take it."

"You still haven't answered the question." Dad smiles. "Are

you boys happy together?"

It's still weird to think of it in those terms. "Yeah. We are." Heat creeps up my neck, and I hunt intently for a lobster chunk, gripping my fork.

"Oh my God. He is *totally* in love!" Rachel shrieks.

"Shut up! I am not!"

"Are too!"

My dad raises his hands. "Girls, girls, you're both pretty."

We all burst out laughing, and I fling a piece of lettuce at Rach. She retaliates with a fried scallop, but my parents shut it down before a full-fledged food fight breaks out. I know I'm an official grown-up and should be above such things, but I'm so not.

Later in bed, I clutch my phone, staring at the screen and waiting for Matt to text, call, tweet—anything. Sam's flight finally arrived, and he's in the shower, his occasional singing murmuring through the door.

I'm about to give up on waiting and force myself to sleep when a FaceTime call comes in, Matt's gorgeous face filling the screen. Heart racing, I run a hand through my hair and plaster on a calm smile. "Hey!"

Matt's eyes scrunch up. "Hey, baby. How are you? Sorry I've barely texted. Today has been crazy." There's a mirror behind him where I can see his broad back and glimpses of a hotel bathroom. He's leaning against the sink with a towel around his hips, and his hair's damp.

The best part—even better than perving on his hot bod—is that he's wearing the worry stone I gave him before we left Toronto. It's a flat, dark rock on a black leather cord, and you rub it when you're anxious. It has a groove that's perfect for your thumb. I told him he should use it whenever he felt guilty about what happened to Mylene, or—duh—he was worried about anything.

He laughed and said I needed to get a worry stone for myself, and I probably should. I love seeing the stone nestled against his chest hair, and wish I could reach out and touch.

"I'm good…Matt." My belly flutters at the way he calls me "baby" sometimes. Shit, should I be calling him something schmoopy too? I totally should, right? But what? He's already calling me "baby." Hmm. Babe? Hon? Sweetie? Pookie?

"Earth to Alex."

Blinking, I focus on him. "Sorry. I was just—"

"Thinking," Matt finishes with a smile. "I know. Your eyes go kind of crossed."

"Oh my God, seriously?" I stare at the little square of my image in the corner of the screen.

He laughs. "No, not really. But you do get spacey. What are you thinking about?"

"Nothing." I'll worry about a pet name later. "The competition. You know, the usual. How are things in Vancouver?"

"Awesome. We did the draw and I'm in the second group, so not too bad."

It's way better than it used to be, but sometimes the judges still hold the really big marks for later because I guess they don't want to blow their wad if there are still good skaters to come. "That's great. How's practice?"

"Really good." He practically bounces, his face alight. "The press are talking about how strong I looked this morning and that I'm a contender for the team. Me! As a *singles* skater. Sometimes it's still surreal, you know?"

"Yeah, I can imagine." A horrible thought snakes through my asshole mind with a low hiss: What if Matt makes it to Salzburg and I don't? I want him to make it so badly, but what if I have to watch him on TV and I don't get to be there myself? What if I fail utterly and never get another chance? I'll be pathetically jealous, and it'll ruin everything.

"Alex? You okay?"

"Yeah, I'm good," I lie with a fake-ass smile. "Sorry, was thinking again. I'm just tired." That's the truth, at least. "I'm so excited for you!"

But the exhilaration in his voice has been replaced by concern. "What's going on? Tell me."

The ache of missing him flares so hot I almost wince. If he was here, we could curl up in bed and obviously have sex, but then we'd cuddle, and God, I could use it right now. "Don't worry. Just freaking myself out about not making the Olympic team." That's mostly true.

"You will. I have complete confidence."

"What if I don't?"

"Unclench, Alex."

I snort out a laugh. "Wish you were here to unclench me."

"Tell me about it." He glances away for a moment and lowers his voice. "You know, if we're quiet, I bet we could—"

"Dude, I stink. Hurry up." The male voice is accompanied by a knock on Matt's bathroom door.

Matt sighs heavily. "Then again, maybe not. I guess you'd better get to sleep anyway since you're three hours ahead. I need to grab dinner."

The door opens in the mirror and Todd the ice dancer pokes his head in. "Sorry to interrupt you love birds, but I need to shower." He calls out, "Hi, Alex! Since I know that's who you're making kissy faces at, no matter how cool you try to play it, Savelli."

I have to laugh and call back, "Hey, Todd!" Guess Rachel's right that people have been talking.

Matt flicks a towel at Todd before gazing into the screen. "Talk soon, okay? You're going to kill it tomorrow. We both are."

"Damn right we are." Looking at his face and his big, brown eyes and sweet smile, affection flows through me. "I l—" Holy shit, wait. What am I saying? I clear my throat. "Later!"

Hitting end before I can embarrass myself further, I stare at the ceiling. Rachel's teasing words whirl around my mind. *Am I totally in love?*

MY FIRST ENCOUNTER with Tanner Nielsen goes better than expected. I guess it's my second encounter, as we were both there to draw for the skate order for the short program. But there were dozens of people and we stayed on opposite sides of the room, so it didn't really count.

We're in the same flight now for practice, and as we take the ice, I can hear the cameras clicking away. I'm sure the media's playing up my rivalry with Tanner, and I'm determined not to give them any more ammunition.

That reporter who made me look like a giant asshole is here and asked for another interview earlier. I managed to politely decline her request without making a scene, which made Mrs. C actually smile, with teeth and everything.

Practice goes fine, although I don't try my quad Sal. I'm doing a quad toe combo in the short, so it's only the long program I need to worry about for the Sal. Besides, I don't want Tanner and the press watching me wipe the ice with my ass over and over. I'm sure they wouldn't mind a bit, though.

There's quite a lot of buzz around a young skater from Florida named Zach Doyle, and I can see why as I casually watch him doing his run-through. He's got amazing jumps—including a quad flip, which is incredibly rare—and really clean lines, and he's suddenly come into his own this year. He's a natural, and I bet he's taken ballet lessons since he was a toddler. I should have started earlier than eleven.

Thankfully, there are three Olympic spots open for the men, thanks to my bronze medal and Tanner's fifth-place finish at

Worlds last year. To get three spots, a country needs two placements that add up to thirteen or less. So my third plus Tanner's fifth equaled eight, and presto—three spots instead of two.

When our practice time is over, Tanner and I reach the door in the boards at the same time. Our coaches hand us our skate guards and there's this weirdly tense moment as we each put them on. Then Tanner motions for me to go first as I do the same to him at exactly the same time. This makes everyone in the vicinity laugh, and I laugh too with my competition smile firmly in place.

Tanner waves me through with exaggeration, and I bow in response, which really gets the fans in attendance going. Then Zach squeezes through between us, saying, "If you two are just going to stand here all day..."

I laugh again—ha, ha, ha, see what a good sport I am?—and Tanner follows him off the ice. Soccer moms Rose and Mary wave, and I go over to say a quick hello. I hug them both and they tell me how wonderful I'm going to do and how fantastic my practice was. Seriously, it's nice to have fans.

While I wasn't too worried about Zach Doyle in practice, I'm substantially more concerned as I skate around the rink that night during the six-minute warm-up for my flight of skaters. I keep telling myself that I'm going to be awesome and do every element perfectly, yet the doubt creeps in.

Zach and his creamy complexion and shiny black hair skate by. I remember what it was like to be at your first senior Nationals, when you're not afraid of anything and there's no pressure. I've heard a million skaters say defending a title is harder than winning one, but I never really believed it.

Until now.

My palms sweat. I'm skating around in circles taking deep breaths, but it's not calming me down. My heart pounds painfully, and I can't think straight. What if I fall? If I miss an element, I could end up way down in the standings. It's not just the jumps I have to worry about. I need to do all the required elements cleanly.

To my left, Zach lands a gorgeous triple Lutz. My throat seizes up and I cough on my next breath. At the boards, Mrs. C hands me my water bottle and says nothing as I cough and drink. When I'm finished and am breathing mostly normally again, she grasps my hand hard.

"Listen, Alexander. You have done perfect short program more times than I can count. You can do it tonight. Forget people."

I nod jerkily and blow out a long stream of air through my mouth. She's right. I can do this.

She loosens her grip and pats the back of my hand. "Breathe. You can do it."

I can do it. I can do it.

The one-minute warning for the end of the warm-up is announced, and I do another couple laps of the rink, bending into my knees, getting a feel for the ice. I repeat the words in my mind like a mantra. *I can do it.*

When it's my turn, the crowd cheers and my heart is going to explode as I take my starting position. The music begins, and I'm off with a smile on my face and a spring in my step.

And I totally do it! I'm *awesome.* Seriously awesome. I don't have to struggle for the jumps—they just flow one after the other. Everything feels right, and when I'm finished, the packed arena leaps to its feet.

The marks are huge, and I'm completely confident they'll hold up. Zach is right after me, and I sit in the Kiss and Cry and watch him skate. He puts a hand down on his triple Axel, but other than that he skates really well. I applaud when he's finished and clear out of the Kiss and Cry so he and his coaches can use it.

Backstage, I hear his numbers and the whole time I don't stop smiling. Good for the kid for doing a great job in his first big competition. But I still did better.

Now I just have to wait through two more skaters before Tanner. With my USA jacket zipped over my costume and sneakers on, I give a few interviews in the mixed zone, keeping my answers completely positive and non-controversial.

Then I stick in my earbuds and pace around backstage, aware of the TV cameras on me. The network has a waiting lounge with couches where we're supposed to sit and smile and pretend we're not freaking out, but I can't do it.

Mrs. C stands nearby with a placid expression, and I crank up Prince and walk the length of the hallway until it's finally time. There are monitors backstage, and while I can't bear to watch Tanner skate, when he's done I check out his body language in the Kiss and Cry.

He's leaning back on his hands, lips pressed together. His coach says something, patting his leg, and my pulse races. Oh my God, he made a mistake. I know it. Or else I would have heard the thunderous applause even with my music on.

The scores come up, and he's in third place. My lead is five points—not insurmountable by any means, but a good cushion.

I share a smile with Mrs. C and wave to the cameras. Now I just need to do it all again tomorrow. Piece of cake.

I MAKE IT to the elevator at the hotel just as the doors are closing, so of course I don't realize Lisa Ackles is in there until it's too late. My breath catches and I try to smile. "Hey, Lisa."

She's as perfectly coiffed as ever, golden hair and makeup flawless. She regards me coolly. "Alex."

Okay, I can't blame her since she thinks I was dissing her to that reporter. "Listen, Lisa, about that article—"

"Where's Matt Savelli? I guess he has something better to do than come watch you compete, huh?"

She catches me off guard. "What?"

"Come on, everyone knows you two are a couple. Figure skating's a small world."

"Well, um, Matt's actually at Canadians this weekend."

She shoots me a withering stare. "You know, I go to college. Stanford. Ever heard of it?"

"I—wait, you go to Stanford? I actually didn't know that."

"I started premed in September. I'm not some ditzy blond bimbo following her boyfriend around and doing nothing but making him dinner and picking up his dry cleaning."

Shame prickles my skin. "I'm sorry. Seriously, that reporter screwed me over. All I meant was that it would be nice to have your girlfriend cheering you on at all the big competitions. I wasn't being sarcastic, and I didn't mean that you have nothing better to do. I really, truly didn't. I wish Matt could be here. You and Tanner are lucky to have each other." I may not like the guy, but it's true.

The elevator pings and the doors slide open at the tenth floor. Lisa's expression has slightly softened, and she holds the door open. "I guess I'm a little sensitive about it. Sometimes I really miss being the one out there competing."

"I can totally imagine."

Sighing, she shakes her head. "Okay, Grady, you're forgiven. I'd wish you good luck tomorrow, but that would be a conflict of interest. I hope you lose. No offence."

I laugh. "None taken."

Lisa cracks a smile before the doors close, and at least I feel a little better about that situation.

There are excited congratulatory texts from Matt, who is skating his own short program later. The men are going last in Vancouver, so it'll be way too late for me to stay up and stream online or check the results.

I call and leave a voicemail telling him he's going to crush it, and that's really all I can do. He'll be in his bubble pre-competition. This week we're both fighting for the Olympics, but we have to do it on our own.

PRACTICE IN THE morning goes smoothly, except for one thing. Well, two things. The first is that I'm stressed about Matt being in fifth place after the short. He's only a handful of points off the podium, so it's still possible. But acid gurgles in my belly. I want him to make it so badly I can taste it. I want to share this with him.

That's assuming I make it myself, because the other problem is that my fucking quad Sal has seriously deserted me and I don't know if I should even try it tonight. Mrs. C and I talk quietly by the boards after I've crashed five times in a row. We decide to try it once more.

As I gain speed, I tell myself that I'm in Toronto, and Matt's here, and it's just another day of practice. I launch up into the jump—and yes! I land it! Okay, I turn out of the landing and can't hold the position, but I did all the rotations cleanly. I resist the urge to pump my fist in the air, instead pretending it's no big deal, which it shouldn't be.

Mrs. C nods her approval, and we move onto a run-through of the first half of my long program. The rest of practice goes by quickly, and I talk to Sue Stabler from the Federation for a minute by the Kiss and Cry.

"That was an interesting interview you gave last week."

Great. "Look, that reporter totally misquoted me and twisted my words. She wanted controversy."

Sue straightens her jacket and smiles thinly. "You always seem able to provide it."

Stay calm, stay calm. "It really wasn't my fault this time. Honestly."

"Mmm-hmm." She exhales long-sufferingly, and I barely manage to stop from rolling my eyes. Oh, the poor Federation. They should be glad for any publicity they can get. TV ratings for skating in the States aren't what they used to be, *Time* cover or no.

"Don't worry, it won't happen again." I know that's what she wants to hear, so maybe it'll move things along.

"We hope not, Alex. You're a wonderful skater and you know we support you, but there's a certain image our skaters have to project."

Anger boils up in an instant. I've never fit their precious *image*, and if they don't like me the way I am, they can bite me. As I open my mouth to reply, Mrs. C is suddenly there. "Of course, Alex has support. He is defending champion and World bronze medalist. It is partly because of him United States sends three men to Olympics. As you say, he is wonderful skater."

Sue smiles, since there's nothing much else she can do in this situation. "Yes, of course! We all want the same thing here. To show the world the very best in American figure skating."

I nod and smile and let Mrs. C do the rest of the talking. Sue wishes me luck in the long program, and Mrs. C and I go backstage. "Thanks for coming to my rescue."

She gives me a sideways look. "Remember politics. In skating, it is as important as what is on ice. Sometimes more. Always has been this way. Always will."

I nod. It sucks, but I have to play the game.

MY COMPETITION SMILE is about to crack my face when I take the ice for my long program. I'm last, and I can tell by the electric atmosphere and Tanner's high marks that he did very, very well. I try to put it out of my mind, but I'm light-headed and nauseous.

It should help my nerves that I'm leaving out the quad Salchow tonight and doing a triple. The quad isn't consistent enough, and if I miss it, it could destroy the rest of the program. Mrs. C has decided the risk isn't worth it, and as much as I want to argue—as much as I want to make that damn jump my bitch—the smart move is to skate clean and go for the grade of execution and component scores.

Breathing in and out slowly, I take my time before hitting my starting position. *You can do this. Prove them all wrong.*

And I totally do! I do it!

I'm utterly in control, all my transitions between elements flowing smoothly as I interpret the soaring music and hit my lines. I don't have to force the jumps, and there's only one little glitch when I have to put my hand down on my triple flip, but that's a tiny deduction. As Pavarotti finishes on a high note, I pump my fist in the air, the audience standing, applause deafening.

When my scores appear, I leap up in the Kiss and Cry, shouting for joy. By the tiniest of margins, I'm the winner. I'm the motherfucking winner!

The crowd cheers, and I soak up this moment of victory. Mrs. C is smiling a real smile and holy shit, I won. I was brilliant. If I do say so myself, which I do. I was freaking *brilliant*! I can't believe this is actually happening.

Now I just need to do it again in Salzburg—with the quad Sal.

Some of my joy fizzles, stress creeping back in like fishing hooks in my gut. I give myself a mental shake and wave to the crowd. *Enjoy the moment. Don't think about the future.*

Backstage, Mrs. C gives me my cell phone out of her purse and I hit Matt's number. He answers right away. "Congratulations!"

"Were you watching?"

"Of course! Alex, you were incredible! I'm so proud of you."

"I wish you were here!" The urge to hug and kiss him and feel his arms around me overwhelms.

"Me too, but I'll see you soon. Go celebrate. I've got to get to the arena."

"Okay. You can do it! You're going to do it!"

Matt says goodbye and I grip my buzzing phone, texts flooding in as Sue Stabler and the other Federation officials come over to congratulate me. To their credit, they seem genuine in their praise.

"That was a classic final! One to remember," Sue gushes.

I thank her and shake one hand after another, and it's all a blur of activity as we get ready for the medal ceremony. Zach Doyle is the bronze medalist, and he and Tanner congratulate me as I congratulate them right back. Tanner is a gracious loser, I'll give him that, his perfect smile in place. But goddamn, it feels amazing to beat Golden Boy.

I did it.

Resting my hand on my chest, I rub my fingers under my right collarbone where the Olympic rings tattoo will go. This is the last step closer to winning gold. I'll be in Salzburg in weeks. I can do it. I'm going to do it.

I practically skip my way back to the dressing room, smiling and thanking the well-wishers I meet. Two-time US National Champion Alexander Grady! Olympic team member! It has a pretty damn great ring to it.

The Feds haven't officially announced who'll make the team yet, but it's usually always the top three or two, depending on the number of spots. There have been a couple of controversial exceptions, but I think Tanner and Zach are a lock. As the winner, I'm guaranteed my spot. I'm going to the Olympics! I made it!

The door to the empty dressing room has barely shut when I hear a muffled voice from the bathroom. I don't pay attention at first, but as I'm unlacing my skates and butt dancing on the bench, I realize it's Tanner.

In my socks, I tiptoe closer to the bathroom. I shouldn't eavesdrop, but the temptation is too strong. Tanner must be *pissed* that I beat him two years in a row. Ha! In your face, Nielsen.

His voice trembles. "I tried my best, Dad." He sniffles. "I'm sorry."

I freeze just beyond the wide entrance to the bathroom, which doesn't have a door. Tanner must be in one of the stalls.

Crying.

"Do you have to fly out tonight? I've barely seen you. Did you already leave for the airport?"

Whoa. His dad's taking off? That's harsh. Really harsh. I mean, I only beat Tanner by two points. It's not as if he didn't make the team. He's still going to the Olympics, and he's still a favorite to win.

"Sure. I understand." Tanner sniffs again, and his voice thickens. "I wanted to make you proud." There's another pause. "I'm not crying. I'm not!" More silence, and I hold my breath, afraid to move. "I promise, I won't let you down in Salzburg." A pause. "Dad? Are you there?"

Then there's only a quiet sob. His dad actually hung up on him. I think of my parents and sister outside waiting to take me out to celebrate. I never thought it would happen, but fuck, I feel sorry for Tanner Nielsen. I guess no matter how perfect someone else's life looks, things aren't always the way they seem.

Which, *duh*, shouldn't really be a revelation, but standing there in my socks in the dressing room at Nationals, inching away so Tanner won't know I was listening, it is. The Golden Boy is human.

I manage to creep to a bench before Tanner walks out. When he sees me, he stops dead in his tracks. His eyes are red, and his blue and black costume is half unbuttoned, hanging off him haphazardly.

"Hey, man." I smile, and I really hope it doesn't seem fake, because I don't mean it to be. "Great competition." Of course, we already said all this and shook hands on the podium, and smiled and congratulated each other as lightbulbs flashed, but this time I really mean it. It's like I'm suddenly looking at him with new eyes. "It's going to be hardcore in Austria."

Tanner assesses me for a moment, like he's trying to figure out if I'm for real or being a dickhead. I guess he decides I'm sincere, and he smiles back shakily. "Yeah, it'll be off the hook." Then he laughs, and it sounds real. "Do people still say that?"

I laugh too. "I have no idea. But it is *totally* going to be off the hook. Yo. We're going to keep it 100." I frown. "Are people still saying that? We spend too much time in ice rinks to keep current."

Tanner extends his fist. "Team USA."

"Team USA all the way." I bump his fist with mine and for the first time, I'm kind of sad they abolished the team event after Sochi. It wouldn't be so bad to be competing *with* Tanner instead of against him.

As he peels the rest of his costume off in silence, he coughs to cover the fact that he's still sniffling. I can't imagine having my father treat me like that. I always knew Mr. Nielsen was tough, but damn. Thank God my parents don't put that kind of pressure on me.

Zach bursts into the room, all smiles and excitement. It's infectious, and before long we're all talking eagerly about what it'll be like at the Olympics. This will be Zach's very first big international competition, and I envy him going into it with no pressure. Sure, he'll put pressure on himself, but no one expects him to even crack the top ten. It's a different world when you've never won a major title.

"I can't believe I'm going to the Olympics!" Zach grins, bursting with joy.

After all the hard work I've done, I know I deserve this, but I can't quite believe I'm going either.

As I'm leaving the arena, tendrils of worry curl through my mind, dissipating the euphoria. Even though the big stuff is paid for, how are my parents going to afford to come to Austria? There's food and transportation and all the incidental costs while traveling that add up so fast. How did they even afford to come to Nationals? I should have thought about it before and told them to stay home, but I was too wrapped up in myself.

I find them outside, and after a round of hugs and kisses, we hail a cab back to the hotel. In the back seat between Rachel and my mom, I go over figures in my head.

"Hello, you're supposed to be *happy* now." Rachel elbows me in the ribs.

"Huh? I am. Ow, stop that."

"Then what are you moping about?"

"I'm not moping!"

Mom shoots me a skeptical glance. "You seem awfully quiet, honey. What's wrong?"

"It's just… Look, if you can't come to Austria after all, I won't be upset."

"*What?* We're not going?" Rachel screeches.

"Of course we're going!" Dad pipes up from the front seat. "Alex, don't be silly. We paid for the tickets a long time ago. The hotel and flight too. You know that. We're doing fine, son. You don't need to worry about it."

"But—"

"No ifs, ands, or buts!" Mom kisses my cheek. "We are going to watch you at the Olympics. You've worked for this your whole life. Wild horses couldn't keep us away! Besides, I got a raise at work and we're doing okay."

"Are you sure?"

"Yes!" My parents reply in unison.

Rachel scowls. "We'd better be going to the Olympics! I've

had to go to enough crappy places to watch you skate."

I laugh. "What, you didn't have a great time in Delaware that one year? Come on."

"Nothing's quite as wonderful as Milwaukee in the dead of winter."

Mom adds, "That was my personal favorite. It was minus twenty and impossible to find cabs."

As we reminisce, I'm feeling better about the money situation, and I remind myself that I won Nationals for the second year in a row, defying the skeptics who thought I'd cave under the pressure. I showed them, and it's an incredible feeling.

I quickly check the online scores from Canadians, but the ice dancers are still on. Now I just need Matt to make the podium so we can share the feeling together.

"OH MY GOD, come on you piece of shit!" I'm about to throw my laptop out the hotel window.

"Language!" My parents scold in unison as Rach rolls her eyes.

We're huddled on the king bed in my parents' room, watching the live stream of the Canadian men. Of course the fucking feed freezes with a minute left to go in Matt's program. He landed his quad toe. He landed his two triple Axels. There was a sloppy landing on his Lutz, although not disastrous. But with only one quad, he needs to be next to perfect.

There's one more major jump in his program, a triple Sal, and then a double Axel before his final spin as Coldplay's "Fix You" crescendos and then eases to a gentle finish. But we're not seeing any of this because the screen is frozen with an image of Matt going into his flying camel, his face screwed up and limbs extended.

His black costume with silver threading and accents looks

perfect on his tall frame, and now if the FEED WOULD JUST FUCKING START AGAIN—

With a stutter, it does, right as Matt is in his final spin. One of the commentators says, "Enough," and oh my God, what was the rest of that sentence? Will it be enough? It was more than enough?? *Aaaaaaah!*

The crowd's roaring and leaping up, and as Matt hits his final pose, standing with one arm extended out and a pensive, emotional expression, I have to think the rest of the program went well. *Please, God. Please!*

Then Matt breaks into a massive grin, and he might cry, but clearly in a good way. "Oh my God. It looks good. I think he did it." I'm talking mostly to myself, but my family chime in that they think so too.

The ice is littered with flowers and toys, and the camera pans to Mylene and her parents in the audience, and they're all crying, and fuck, my eyes are burning, and I can't breathe, and we need the scores already!

Chantal is a wreck as she hauls Matt into a hug, and the replays start. Slo-mo has never seemed so slow as we watch Matt's jumps. He's got the rotations, and I think everything in the last minute was clean too, and I'm digging my fingernails into my palms so hard I'm going to draw blood.

"Come on, come on, come on," I mutter.

"Now you know how we feel." Mom squeezes my shoulder.

Matt and Chantal are on the bench now, and Matt looks into the camera. "Hi everyone at home! Miss you all, thank you for everything. Hey baby! So proud of you today!"

The flood of heat to my cheeks might make my head pop clean off my neck as my family "Awww!" in unison, even Dad. I wonder who Matt's parents will think he's talking to? They're there in Vancouver, so maybe he's banking on them not watching the broadcast later. Or maybe he'll lie and say it's some girl.

My skin itches with a prickly shiver of hurt. If I really mean something to Matt, how can he keep me a secret from his family? It's not like he's estranged from them. He *lives* with them. He sees them every day. And I know it's about his own issues, but...

The scores come in, and I push everything else away, shoving it down deep. My brain's trying to process the numbers and holy shit! He did it! He's second overall with one more skater to come! He's on the podium!

The ordinals come up in the arena, and it erupts. Matt and Chantal leap and hug again, and Matt stands there in shock with his hands in his hair and mouth open.

We're going to the Olympics.

CHAPTER SIXTEEN

WHEN I GET back to Toronto, Matt picks me up at the airport in his little beat-up Ford. He's waiting outside baggage claim holding up a sign that reads, *Two-time US National Figure Skating Champion Alex Grady*. Every time I'm reminded, a thrill of delight whips through me.

Before I can worry about anyone filming us with their phones, I plant a big kiss on him. "Hey, Canadian National Figure Skating Bronze Medalist Matt Savelli. How's it hanging?"

He laughs and murmurs, "Aside from my blue balls, pretty fantastic."

We kiss again and hug, and the people around us don't blink an eye, which is one of the great things about Toronto. I've seen guys holding hands in the Eaton Centre, the big mall downtown, and no one cares. And if they do, they keep their traps shut.

Mrs. C is behind me, and Matt greets her and offers a ride, but she politely declines, leaving to hail a taxi. I'm guessing she's seen Matt's crappy car in the arena parking lot, and she's going farther north anyway.

Matt stuffs my bags in his trunk and before long we're on Highway 427 heading south and then into Toronto on the Gardiner Expressway. I demand to know where we're going, but Matt won't tell. Going with the flow, I sit back and enjoy the ride, reaching over to rub his thigh, just happy to touch him and have him near.

He exits into the downtown core on Yonge Street, and after paying too much for parking, soon we're sitting in a cozy booth at a wood-paneled Italian restaurant on Front Street, sharing all the details from our competitions.

The food is amazing, and I go crazy on the carbs just this once since we're celebrating. Although we have to be up early, so we don't drink any wine. I treat myself to a Coke instead, and Matt cracks me up by doing an imitation of what Mrs. C's expression would be if she could see me drinking sugar water.

Matt twirls spaghetti on his fork. "We're going to the Olympics! The *Olympics*!" He grins. "It's incredible that we're going to get to take part in something that so few people do. It's going to be so much fun."

"Fun?" I snort. "Sure, *after* I've won. It'll be fun having that gold medal around my neck."

"But it's the whole experience." His smile falters. "Alex, only one man gets that medal every four years. You know the odds, right?"

The buttered bread I wolfed down suddenly feels like it's jammed in my digestive tract. "You don't think I can win?"

"I'm not saying that." He reaches across the table and squeezes my hand. "Just that you never know what's going to happen. What if you don't win? You have to be ready for that."

Pulling my hand away, I gulp some Coke, my blood running cold. "Failure is not an option." I have to believe I can do it. I've worked my whole life for this. To compete. To *win*. And winning the Olympics is the ultimate. I need to do it."

Matt smiles. "Come on, relax."

"Don't tell me to relax," I snap. "It drives me crazy when people do that."

His smile is strained now. "Okay. But we're supposed to enjoy this, remember? It's about the journey. The Olympics are only one competition."

"Uh-huh. You're right." I know that's what he wants to hear, even if I don't believe it. "Sorry."

"Don't be sorry. I worry about you." He reaches for my hand again, and I let him thread our fingers together. It feels safe and warm and good, and I shove away my fears and let myself return his smile and forget about everything else, just for a little while.

After dinner, we drive to my apartment, and my hand goes higher on Matt's thigh. I can't wait to get him into bed. When he touches me and I touch him, my mind turns off and I can just be.

He bats me away playfully. "We're almost there. We won't go to the Olympics if we die in a fiery wreck." He puts on an announcer baritone. "Remember, distracted driving kills." Dropping the low voice, he smiles slyly. "And you, Alex Grady, are a huge distraction."

He's only joking, but the word "distraction" pinballs in my brain, rattling around. My blood pressure rises with each mile as I think about how much work is still left to do before Salzburg, and that we really shouldn't be distracted by anything.

This is the most important competition of our *lives*.

The pasta, bread, and Coke—and fuck me, why did I have that cheesecake?—sit like lead in my gut as Matt pulls into guest parking at my building. My quad Sal is still not consistent enough. Pulse thundering, I squint at the time on the radio display. Maybe I can bribe the janitor to let me into the rink. I need to practice. God, why aren't I practicing?

"Alex?"

Breathing hard, I whip my head toward Matt. The car's off, and he's watching me with obvious concern, his brow deeply creased. I croak, "Huh?"

He reaches out and strokes a hand over my head as I sit rigid. "What happened? Where did you go?"

"Going to the Olympics. I'm not ready." An iron band constricts my chest. "Need to focus. There's so much to do!"

"Hey, it's okay. Breathe, baby." He leans over and draws me close, but I slap his hands away and jab at the seatbelt release. I trip out of the car onto the frozen ground, ice and pebbles stinging my bare palms, the razor-sharp, subzero air grating my throat and lungs.

I shove to my feet, breath coming in rapid plumes in front of my face as Matt rounds the car. "What are we doing? We need to be focused on skating! There's no time! We're going to Europe in two weeks! The Games start in three! There's so much to do."

"Shhh, it's okay." Matt reaches for me, but I stumble back. He holds up his hands. "Alex, it's okay. Let's go upstairs. Everything's fine."

"No. Need to sleep! Sex can wait." Shivering, I hug my lurching stomach.

"I just mean let's get inside where it's warm." He steps closer. "You're panicking. It's okay."

"But it's not!" My lungs won't inflate, and pain stabs my sternum. "We should have gone straight home from the airport. Should have eaten lean protein and whole grains, and done my stretches and already be sleeping."

Matt shakes his head. "It's *one* night. We're fine! You just defended your title, and I made the Olympic team. We did it, even though we've been seeing each other for months. We're allowed to have one night off."

"No!" My hands fly through the air, my heart about to explode. "We're distracting each other! This is an Olympic season. There's so much still to do."

He jolts a little, his face creasing. "Alex, you're not a *distraction*. Don't you know how important you are to me?"

"I don't know? Do I?" My hands flail. "Where were you going to tell your parents you're sleeping tonight?"

Shrugging with a tense jerk of his shoulders, his gaze drops. "A friend's place."

"Right. Because you're ashamed of me." *Lungs won't work. Throat closing. Going to die.*

"Breathe!" He takes hold of my shoulders, and I'm able to gasp in some air, my head spinning and pounding like a steel drum. "I'm not ashamed of you! I want to tell my parents, I do. But this isn't the right time. They're so happy after Nationals, and I don't want to ruin that. Not before the Olympics. You want to talk distractions? Coming out to my parents now would be a massive one. I need to focus on training."

"Right!" I push his hands away and pace, almost slipping on an icy patch of concrete, old snow crunching under my sneakers. "Okay, I get that. I understand you don't want to tell them now. We need to focus on training, absolutely. That's what I'm saying! That's why I can't land the Sal consistently. I should be able to by now. I should have it."

"Taking a break for one night isn't going to make the difference. Quad Sal is a hard jump. There are plenty of guys who can't land it. I can't even come close!"

"You're a *pairs* skater. Of course you can't land it!"

His spine straightens, and he blows out a long, white breath in the frigid air. "I know you're upset and panicking right now. But you're getting worked up over nothing."

"*Nothing*? It's the Olympic gold medal! I should be ready, and I'm not. I wasn't ready at Nationals. I had to take out the quad!"

"You still won, remember?"

"So what? So I won Nationals! All that means is more expectations on me going into the Olympics."

Matt shakes his head. "Alex, you're putting these expectations on yourself."

I bark out a laugh, bitter and nasty. "Easy for you to say. No one expects you to do *anything*."

"That's not true." He clenches his jaw.

"Of course it is! Everyone knows you don't have a prayer of medaling unless half the field is assassinated before the long program. No one expects anything from you—you're the feel-good media story. A great press angle for the team." The words are bursting out of my mouth like machine gun fire, and I don't even know what I'm saying.

"So you think that's why I made it? Because it's a good story? I worked my *ass* off to make that team. I got that spot fair and square."

"I know you did! But everyone still feels sorry for you for dropping Mylene."

Eyes widening, he jerks back like I slapped him, and when he speaks again, it's eerily calm. "You know what? You're right. This obviously isn't working out. We should stick to training. Focus on ourselves. You're an expert at that."

He marches around to the trunk and yanks out my suitcase, throwing it on the ground, where it totters on its wheels. I reach for it automatically, and then Matt's already in the car with a slam, and the engine guns as I try to make it to the surface of the anger and panic boiling over.

Wait, what just happened? What did I say? Fuck, I need to fix this! I cry out, "Matt!" but his taillights are already zooming away, accusing red eyes in the night. Then I'm alone, and it's exactly what I deserve.

MATT'S ALREADY ON the ice when I arrive the next day, and he steadfastly ignores my presence. Instead of water, I'm drinking my second coffee of the morning, even though I know Mrs. C does not approve. If she doesn't stop giving me the stink eye, I'm going to get a can of Coke, and we'll see how she fucking likes that.

I tossed and turned most of the night, replaying the argument in my head and wincing at the terrible things I said. I don't know why I panicked that hard, or how everything spiraled out of control so quickly.

How did I ruin everything in a blink?

I run through chunks of my programs in a haze, wishing I could wake up from this surreal nightmare. Because I think we broke up. I think that's a thing that happened. Just like that, I don't have a boyfriend anymore, and he's *right here* but miles away.

I ache to apologize, but every time we're close on the rink, he skates off in the other direction. I can't blame him after what I said about dropping Mylene. Why the fuck did I say that?

When his morning session is over, I wait for him at the exit in the boards, since it's the only way he can get off the ice without clambering over. As soon as he gets near, I say, "Look, I'm an asshole."

Matt gives me a long stare. "Yeah. Sometimes you really are." He tries to brush past me, ripping his arm away when I touch it.

"Can you give me a chance to explain?"

"No. No, I can't. You know how much it kills me that Mylene got hurt because of me. You *know*."

Shame corkscrews through me, and I hate myself. "It wasn't your fault. I didn't mean it to sound like that." I don't know how to apologize for this. I don't know how to fix it.

His eyes shine with hurt, but he speaks coolly. "When I first met you, I thought you were an egotistical jerk who always put himself first. I guess I was right after all."

Now it's my turn to be hurt, and my voice sounds pathetically small. "You know there's more to me than that. Don't you?"

"I thought I did. But I think we should take a break. Focus on the Olympics with no distractions. That's what you want anyway." He slaps on his skate guards and clomps out.

I face the ice in time to see everyone's heads snap away, pretending they weren't watching. After a few strokes to gain speed, I spin in place as fast as I can, making the world a blur, my guts feeling like a bloody, shredded mess.

Getting what I want has never ripped out my soul like this.

CHAPTER SEVENTEEN

T HIS IS IT. I'm finally here.

The Olympic Games.

I mean, I've been at the Olympic Games for days, but this is the day. *My* day. Okay, the short program is tomorrow, but we're doing the draw. I'm weirdly nervous as I walk into the plain room where it's taking place. It looks like any hotel conference room, with chairs and a main table at the front.

But this isn't just any conference room. This is the *Olympics*. Like most people, I've watched the Games on TV since I was a kid. *Unlike* most people, I knew one day I'd be here. That it would be me walking behind the Stars and Stripes into the stadium, waving to the crowd, wearing a matching team jacket and hat that I hoped wouldn't be too ugly.

I didn't expect to be vainly searching the crowd of Canadian athletes when the USA walked by them, desperate for a glimpse of my ex-boyfriend, dying to see his face again after more than a week since leaving Toronto.

Now, despite the cheers and fireworks and spectacle of the Opening Ceremonies, so loud and bright and *huge*, it hits me much harder that *I'm at the Olympics*. I've done about a million draws for order of skate in my life, in boring rooms like this all over the world.

Yet the number I draw in *this* boring room will play a role in my destiny. My fate. My future. My *everything.* Scanning the room, I recognize skaters I've competed against for years. Skaters I've toured with in the summers between seasons. Skaters who—

My heart lurches into my throat. A skater who was my boyfriend until recently.

Matt's sitting with one of the other Canadian guys, and I can only see the back of his head, but I know it's him in an instant. He laughs at something, and pain and resentment needle my spine. Clearly he's doing just fine without me.

We trained in the arena for weeks, ignoring each other, and there's no reason why it should be any different here. Still, I long to go over and wish him luck. I really want him to skate well. He should be so incredibly proud of himself for getting here, and I hope he can enjoy every second. I hope he has the fun I can't.

There are too many people around, though. It would be awkward, especially if he ignores me. I don't think I could take that. Ugh, here I go again, worrying about Matt instead of focusing on the whole reason I'm here. Clearly it's a good thing we're not together, because I need to get my priorities in order.

Determined, I turn away and plop down on the first available chair, safe on the other side of the room. At least Canada and the US are on different practice sessions, so I've been able to train without distraction. I can't think about Matt anymore.

Focus, focus, focus.

Kenny sits beside me, jiggling his foot nervously, and Hiro Kurosawa sits on Kenny's other side, saying something in Japanese. Tanner Nielsen's hair gleams out of the corner of my eye, and I see him and Zach Doyle walk in together. Tanner and I might never be best friends or whatever, but after Nationals I don't hate him the way I used to. I still want to beat him. Obviously.

Last and certainly not least, Vladimir Sidorov makes his entrance, all square-jawed and steely-eyed handsomeness, with the other two Russian skaters in tow. They train in Moscow with the same coach, and Vladimir is definitely the favored son. Gregor and Oleg probably have to walk three paces behind at all times and only speak to him when spoken to.

As the officials get everything ready, I take a look around the room. There's a bond you have with your competitors that's hard to describe. The thing with guys like Tanner and Vladimir is that even if we're not best friends, or even really friends at all, they understand me in a way that very few people do. They get what it's like to be under this intense pressure. They get what it is to be an Olympic athlete. How hard you have to work.

My eyes find Matt once more. He laughs again, head close with Chris Montoya, the Canadian champion. It sucker punches me in the solar plexus that after everything we've been through and how close we became, I'm really not sharing this experience with Matt. I have to swallow hard over the lump in my throat.

Focus, focus, focus.

One of the officials calls for attention, and I force my gaze to the front of the room. There's only one thing I need to think about right now: winning.

When they call my name to come up and pick my number, I make sure not to even glance Matt's way. After I get to the front, I smile at the officials and thrust my hand into the bowl. I always pick my number the same way: it's got to be the first piece of paper I touch. If I touch more than one, I go with the piece on the right. Never the left.

My fingers close around a folded slip, and I pull it out and open it.

30

Oh. My. God. I'm the final skater. The stage is set for me to go out there and kill it.

I hand the paper to the woman, who reads it out to the room.

There's a smattering of applause, and I smile. "Saving the best for last."

Most people laugh, and on my way back to my seat, I glance at Matt before I can stop myself. A tiny smile tugs at his mouth, but he isn't looking my way.

OF COURSE GOING last means you have all damn day to freak the fuck out.

I don't get to the rink until more than an hour after the event starts, and even then I still have what seems like forever to wait. Mrs. C tells me things I already know. I listen and nod, glad of the distraction.

The rest of the time, I have my earbuds jammed in my ears, trying to ignore all the other scores. I don't want to know how anyone else does, and I don't want to know who's winning. About twenty minutes before my time, I spot Matt on his way to the dressing room. He doesn't seem to notice me tucked away into the corner, and even though I want to chase after him, I stay put. Although I guess I do want to know how *one* skater did after all.

I can't tell anything from his body language because Matt's so unruffled most of the time. He could have the best short program of his life or the worst, and he'd probably just smile peacefully and act the same way. The only time I've seen him come undone was in Philadelphia after the accident and when he made the team at Canadian Nationals.

I quickly shut down thoughts of Matt by closing my eyes and turning up the volume on Eminem. I imagine my short program, and how amazingly I'm going to skate it. How I'm going to be in first, and how I'm going to win gold in two days.

The warm-up isn't great, but it isn't a disaster either. I go down on my trusty triple Axel, but try another one near the end of the six minutes that I land beautifully. The crowd applauds in appreciation.

Now that I'm all warmed up, I get to hurry up and wait. Mrs. C sits silent and still in a chair as I pace around, singing along in my head to my playlist, eyes on the ground, resisting the urge to fiddle with the hooks closing my gray costume pants. I zip up my team jacket over my dark purple sweater vest, then take it off again.

Finally it's my turn.

The Finnish skater on the ice will be lucky to even qualify for the long program, so I don't care about hearing his marks. I make sure not to look when the leader board is shown, instead keeping my eyes on Mrs. C, who tells me to remember my training and pretend we're at home.

The thing is, I can tell myself that all I want, but I'm at the freaking *Olympics*. I'm standing on *Olympic* ice. The arena is huge and filled to capacity. It's all so much bigger than I'm used to. The crowd is raucous and the butterflies flapping in my stomach are freaking birds of prey at this point.

The announcer introduces me, and with a final look at Mrs. C, I glide out to center ice, arms spread as I acknowledge the applause. I skate around for a few seconds, breathing deeply and calming myself before I take my place.

This is it. This is what I've been working for my entire life.

When the music starts, I pour all my focus into what I'm doing. I think through every single movement, never rushing ahead, always keeping in the moment. My triple Axel goes up and it's huge, the landing smooth as silk.

Combination jump is next—quad toe-triple toe. Textbook. Everything feels perfect as I move through the required elements while smiling and playing to the crowd, getting them clapping along with Benny Goodman.

Into my straight-line footwork, going from one end of the rink to the other, twirling and leaping fast and smooth, using my edges and the run of the blade.

Up, down, side, back, kick, turn, up, side...

Suddenly my ass crashes onto the unforgiving ice, the gasp of the audience like a gunshot. I automatically jump up and stroke quickly to catch the music, finishing the footwork at the other end of the rink. I skate backward around the corner, heart thumping against my ribs, blood rushing in my ears as panic sets in, the crowd applauding to support me.

What just happened? What the hell just happened?!?

My body is going through the motions of my program as it has thousands of times in training, and I do the connecting steps into my triple Lutz.

Breathe. Concentrate.

The music builds, and I push off my toe pick and spin in the air. Then I'm landing, flowing out of the jump with my free leg and arms extended beautifully. Everyone roars, and I etch a smile on my face as I step into my final spin.

Crouching low on one leg in my sit spin, my brain finally catches up with my body again and the truth hits me with a fresh swell of nausea. I fell. I fell on my footwork. *I fell on an element in the short program.*

Oh my God. It's gone. The gold is gone.

A sob threatens to tear up through my chest and suffocate me. The music's still playing and I have ten seconds left in this program. I want nothing more than to just stop and run away, but I have to finish.

I lost the gold medal in a split second. It's done.

Through the fog of despair, the audience is clapping, urging me on as I skate into my final pose. The music stops, and I'm down on one knee with a playful expression on my face. At least, it's supposed to be playful. I don't know what my face looks like right now, and I keep telling myself to *smile, smile, smile!*

Everything moves in surreal slow motion as I take my bows to each side of the jam-packed arena. Millions of people around the world are watching as I wave to the crowd. Millions of people watched me trip on my footwork.

This is really happening. I'm not dreaming. I fell in my short program. I'm not going to win gold.

I skate toward the Kiss and Cry, because that's where I have to go. There's no other way off the ice, even though clambering over the boards might be a better option than facing Mrs. C. She might just kill me on live TV.

Inevitably, I reach the end of the rink. Mrs. C is standing there like always, ready to hand me my skate guards. As always, I take them, bend over, and slide them over my blades. Then I stand up, step off the ice, and move my arms around Mrs. C for the obligatory hug/pat.

This time, something really weird happens. Her little arms reach around me and squeeze, holding me so close. It's like she's really *hugging* me.

I cling to her, standing in the doorway to the Olympic ice, where I just destroyed my dreams. Mrs. C rubs my back and I grip her as tears threaten. We've got to go sit in front of the cameras and the whole freaking *world* to get my marks, and she holds my hand the whole time we walk over.

"How did this happen?" I can hear the question come out of my mouth, but the words sound very far away. I think I'm having an out-of-body experience without dying. Or maybe I am dying. I'm not sure it could feel worse.

"You didn't give up." Mrs. C pats my knee as we sit.

I stare at her, stunned. "I fell on an element. I lost all my GOE on it, and the base mark is going to be screwed."

"Yes. There was probably rut in ice. This happens, Alexander. Most important is that you didn't give up. You landed Lutz. You had good spins. Good expression."

"I did?" I honestly can't even remember, even though it's only been minutes. The replays are on the monitor in front of us, and my chest tightens as I watch how perfect my jumps were.

"Fall was bad luck."

"You're not mad?" I blurt, even though everyone can hear. Seriously, this has *got* to be a dream.

Mrs. C peers at me sincerely. "You work hard. You are good student. It's okay."

My heart leaps. Maybe the other guys fucked up too. If everyone had a bad day, I might still be okay. I might still be in contention.

The announcer comes on. "The scores please for Alexander Grady of the United States of America."

I'm going to explode, my heart thumping out of control. Do I still have a chance?

"The short program score please." Another pause, and I grip Mrs. C's hand. "He's earned 90.47 points in the short program."

Oh my God, it's not that bad. What matters now is how everyone else skated. If it was a shitty night...

My heart sinks as I squint at my placement, the announcer saying it in his smooth baritone: "He is currently in sixth place."

Sixth place.

Any lingering hope crashes and burns. I'm done. Vladimir is in first, Tanner in striking distance in second. Kenny's in fourth. I quickly scan the list and find Matt's name. Tenth, which is freaking amazing for him in singles. I should feel happy for him, but I don't feel anything at all. It's like I'm watching someone else's life instead of living it.

Vladimir's twelve points ahead of me with his quad toe *and* quad Sal, the son of a bitch. Tanner is eight and a half points up. Hiro Kurosawa's seven. Too many points.

There's a tug on my arm and Mrs. C leads me backstage. I follow obediently, my legs moving as they should. *Left, right, left, right.* Vladimir is on his way out, smiling and laughing, brimming with confidence. He doesn't so much as glance at me as I pass.

I can't believe this. The short program is over. So is my chance of gold. A mistake in the long program can be overcome. Not in the short—not when the field is this strong.

Mrs. C has Kenny to deal with too, and I tell her I'm fine. I tell him that too when he hugs me silently. He had a good skate and still has a legit shot at the podium. I'd need some serious implosions from the five guys ahead of me.

Talking to the media is torture. *Am I disappointed in my performance?* I just fell in the short program at the Olympic Games. Gee, I fucking wonder.

I try to smile and give them the answers they want, like how I'm not giving up and I'm going to have a great long program, and it's not over until it's over. It's all bullshit. I'm talking, but I have no idea what I'm saying, hovering outside my body, watching this all unfold.

Then Sue Stabler is there, and she's talking, her mouth moving, and I can't hear over the rushing in my ears. I can only stare, and Sue reaches for my arm, squeezing lightly.

"It's okay, Alex. Good job keeping the program together after the fall. We're proud of you."

I stand there, and I'm either going to burst into tears or just float away into nothing.

Her face softening, Sue pulls me into a hug that smells of citrus flowers. "Skating's a slippery sport, Alex. You did your best."

She's called away, and I watch her go, staring dumbly. Then I walk to the dressing room, because that's what I'm supposed to do next. *Left, right, left, right.*

Rachel and my parents are waiting outside the arena. They take turns hugging me and telling me it's okay. I wish it was true, but there's no way it can be. I ruined everything. All those years of work. All my parents' money. All my dreams. I should be a sobbing mess, but I'm empty. There's nothing here anymore.

A shuttle bus is leaving for the Athlete's Village, so I use it as an excuse to escape my family's kind eyes and sympathetic smiles. I put in my earbuds and stare out the window, lights and old brick buildings blending together, snow drifting down. My phone's off in my pocket. I can't deal with messages.

This can't be happening. All these years. All my dreams. It can't be over, just like that.

It's not fair.

A sudden scream claws at my throat, and I race off the bus to my little dorm room in the village with hotel art and a big window. My roommate Sam takes one look at my face as I burst in the door and grabs his coat. He clasps my shoulder sympathetically on the way out.

I drop my bag and sit on my single bed, my team USA coat still on. Then the tears finally come. There's this old saying in skating: You can't win it in the short program, but you can lose it. Well, I sure proved that true tonight.

CHAPTER EIGHTEEN

BLINKING, I SIT up in bed in the dark in my clothes, trying to remember where I am and what time it is and—

I remember.

My stomach clenches as the reality hits me all over again. No gold medal. I'm not going to win. I cried myself to sleep, which is all kinds of pathetic, but it was all I could do.

How can I go on? How am I supposed to get up tomorrow and get dressed and go to practice? I'm hollow, like someone's scooped out my insides.

There's a knock at the door that's more like a scratch. Poor Sam probably wants to get back in the room, although this morning he was talking about hooking up with some Swedish skier. She does that weird cross-country event where they stop and shoot targets.

He knocks a bit louder, and I call out, "It's okay, you can come in."

There's a pause before the door opens, and when I look up, Matt's there, backlit from the hallway. I stare at him, and then I have to turn my head, because I'm crying all over again. The door closes and the bed dips, and his arms pull me close in the faint white light of the moon. Even though I'm ashamed for so many reasons, I turn to him and let him hold me.

Matt makes reassuring little shushing noises, and I bury my

face in his neck as he hugs me tightly and tells me to let it out. I'm amazed there's anything left, and I try to breathe until the tears stop, inhaling Matt's vaguely minty, reassuring scent. Sniffing, I lift my head so I'm not snotting all over him.

He brushes my hair back and swipes the wetness from my cheeks with his thumb. We're staring at each other, and the only sound is my sniffing and heavy breathing. He's so close, and looking at me so tenderly, and the need to kiss him overwhelms.

At first it's just nice and slow, our tongues winding together. I'd say I'd forgotten how good it was to kiss him, but the truth is I wouldn't let myself think about it. I'd only thought about—

A pulse of grief expands in my chest, and I cling to him tighter, kissing him hard, my fingers in his hair. He tugs at my team coat, and I shake it off, tossing it wherever. My sweatshirt follows, and then his hands are on my skin, peeling my T-shirt over my head.

I do the same for him, and as his shirt sails onto the floor, I see the black necklace against his pale chest and the dark hair scattered there. Reaching up, I rub the worry stone, amazed that he's still wearing my gift after what a jackass I've been. Our eyes meet, and I know without a doubt that this is more important than any piece of metal I could win on the ice.

"I'm such a fucking idiot. I'm sorry, Matt. I'm so sorry." Tears burn my puffy eyes again. "Can you forgive me?"

"Of course. Shh, it's okay. I'm sorry too. I shouldn't have held a grudge. I know you didn't mean it about the accident. And you're right, I need to tell my parents. I'm not ashamed of you. I'm so proud of you. The way you kept going tonight? I couldn't be prouder."

"But I blew it."

Matt smiles sadly. "Sometimes you just catch an edge."

I recognize my own words, and images of Skate America and Matt covered in his best friend's blood fill my mind. I know I'm lucky in comparison, and this isn't the end of the world even if it feels like it. "I wish it didn't fucking suck so hard."

"Me too, baby." He presses kisses all over my face. "I wish I could fix it."

I lunge at his mouth, holding his face in my hands as I kiss the hell out of him. Gasping, I mutter, "Need you. Need to feel you. Fill me up." *Make me whole, at least for right now.*

Nodding, he digs in his wallet as I strip off the rest of my clothes. When we're both naked, the covers kicked aside, he presses me back on the too-narrow bed and kisses all over my body, my nipples tingling as he sucks them one after the other.

I'm moaning too loudly, but I don't care. All that matters is Matt's hands on me, his hot breath on my skin, his mouth on my cock.

When he pushes inside me, my legs up over his shoulders, he kisses me tenderly, our eyes locked together in the moonlight. It burns as he stretches and fills me perfectly, so deep I swear he's touching my broken heart, making it whole again.

"I love you so much." The words escape my lips in little puffs, and I imagine I can see them hanging there between us like hot breath clouding in a cold rink.

Rocking his hips, buried all the way inside me, Matt cups my cheek. "I love you too." Tears glisten in his beautiful brown eyes, and he kisses me deeply, moaning into my mouth.

There's no more talking after that, just our grunts and cries and groans as Matt fucks me hard. I dig my fingers into his broad back, letting everything go as he thrusts, sweat on our skin, messy kisses on our lips.

My orgasm slams through me as Matt reaches between us and strokes my leaking dick, and I bang my heels on his back, gasping, all the pain wiped away clean. I know it'll be back, but for now, all I care about is Matt and seeing his face when he comes.

"That's it. Fill me up," I murmur, even though he's wearing a condom. As he shudders and goes over the edge, his mouth open on a cry of ecstasy, I squeeze his cock with my ass. "Never going to let you go again."

Matt collapses on me, my splayed legs thumping down to the mattress. Pressing wet, breathy kisses to my neck, he whispers, "You're stuck with me now."

After cleaning us up, he squeezes beside me on the single bed, our legs tangled, heads close together on the pillow. I trace circles on Matt's chest and caress the worry stone. "You're still wearing it."

"Figured it might come in handy."

God, I'm so lucky to have met him. So lucky that he actually likes *me*. "This is the best worst day of my life."

A laugh rumbles up from Matt's chest, and he kisses me again. "Silver lining, at your service." He traces my lips with his fingertip. "I know what you mean. As glad as I am to be here with you, I'm sorry it had to happen this way."

Stark reality returns with a vengeance, and I burrow closer into his warmth. "I can't believe it. All those years of training. How could I fall on my footwork?"

"Sometimes you just catch an edge."

Our lips meet again, bodies pressing together as we shift closer. Right now, I don't want to think about anything else but Matt, kissing and holding me. The Olympics will still be here in the morning.

THE OLYMPICS ARE *definitely* still here in the morning. I blink awake, my arm numb from being trapped beneath Matt. I glance at the other bed, but Sam must have gotten lucky with his skier.

Then my brain replays everything from yesterday in fast forward—the fall and getting my marks, being sixth. I wait for the sick, gut-wrenching sinking sensation to hit me. It does, but after a few deep breaths, it fades.

I don't know how, but it's okay. I think I'm okay.

Matt's still asleep, his lips parted slightly, face utterly peaceful. I manage to slide my arm out without waking him, and I grin like an idiot. I can't believe I got him back. I can't believe he wants to be with me. I must admit, this really, really helps with the being okay. After a while, I contemplate the ceiling.

So.

Here I am, the day after I screwed up my Olympic short program. The world has kept on turning, even though I'm not going to be the gold medalist in Salzburg. I wait again to feel the terrible sense of loss I did last night—for tears to well in my eyes, sobs to choke me. But a weird thing happens.

I don't feel that bad. In fact, I almost feel *good*. Relieved that the pressure's off.

I'm not going to win. At least, not at this Olympics. The next Games are in Annecy, France, and I'll still only be twenty-four. Plenty young enough. I'm going to keep training.

It's not over. What would I even do if I didn't skate? That's the thought that sparks panic, and I inhale deeply. I still have skating. No matter what happens with the judges and the scores and the medals, I still have my blades and the ice.

I still have *me*.

Worlds are in three weeks, and I'm going to work my ass off to prepare. But one step at a time.

Normally, I'd be feeling sick about my quad Salchow right about now. Visualizing landing it perfectly, mentally preparing for practice. But you know what? It needs more work. I need more time with it. So I'm not going to do it tomorrow. I'm not going to torture myself and my body. I'm going to be the best skater I can be, even if I can't land that one jump.

Yet.

Because I'm going to master the damn quad Sal. Then maybe I'll go for the Lutz or flip. Or even the Axel. Ha! I try to swallow a burst of laughter. Okay, no need to get carried away with the quad Axel fantasies, but I'm going to keep training my ass off regardless.

"Alex?" Matt raises his head, blinking blearily, hair standing up. "It's okay, sweetheart." He draws me close before doing a double take. "Wait. You're smiling."

I brush his cheek. "Morning."

Matt smiles back, and warmth expands in my chest, ready to break my ribs. "No regrets?"

"Huh?" Eloquent as ever.

"You were really upset last night, and you needed comfort. Now in the light of day… You haven't changed your mind about us?"

"About being in love with you? Actually, now that you mention it, eh. I dunno. Sure, you're sweet and caring and gorgeous and—"

He rolls on top of me with a kiss. "Okay, okay. Wait, what am I saying? Go on."

But we're both laughing too hard, and then we're kissing, and I really want to get used to waking up with Matt. We should totally move in together. We can carpool to the rink, and he wouldn't be trapped at home and—

Sucking on his neck and grinding my hips up, I refocus. One step at a time. Then my heart lurches. "Oh my God, I didn't even congratulate you! Fuck, I'm sorry. You did so great! I'm so proud of you. Tell me all about it."

"I will. Later." Licking around my belly button, he heads down…

And of course his phone buzzes. He answers it with a wide grin. "*Salut!*"

I can hear the murmur of Mylene's voice on the other end, but not what she's saying. Matt glances at me, still smiling as he draws a circle on my bare hip. "Yeah. You were right. Yes, it was a good night." There's a pause. "No, I'm not giving you the details!"

Laughing, I say, "Tell Mylene hi, and thank you."

Matt relays the message and listens. "She says you're welcome, and to have fun in the long program."

Fun. There's that concept again. I think about that while Matt finishes his conversation and puts his phone back on the side table.

"Alex?" He strokes my inner thigh, sending a tremor over my skin.

"You know, I don't think I've ever really enjoyed skating in a competition. I mean, I love winning, don't get me wrong. But it's always been work. Not fun."

"It's never too late."

"I guess it isn't."

Matt's fingers trace my spine as he presses his lips to my collarbone. "First time for everything."

Lifting my hand, I touch the strip of skin there. "I guess I can't get my tattoo. Not yet, anyway."

He frowns. "What tattoo?"

"It's so cheesy, but I've always dreamt of getting the Olympic rings right here after I won gold." I rub the empty skin.

"Alex, you're still an Olympian. Get the tattoo! You know how few people actually compete at the Olympic Games? You've earned it, no matter what."

"Huh. I guess I have. Also, have I mentioned I love you?"

He grins, eyes crinkling. "That rings a bell."

Whistling, Sam walks in and freezes in the doorway. He takes one look at us and rolls his eyes with exaggeration. "Geez. Get a room, you two."

We all laugh, and it's so crazy that I'm *laughing*. The world really didn't end.

I TOTALLY FORGET that Rachel and my parents are meeting me outside the Athletes' Village before practice, and I stop in my tracks when I see them. Matt follows my gaze. "Do you want me to go? It's okay if you do."

They haven't noticed us yet, but I don't hesitate. "No. Come meet my family." Smiling, I tug on Matt's red Canadian team jacket.

"Are you sure?" He lags behind. "I understand if you don't want me to meet them. Especially considering my situation. Speaking of which…" He takes a deep breath. "I'm going to tell them. About me. About me and you. All of it. As soon as I get home."

"Yeah?" I can't hide my smile.

He returns it tentatively. "Definitely. I mean, they already know. I know they do. At Christmas, they asked a bunch of questions about you and complimented your skating. My dad said your quad toe combo's perfect. Mylene thinks it was his way of saying he's okay with it. Okay with you. She thinks they're more ready to accept me being gay than I give them credit for." He laughs softly. "And she's usually right."

"Well, she's a very intelligent young lady." I reach for his hand and squeeze. "And no matter what happens, we'll get through it. They must be so proud of your finish here, right?"

He beams. "Yeah, they are. My dad's posts on Facebook are hilarious. Never seen him gush like that." He glances over at my family. "Are you sure I'm not intruding?"

I tug gently. "You're my boyfriend. Trust me, this is going to make their day."

When my mom notices us, her whole face lights up and she practically runs over. "Matthew! So nice to meet you!" She shakes his hand as my dad ruffles my hair and I squirm away, our same little routine as always before Dad pulls me into a tight hug. Then he pumps Matt's fist enthusiastically.

"Hi. Nice to meet you too." Matt smiles nervously.

Rachel clears her throat. "Hello, you're forgetting someone."

I wave my hand in her direction. "Oh yeah, this is my annoying little sister, Rachel."

"Gee, I love you too, Alex." Rachel sticks out her tongue, and I sweep her up into a big hug in retaliation. She squeals and tries half-heartedly to get free.

When I put her down, emotion clogs my throat. Shit, when I think about how much my family has sacrificed for me to pursue my dream, I wish I could give them a medal, and that they could stand on a podium and be applauded by thousands of people. They deserve it as much as I do.

Rachel gives our parents a nervous look. "Alex, are you okay?"

Mom steps in smoothly, rubbing my back. "Honey, if you want to cry, go right on ahead."

"No, no." I exhale a big breath. "I'm good. I am."

My mom peers at me closely. "Are you sure?"

I nod. "I'm okay."

My family looks at me, then at each other and Matt, like they're trying to decide if I'm about to snap. "You're handling this all very well, Alex." My dad's watching me with this odd expression that I can't figure out.

"Seriously, I'm okay. This is one competition. I love skating, and I'm not giving up. It has to be about the journey or whatever. You know? I'm not saying this doesn't suck, but I can't change it. I can only move forward."

Mom stares at me, and then a tear slips down her cheek. Whoa. Totally not the reaction I was going for. "Mom, it's okay, really!" I hug her tightly. "I'm fine."

She sniffles as she pulls back. "I know. I'm just so proud of you."

"Then why are you crying?" I seriously don't get parents sometimes.

Dad kisses her cheek and ruffles my hair. "We're so proud, Alex."

Rachel sighs dramatically. "Can we get breakfast now? I'm starving."

Laughing, we head off to find a restaurant, and here I am on the day after I lost my lifelong dream. It's really not so bad. Maybe I didn't lose it after all. Maybe the dream just evolved.

I'M GETTING CHANGED into my fancy, coordinated practice clothes in the locker room when Kenny walks in. He smiles uncertainly, apparently afraid to get any closer. I chuckle. "I won't bite."

Kenny peers at me with deep concern. "You are okay, Alex?"

"Yeah. I am."

"You missed element in short program," he reminds me gravely.

This makes me laugh. "I know, I was there."

"I thought you would still be very, very upset." He sits beside me.

"I was. I mean, I am, but it's okay. I'm going to be okay."

As he pats my arm, Kenny smiles. "Glad to hear."

"Hey, you're in fourth. Still within reach of the podium. Great job, man."

He bobs his head. "Thank you. You are still in reach too. It's happened before, Alex. Don't give up hope."

Mrs. C will be waiting, so I tell Kenny I'll see him on the ice. It's true that skaters have landed on the podium after being back in the standings, but I'm not holding my breath.

Before I get on the ice, Mrs. C and I go into a quiet corner.

"Ready for practice, Alexander?"

I know this is her way of asking me if I'm okay. "I'm ready. Just one thing, though. I'm not going to do the quad Sal today."

She doesn't say anything, and the silence stretches out. Then she nods, a curt movement of her head. "Focus on rest of program. Make it best ever."

"That's the plan, Mrs. C."

She claps her hands together imperiously. "Enough talking. Get on ice."

I do, and start reeling off triple jumps after a few minutes of warm up. After I go down on my Lutz, I glance over at Mrs. C and don't even need to read her lips to know what she's saying. *Again.*

Back on my feet, I take another lap of the rink and try again.

GOD, I'M NERVOUS.

Matt just skated, and I watched on the monitor backstage. He two-footed his quad and touched down on his Axel, but the rest was strong. We high-five as he passes by, conscious of the cameras on us. He's not out to his folks yet, and endorsements are still a factor. We're not going to hide in a dark closet, but we're not rushing into public declarations yet.

And now I wait for my turn, pacing while Mrs. C stands by the wall, calm as ever. I should listen to my music, but for some reason it's not helping tonight, and I give my iPod to Mrs. C to put in her purse.

The pressure to win is gone, but this is still the freaking Olympics. The world's watching, and I want to skate well. I want to show everyone I'm still a champion.

"You know where my gold medals are?"

I glance at Mrs. C in surprise. Usually she doesn't say anything at these moments in competitions. "On your mantel?"

A tiny smile escapes. "In box under bed."

"Seriously?"

She nods. "Many years of work, and thinking medals were most important thing. They are good things. But not everything."

This is all really deep, and the most personal she's ever been with me. I have no idea what to say. I think about what Maxim told me about how good Mrs. C is to him and Oksana, and I wonder if she talks to them like this.

She goes on. "Victory depends on four and a half minutes on ice. Life cannot." She looks down at her left hand and twists the diamond band on her ring finger. "Life with Boris was more important than medals."

I have no idea what to say. "Um, you must miss him." It's kind of blowing my mind that Mrs. C really does have *feelings*.

"I push you very hard. Do your best now. Be happy."

Extended applause fills the arena, which means the current skater has finished. I hug Mrs. C quickly. "You're the best coach I've ever had. Thank you for everything."

She nods, and we walk to the rink entrance, waiting for the Swiss skater to bow and leave the ice. The ritual begins.

I hand my skate guards to Mrs. C and step on the rink. We look at each other, her on one side of the boards, me on the ice. She hands me a bottle of water, and I take a couple of sips before giving it back.

Deep breath.

Enjoy this.

Have fun.

"Please welcome the next competitor, representing the United States of America: Alexander Grady."

EPILOGUE

"**Y**OUR TOQUE DOESN'T cover enough of your ears," Matt says, stamping his feet to keep warm and moving as we wait for the bus outside the Athletes' Village. The sun is out, but the temperature has plummeted, and I pull my wool hat down further.

"My what?" I love Matt's little Canadianisms. I also love him. And he loves me. Every time I remind myself, joy bursts in my chest like fizzy pop rocks.

"Shut up, you know I mean your hat."

"Eh? What are you talking *aboot*?"

Laughing, he says, "We don't sound like that. Well, maybe sometimes."

"Hey, have you talked to Mylene today? I've got to call her. She left me a really sweet message."

Matt's whole face lights up. "Yeah, I talked to her last night. Didn't I tell you the news?"

"No." I inch closer and leer suggestively. "It must have slipped your mind while we were celebrating."

I wish I could say we celebrated my miraculous podium finish, but alas. While I did lay down a fantastic program, it only brought me up to fourth. So close, but so far. Still, I'm grateful for a clean skate. It was *fun*, and I got a huge standing ovation. Poor Kenny screwed the pooch and ended up twelfth, and I need to text him again to check in this morning.

"Mmm, must have." Matt nudges my shoulder. "Can't imagine why I was distracted."

"Wait, what were you supposed to tell me?"

Matt vibrates so much he nearly levitates right off the snowy sidewalk. "The doctor said she can start training as soon as her arm is fully healed and rehabbed. Her head is totally fine. Should be six more weeks for her arm, and then we're back in business."

"That's awesome!" I can't wait to see Mylene at the rink, and I'm not going to be stupidly jealous like I was last time.

"I can't wait to come here with her. I mean, not *here* to Salzburg, but in four years, Mylene and I are going to the Olympics. Skating singles reminds me of how much I love pairs. I can't wait to have her back with me. We're going to make it next time. I know it."

"You will. We both will."

Just then, someone shouts my name, and I spot Tanner and Lisa coming out of one of the buildings. "Hold on, I'll be right back. Call me if the bus is coming!" I jog over to them.

Lisa practically blinds me with her grin. I can see why she has a toothpaste endorsement. "You guys make a cute couple. You going to the short dance this aft?"

"Nah, we see enough ice dancing. We're going into the city to be tourists."

Tanner glances over at Matt and back at me. "Try not to screw it up this time, dude. We heard it was *frosty* at your rink in Toronto after Nationals."

My hackles automatically rise, but I bite back my knee-jerk response. Tanner's only joking, and besides, I did screw it all up pretty epically. "I'm hoping I can at least wait until after Worlds to cause more drama. Hey, speaking of which, will I see you there, or are you going to rest on your laurels?"

Tanner and Lisa give each other a look and communicate

silently. After a moment, Tanner shrugs. "I guess I can tell you. I'm not going to Worlds. I'm retiring."

Whoa. "Wow. Congrats, I guess?" It's going to be *so* weird not competing against him anymore.

"Thanks." He heaves a happy sigh. "I'm done. I'm so done. I'll tour, and then I'm going to school and spending more time with Lisa." He slings an arm around her, squeezing.

"But aren't you going to miss it? Competing?"

He shakes his head. "I've won Nationals, Worlds, and now Olympics, by the seat of my pants." He lowers his voice. "I should send good ol' Vlad a thank-you note for falling apart."

I whistle. "Seriously. That was like watching a nervous breakdown." I think of Tanner's phone call at Nationals. "Your parents must be so happy, huh?"

His smile's a little strained. "Yeah. They are. I'm just relieved I didn't let them down. I guess part of me will miss it a bit, but I just feel...done. You know? It's been a great career." Tanner slaps me on the shoulder with his mitt. "You really pushed me to be my best, Alex. Thank you. It'll be you wearing gold in four years. I know it."

"From your lips, etc."

"Tenacious little bulldog like you? Oh yeah. You're going to be world champion, and my money's on you in Annecy."

"If you're not careful I might actually start to like you." Oh shit, did I say that out loud? As Tanner and Lisa laugh, I realize I did, and all I can do is laugh along. "You really pushed me too. Thanks, Tanner. And congrats. You earned it."

Matt calls over, and I say goodbye before jogging back. We climb on the bus, heading away from the Olympic venues this time, into old Salzburg. We pass beautiful mountain vistas I never would have paid attention to in the past. Now I soak them in, determined to enjoy the little moments.

Annecy's going to be gorgeous too. The Games were supposed

to go to Russia, but there was a big scandal and Annecy stepped in. We'll be back in the Alps, and even though I'm taking it one step at a time, my spine tingles as I peer past Matt at the mountains soaring into blue sky.

I'm coming back. I know it in my bones.

Soon I find myself watching Matt instead of the scenery. He glances over. "What?" He takes my hand on the seat between us.

"Just thinking."

"About how handsome and wonderful I am?"

I chuckle. "Absolutely. About the next Olympics too."

He squeezes my fingers. "Ready to do it all over again?"

Four more years.

Four more years of dark, cold mornings, and sore feet and muscle strains, and falling on my ass over and over and over again. Four more years of trying to be perfect. Four more years of doing what I love, and I'm going to have *fun* this time.

Despite Tanner's optimism, I know the odds are against me in Annecy. One man every four years isn't a safe bet to make, but I'm going to try my best.

Looking into Matt's eyes, I nod. "I'm *so* ready."

We grin at each other and lean in close to steal a kiss. The driver announces our stop, and I keep hold of Matt's hand as we slip and slide down the icy cobblestone street, our laughter echoing.

Maybe I won't win Olympic gold, but who knows? I just might.

THE END

About the Author

After writing for years yet never really finding the right inspiration, Keira discovered her voice in gay romance, which has become a passion. She writes contemporary, historical, paranormal, and fantasy fiction, and—although she loves delicious angst along the way—Keira firmly believes in happy endings. For as Oscar Wilde once said, "The good ended happily, and the bad unhappily. That is what fiction means."

Find out more about Keira's books and sign up for her monthly gay romance e-newsletter:

keiraandrews.com

Made in the USA
Middletown, DE
14 January 2021